PAMELA BRITTON

titles in the NASCAR Library Collection

And also by Pamela Britton

PAMELA BRITTON

slow burn

HQN™

Recycling programs
for this product may
not exist in your area.

ISBN-13: 978-0-373-77400-5

SLOW BURN

Copyright © 2009 by Pamela Britton

NASCAR® and the NASCAR Library Collection® are registered
trademarks of the NATIONAL ASSOCIATION FOR STOCK CAR
AUTO RACING, INC.

All rights reserved. Except for use in any review, the reproduction or
utilization of this work in whole or in part in any form by any electronic,
mechanical or other means, now known or hereafter invented, including
xerography, photocopying and recording, or in any information storage
or retrieval system, is forbidden without the written permission of the
publisher, Harlequin Enterprises Limited, 225 Duncan Mill Road,
Don Mills, Ontario M3B 3K9, Canada.

This is a work of fiction. Names, characters, places and incidents are
either the product of the author's imagination or are used fictitiously,
and any resemblance to actual persons, living or dead, business
establishments, events or locales is entirely coincidental.

This edition published by arrangement with Harlequin Books S.A.

® and TM are trademarks of the publisher. Trademarks indicated with
® are registered in the United States Patent and Trademark Office, the
Canadian Trade Marks Office and in other countries.

www.HQNBooks.com

Printed in U.S.A.

Dear Reader,

As the dedication page states, this book is for you! My life has been a constant series of ups and downs—from losing my father three years ago to dealing with a mom with Alzheimer's. Throughout it all, you guys have been there for me; I can't tell you how much I appreciate that.

I hope you enjoy *Slow Burn.* I'll be honest: there have been times in my life when all I've wanted to do was escape, and so I thought it would be neat to write about a heroine who does exactly that—runs away…to a NASCAR race. It was so much fun sending that heroine on adventure after adventure. But my heroine must also learn to confront her own fears and insecurities—something I'm intimately familiar with, too. Believe it or not, I consider myself the world's worst writer. Your letters might tell me otherwise, but I can't seem to stop myself from thinking Shakespeare must be rolling over in his grave. Your letters always lift me out of those writing funks.

So, once again, I'd like to thank each of you for taking the time to drop me a line, and for supporting me on the Internet and for…well, just being there whenever things get a little crazy. You might love my books, but I love all your letters just as much! Visit me at my Web site, www.pamelabritton.com.

Pamela

slow burn

This book is for my readers.
You guys are so flippin' amazing, it's not even funny.
Your notes always cheer me up.
Your letters always bring a smile to my face.
Your kindness knows no bounds.
Bless you, one and all!!

Michael, I know you're reading this page, too.
You're such a goof. *Every* book is dedicated, in part, to
you...and to Codi, our little miracle child. xoxo

CHAPTER ONE

"I'D SELL MY *SOUL* to win a date with Braden James."

Dana glanced at the woman who'd spoken the words and wondered, not for the first time, if alien beings had invaded Alysa's body.

"I mean, can you imagine anything better than spending two days with *that* man?" Alysa asked, her blue eyes wide and full of wonder as she stared up at a picture of her idol perfectly illuminated by Las Vegas's hot afternoon sun.

"Actually," Dana said, having to practically yell the words in order to be heard over the hundreds of people—mostly women—gathered in front of the Braden James souvenir hauler at the speedway, "I'd rather spend time with my dog."

Her stomach curdled in an all too familiar way. She fought against the sensation, fought against remembering.

"Oh, Dana," Alysa said, obviously catching a glimpse of her face. "I'm sorry. What an idiot I am to talk about dating someone when just last week…when less than five days ago you were about to get—"

Married.

Dana almost said the word out loud, but she couldn't. If she said it, it'd be putting a name to one of the most heartbreaking and miserable experiences of her life.

"You want to go back to the hotel?"

"No, no," Dana said. Standing between a row of big rigs and feeling like a gum ball in a bowl was okay with her. It beat being at home, dealing with the phone calls, the people dropping by, a stack of wedding presents that needed to go back. Dealing with the ever-present worry that something must be wrong with her since she'd almost married a man like Stewart, something that she feared had to do with her past.

Yeah, like maybe watching her mom pick loser after loser.

Thank God Dana had done something about her situation before it was too late.

Nausea threatened again. "I'll be fine."

"You sure?" Alysa asked.

Dana would have to admit Alysa had been wonderful during the past few days. Initially, Dana hadn't wanted to go anywhere, but Alysa—a coworker at Steele & Steele and someone she'd become friendly with over the past a couple of years—had dangled an extra ticket and the promise of a good time and

Dana had been too desperate to resist. Granted, she'd never seen a NASCAR race in her life, but it looked interesting on TV, and Alysa swore they were exciting. She just hoped she didn't regret dashing off to Vegas with someone she'd only ever spent a few evenings with at the movies.

"Positive," Dana said, determined to stick it out.

She glanced around. Even though the race wouldn't run until Sunday, fans swarmed the outside of the track like ants on a soda can, not surprising since the great Braden James was about to make an appearance. This, Dana had learned from Alysa, was tantamount to one of the Beatles arriving. But the situation today was compounded because in exactly ten minutes, Braden would select the winner of the *Win A Date With Braden James* contest. That person, probably a woman, would enjoy a trip to California's wine country where they'd get a chance to—*ohmigosh*—have dinner with Braden James.

Dana inhaled deeply, catching a whiff of new T-shirt smell from the souvenir hauler. She wouldn't be dating anyone anytime soon. She was avoiding men like the plague. They were all no good. Not to be trusted. Avoided at all costs.

But she *had* entered the contest.

Well, technically Alysa had entered for her, secretly filling out the form as a surprise.

But Dana had eventually put her signature on it, and let Alysa drop it in the box.

She'd done it to spite her ex-fiancé, she admitted, a man who had long discouraged her from doing anything "spontaneous." The man had planned out every moment of his day, right down to what Dana should wear when they went out. God forbid some-one should disrupt his schedule. Or disagree with him. If they did, it was not…pleasant.

She squeezed her eyes closed. Tight. Heat burned behind her lids because she'd done it again… thought of him.

He'd hit her.

Damn it, Stewart had actually hit her again. Even after begging him not to, he'd done it a second time.

The last *time.*

She sucked in a breath. She was not going to cry. She was done with Stewart. The man could rot in hell.

"We can go eat after this," Alysa said, patting Dana on the back, something that was hard to do amid wall-to-wall people. "At that Mexican food restaurant across the street from our hotel. You look like you could use a margarita."

Or two. Or three.

"Sure," Dana said. Not that she was hungry. She hadn't been hungry since the day Stewart had knocked her to the floor. Plus, it was hot where they stood. Someone should bottle Las Vegas's heat and sell it as an appetite suppressant. How in the heck it could be eighty-something degrees the first week of March was beyond her. She was sweating, miserable and wondering why the heck she'd agreed to go to a NASCAR race when she knew nothing about the sport.

You wanted to leave town, remember?

More like run away, she admitted. She hadn't told anyone where she was going. Heck, she hadn't even told her mom that she was leaving town. She didn't want Stewart to know where she was because there'd been a look in his eyes after he'd hit her, a look that told her next time she might not be lucky enough to get away.

And she *worked* with the man. They were both employees at Steele & Steele. But come Monday things would change. She was quitting her job. Until then, by God, she would have a good time.

That, she realized, was why she'd entered the stupid contest. She was determined to have fun, and to forget about Stewart. Then, too, there was the prize money and the new laptop she might win.

She glanced around, trying to distract herself by looking into the eyes of the man that Alysa so ardently admired.

The image of Braden James stared down at her from the lofty heights of his souvenir hauler, plastered across a ten-by-twenty strip to the left of a portable store's open window. Braden's arms were crossed, his shoulders thrown back, a haughty look of disdain on his face as he stared down at lesser mortals, i.e. herself. He wore a red uniform, a color that would have looked silly on most men but, Dana had to admit, looked great on Mr. James. Gorgeous green eyes stood out like twin neon signs. High cheekbones set off a masculine chin, one that was really, truly square, and had a tiny cleft in the center. The lower half of his face was covered with a five-o'clock shadow, one that matched his jet-black hair.

Oh, yeah, he was handsome, all right…and he knew it. Just the type of man she always sought to avoid. Her mom had favored the handsome, athletic type, and look where that had gotten her—in and out of the hospital for the first eight years of Dana's life. Dear old Dad had been a real winner before their divorce, as proved by the fact that Dana hadn't seen hide nor hair of him since.

"There he is!"

Dana jumped. The crowd around her had come alive. Even Alysa honed in on the red-and-white golf cart that picked its way through a never-ending stream of people, Las Vegas's massive grandstands in the background. The word *My-Lovematch.com* was printed on the front of the vehicle. This, Dana had learned, was Braden's sponsor. A Web site geared toward helping people find their one true love.

As if such a thing even existed.

"Oh my gosh, he's even cuter in person," Alysa muttered.

How could Alysa see *anything?* All around them women were jumping up and down like hyperactive aerobics students. Braden appeared to have an equal number of male fans, too, because she noticed more than a few of them doing the same. And most of the fans were dressed in red and white, like their idol.

Just like Alysa, who appeared to be as fascinated by Braden as the rest of the crowd. Alysa, who was one of Los Angeles's most successful CPAs. Not that you'd know it from her colorful race attire that included a Braden James T-shirt (red and white), a red ball cap (Alysa's long blond hair streaming out from the back), and a fanny pack that carried all the necessary accoutrements of the truly dedicated Braden James fan. Sunscreen, lip balm, scanner frequencies (whatever that was), and a miniature hand-held fan that could be used to cool one's face (red and white, of course). Dana could never, not ever, imagine being that fascinated by a man.

And to think Alysa had graduated magna cum laude.

"Please, God, let this be over fast," Dana muttered.

A few minutes later, the big man himself entered the hauler, a gaggle of people trailing in his wake, most of them wearing red polo shirts with the *My-*

Lovematch.com logo on the pocket. Braden ended up only a few feet away, although the lower half of his body was obscured by a glass display case filled with various racing paraphernalia. Dana spied her sweaty reflection in the glass surface. Her long brown hair appeared to be glowing thanks to the sun's rays. Maybe that's why her head felt as if it was on fire. At that moment she wished she had a red hat…any hat.

Someone handed Braden a headset with a mic, the earpieces brushing against his black hair, his five-o'clock shadow already in place even though it was barely two. He turned and faced the audience and gave them all a smile. And, all right, he was every bit as dazzlingly handsome in person. With a red polo shirt hugging his wide, muscular frame, Dana thought he looked more like a boxer than a race car driver. She could see veins popping out on his arms, as if he'd just worked out or something. And, all right, he looked good standing there. She was woman enough to appreciate that fact—and to feel her body tingle in response when their eyes connected, however briefly.

"Ladies and gentlemen," someone, a male assistant maybe because he couldn't have been much older than Braden's twenty-something years, said, "can I have your attention?" He held up his hand, his cordless mic emitted a high-pitched squeal until he lowered his arm.

"Sorry about that," he said, but the sound was an instant crowd silencer. "We'll be drawing the name of the *Win A Date* contest in just a minute."

The crowd cheered. Dana looked down and thought about asking Alysa if she could borrow her fan. When she looked up, she was almost certain Mr. James himself stared down at her. A trick of the light, obviously.

"After the winning name is drawn, we'll move right into autographs," the assistant said. "Unless the sweepstakes winner is actually present at which time we'll ask him—or her—to come up here for a presentation."

"Get on with it," someone yelled.

"Okay, okay," the assistant said with a laugh. "Braden, you ready?"

Unbelievably, Dana's heart actually quickened. It wasn't that she expected to win. She'd never won anything in her life. Not even at her company Christmas party. Five years of working as a CPA and she'd yet to bring home so much as a gift certificate. And, really, what would she do if she *did* win? Sure, the trip to Napa would be nice…but to actually have to go on a *date* with Braden James? A man who reminded her in so many ways of all the wrong men her mom had brought home over the years. Thank God Roger—an engineer at the office where her mom had worked, and now Dana's stepfather—had convinced her mom a few years ago that geeks made great lovers. He was the kind of man Dana needed to find. Someone down-to-earth and maybe just the tiniest bit uninteresting...not a *superstar.*

"Hello, everyone," said a man with a deep Southern accent. Dana looked up and realized it was Braden. "I just want to say how much I appreciate y'all coming out."

"We love you, Braden," a woman yelled.

Braden looked right at Dana. Worse, his face was filled with wry amusement, as if he thought *she'd* spoken the words.

He smirked.

She shook her head, looked away, feeling even *hotter* suddenly.

"He's looking *right* at you," Alysa hissed.

"No, he's not," Dana said. "He's looking at someone else."

"You're blind," Alysa said, and was it her imagination, or did Alysa sound the tiniest bit peeved?

Dana shot her a glance, but then Braden said, "Are we ready to draw a name?" and the crowd went crazy, including Alysa. Dana glanced around, amazed that one man could evoke such a strong reaction. She peeked up at him, wondering if there would be physical evidence that Braden James's head had just expanded by a few feet.

He stared right at her.

"He *is* looking at you," Alysa insisted, blue eyes full of...what was it? Dismay? Jealousy?

"Maybe he's sensing my man-hater aura."

"You don't hate men," Alysa said with a shake of her head. "You just hate Stewart. But you need to forget about him, Dana. Go on. Smile back at Braden. Flirt with the man. Have a little fun. *I* would if he was staring at *me*."

And, yes, that was very definitely envy she saw in her friend's eyes, but not so much of it that Alysa didn't mind her making a play for her favorite driver. As if going out on a date with a man like him was in her future. Ha.

Dana shook her head.

Someone, she would bet a corporate representative of *My-Lovematch.com* judging by his suit and tie, held open a giant white sack. Inside there must have been thousands of entry cards. She watched as Braden stirred them up a bit.

And, yes, Alysa was right. She didn't really hate men. She just...she just....

Didn't trust the good-looking ones.

Especially one man in particular. Jeesh. Two years of her life...wasted. She should have dumped him the first time he'd lost his temper—two weeks after they'd started dating. He'd gotten angry when she refused to change out of a dress he didn't like, ripping it just to spite her. That should have been her first clue. But, oh no, she'd stuck it out. Forgiving him one time too many. She just hoped he wouldn't make good on his most recent threats, and that he would leave her alone. Let her start a new life, because that's what she was facing. A new job. Maybe even a new city.

"Here we go," Alysa said, patting Dana on the arm and thankfully distracting her from thoughts of Stewart.

From inside the souvenir hauler Braden said, "I think I've got one." The crowd had grown absolutely quiet. Alysa tipped forward a bit.

"Wouldn't it be wild if you won?" Dana mused.

"Yeah. Wouldn't that be *great*," Alysa said, dreamlike. "I've been waiting my whole *life* to meet a man like Braden James."

Dana shot her a glance. Alysa had sounded a bit too serious. Downright stalkerlike. But Alysa was smart. Too smart to be fixated on a celebrity.

Right?

"And the winner is…" Braden paused for a moment. Both women turned. "Todd Peters!"

Someone booed. Alysa groaned, and ironically, Dana felt let down.

"Todd Peters," she heard Alysa say. "He's *got* to be kidding."

"Just pulling your leg," Braden said as if hearing Alysa's remark. "Wanted to see if y'all were paying attention."

Alysa laughed, and the relief Dana could hear in that laugh was unmistakable.

"Who's Todd Peters?" Dana asked, wanting to get a peek into Alysa's eyes.

"Todd Peters is another driver," Alysa said quickly, but she never looked at Dana. Another card was being pulled from the bag and that had all of Alysa's attention.

"Actually," he said. "We'll be calling out the names of the third- and second-place winners first. The third-place winner of a brand-new laptop, compliments of *My-Lovematch.com,* is…"

Now *that* she wouldn't mind winning, Dana thought.

"Now, let's see if I can read the writing… It looks like Frank Williams," Braden said with a wide smile as he scanned the crowd.

There were groans all around. Dana looked left and right, hoping to spot the winner, but she didn't. When she looked up again, Braden was staring at her once more. "Frank Williams?" he asked. "That you?"

Dana glanced behind her.

"He's playing with you," Alysa said.

She shook her head again.

"Okay then," Braden said. "Let's do second place."

"He *is* talking to you," Alysa said, sounding more and more peeved.

"Alysa, please, he's joking around with everyone."

But Dana knew it was a lie, and maybe a couple months ago she'd have been flattered. Now she didn't want anything to do with *any* man, sexy race car driver or no.

"Okay, second place and the winner of a trip for two to the NASCAR race in Bristol, Tennessee, is... Sandra Mullins," Braden said, looking right at her again.

But Dana didn't hold his gaze. Alysa, however... well, Alysa nudged her. Actually, it was more like a shove. Alysa was trying to step into Braden's line of sight, Dana realized. Unbelievable. Alysa was *obsessed*.

"Now the moment we've all been waiting for," Braden said, smiling at the crowd again. Dana made sure their eyes didn't connect. Instead she studied the colorful T-shirts hanging behind him, most of them featuring his car number, more than a few of them with Braden's image on the front. No wonder he had such a confident smile. Although to be honest, it was a *nice* smile.

"The winner of a five-day, four-night trip to the Sonoma wine country," Braden said. "*And* a two-thousand-dollar cash prize..."

Now *that* she wouldn't mind winning, either.

"And pit passes for not just the Sonoma race, but for *this* race, as well, right here. Right now." He pointed toward the grandstands in the distance. "And most importantly," Braden added with another smile. "Dinner with *me* at Vino, one of Napa's most premier restaurants…."

Alysa clapped excitedly. And Dana's breath caught. But odds were, *neither* of them would win.

"Okay, so here we go…"

Yet *still* her breath log-jammed in her throat. She dared to meet Braden's gaze. He was looking right at her—again.

That was probably why she imagined hearing her name. Why she stood there like an idiot, even when he repeated the familiar syllables.

It wasn't until Alysa grabbed her arm and jumped in front of her, a mixture of awe and dismay on her face. "You won!" she screamed. "Oh, my gosh, Dana," Alysa said, shaking her. "You *actually* won. You lucky, *lucky* woman, you!"

CHAPTER TWO

BRADEN WATCHED THE WOMAN he'd been eyeing shake her head. "No, I didn't," he heard her say.

Well, I'll be damned, Braden thought. The brunette he'd been studying for the past five minutes would be his date. What terrific good luck. She was *hot*.

"Looks like our winner is present," John, his PR assistant, said, pointing. "That's fantastic. Dana Johnson, come on up here."

"If I didn't have to work with you on a daily basis, I'd have to kill you," he thought he heard her friend say.

"Don't be shy," his PR assistant called out.

"I didn't actually think I'd *win*," he could have sworn he heard her say back. She glanced up at him and there was no mistaking it. She looked a little frazzled, maybe even taken aback.

Taken aback?

Yup. But by now, others had caught on. People clustered around her, clapping and urging her forward.

"Go!" one of them all but yelled, giving her a shove. Braden watched as, reluctantly, Dana Johnson made her way toward the souvenir hauler.

"You're in luck," John said, covering the mic. "At least it's a woman."

"It wouldn't have mattered if a man had won the 'date,'" Braden said, having covered his mic, too.

"Yeah, but it sounds better to the press if it's a woman."

"Yeah, I suppose." But what would the press do if they knew that woman didn't *want* to spend time with him? Or did she? It was hard to tell because she looked both dumbstruck and flustered.

"She's cute, too," John said with a wiggle of his brows.

Cute? She wasn't just cute. She was a damn knockout with her long limbs and gorgeous reddish-brown hair, with her olive complexion, almond-shaped eyes and sweeping brows. *Exotic.* That's the word that came to mind. He'd noticed her right off the bat, even in the middle of the crowd. But he'd noticed something else, too, something that'd drawn his attention back to her time and again.

She'd had tears in her eyes.

Why?

"You want a moment alone with her to congratulate her?" John asked with a suggestive tip of his eyebrows.

Braden wasn't sure. Something wasn't right here,

but he didn't know what, or *if* he wanted to find out what it was. He had a habit of sticking his nose where it didn't belong.

"I'll settle the crowd while you do," John added.

But Dana looked up at him just as she reached the corner of the hauler, and it was the final meeting of their eyes that settled the matter. In her big brown gaze was a combination of dismay and dejection.

He had never been able to resist a damsel in distress.

Braden took off his headset. "Give me five minutes," he told John.

"*Two* minutes," his PR rep said. Braden and Dana headed toward the mini-office located at the front of the hauler. "We really need to get started on those autographs. The troops will be getting restless if we make them wait too long."

"Got it."

Less than a minute later, Dana was shown inside the tiny little room and Braden had to admit, she was every bit as stunning up close. He liked women who didn't wear a lot of makeup. Women with natural good looks and long, lean bodies—women who looked like Dana Johnson.

"Congratulations," he said as the door closed behind them with a click.

"Uh, yeah. Thanks," she said, swiping a lock of hair away from her face.

It was the hair, he admitted to himself. It was gorgeous. Long and curly in a way that had to be natural. And the pretty brown eyes, ones that were set off by a gorgeous golden tan.

"You excited about winning?"

"Um, yeah, about that," she said, attempting a grin. He wouldn't call it a smile because there was no way in hell anyone could call the sickly grimace she gave him a smile.

"I, uh, and please don't take this the wrong way, but I think I should probably tell you straight up that I don't want to go on the date with you."

"Excuse me?"

"I know that might present difficulties, but it'd be great if I could win the trip to Napa and you could give the date to someone else, maybe my friend Alysa. She's a really big fan."

"You want to give our date away?"

"Well, I, ah…I don't really know a whole lot about NASCAR and so I don't think I'd be a good date, especially right now," she said quietly. "But Alysa *adores* you. She'd be better."

He couldn't believe it. All the hype about winning a date with him and the person who won didn't want to spend time with him. Frankly, his feelings were kind of hurt. "Why were you crying earlier?"

Her brows shot up. "Excuse me?"

"When I first spotted you in the crowd, you had tears in your eyes. And then later…you looked sad."

Brown brows stretched even higher. "You *saw* that?"

"Yeah. So why?"

Those brows settled back into perfectly formed arcs. "That's really none of your business."

He shook his head, pushed away from the small table he'd been resting against. She might be hot, but there was something going on with her. He hadn't spent his childhood in and out of foster homes without learning how to sniff out trouble. "Look, I just met you and the first thing out of your mouth is that you want to give our date to someone else. Forgive me for being nosy, but I'm kind of curious about why. Does it have something to do with you crying. What happened? Some guy leave you at the altar?"

"No, of course not."

But something about her expression made Braden's spine snap to attention. "You didn't really get left at the altar, did you?"

"Thank you for taking the time to meet me in person, Mr. James," she said, starting to turn away. "I'll see you in Napa."

"No, wait." He stepped in front of her and tried not to chuckle. He could not believe his stab in the dark had hit home. "Look, I'm sorry. That was just a wild guess. I mean, I can't believe it actually happened. I've never met someone who's been jilted.

Although I suppose it *does* happen, I never expected it would happen to someone who looks like you."

"Excuse me?"

"You have to know you're gorgeous."

"I'll just be on my way."

She tried to turn away again. He stepped in front of her, placed a hand on her bare arm. It was hot and smooth, and frankly he wanted to stroke it, had to fight a sudden urge to do exactly that.

She gasped and pulled back. "Don't touch me."

She looked furious. And scared.

What the hell was going on?

"Sorry," he said, trying to show her with his eyes that he really meant it, and having to clutch his hand into a fist to avoid touching her again. "It's a habit of mine, touching people." Although he usually tried to avoid touching his fans. They might get the wrong idea. "Please don't misunderstand. I wasn't trying to hit on you or anything."

Then why'd you touch her, Braden?

Because he hadn't been able to stop himself.

"Cripes, there's a whole boatload of women outside who'd date me if I asked. But you? You look like someone who needs to talk. I once had a woman come through my line with a black eye and bruises all over her arms. One question led to another and that same day we had the bastard who'd hit her behind bars."

"It's nothing like that."

"No?" One of his foster moms had looked at him in that exact manner when he'd confronted her about her husband's abuse. But maybe he was wrong. Maybe she was telling the truth. God knows, he'd just met the woman. She might have a perfectly good reason to act so jumpy.

"Well, okay. Obviously, I've overstepped my bounds. I'm sorry about that. And I'm sorry about your being jilted, I really am, but I've got a bunch of corporate execs from *My-Lovematch.com* out there and they want to meet their contest winner, not to mention the media who's all set to cover our date when it happens. Imagine what they'll say when I tell them you want to give that date away, although to be honest, I don't think that will be allowed." That wasn't precisely the truth. His sponsors were a pretty easygoing bunch. But as he stared down at her, he admitted to himself that he didn't want to give up his date with her.

"The media?"

"Yeah," he said. "This contest is a big deal. The press is all over it. My sponsors are going to blow a gasket when they hear you don't want to spend time with me. They've spent hundreds of thousands of dollars setting this thing up, you know, hyping me and this big, important date. I can't imagine what they'll do if you tell them to give the date to someone else." Frankly, he wouldn't be surprised if they weren't hoping he might want to date the winner of their contest more than once. He just might, too, he thought.

She didn't say anything, but he could tell she was listening. No more prickly pear. Thank God.

"But I have an idea," he said. "Why don't you try to *act* like you're happy you won, you know, go out and smile and wave. You'll have to pretend to be happy in front of the media, too, but I'm sure you can do that. Later on I'll ask my sponsors about giving our date to your friend. I don't think they'll go for it, but it's worth a try. Maybe if you play along now, they'll be more willing to cooperate." And if he did something nice for her, maybe that'd put a smile on her face.

She didn't say anything for a long moment.

"I'll throw in some pit passes for your friend, too," he said. "I bet she'd love to see the inside of this place," he added with an even bigger grin.

Her pretty eyes were staring at him unblinkingly. He thought she was mulling over his offer, but then she tipped her head sideways and asked, "Did you really help that woman? The one with the bruises?"

Now it was his turn to mull things over. She seemed…nice, and not the least starstruck. He liked that about her. "I did."

She studied him for a moment and then finally, reluctantly, said, "Okay. I'll play along. For now."

"Terrific." He was surprised at just how happy her agreement made him feel.

"As long as you promise to ask your sponsor about our date as soon as possible."

"Of course. But you know, I'm starting to think there might be something wrong with me, since you don't want to go out with me."

"No, no," she said, lifting her chin. "It's nothing like that."

"I mean, do I smell?"

"No. Of course not."

Was that a tiny smile he saw? "Good 'cause I was starting to worry." He smiled.

She looked away as if embarrassed by his grin. Shy, he thought. He liked that about her, too.

"Look," he said. "I want you to have a good time today. I'll even give you a personal tour of the garage once you get your credentials. You'll enjoy seeing what goes on behind the scenes. I promise. *For sure* I know your friend will…since she *adores* me."

She tipped her head the other way.

"Unlike you," he added, trying to tease another grin out of her.

"My friend Alysa would go nuts if you did that," she said, completely ignoring his teasing.

"Good," he said. "It's settled then."

But she looked lost again, and he hated that.

"Well," he said. "I guess we better go outside and get the presentation over with."

"Yeah," she said before starting to turn away.

"Dana," he said, catching her hand.

She gasped, tried to pull away.

He held firm. "Thank you for doing this."

Her expression grew as frightened and uncertain as a newborn pup's.

"Please let me go," she murmured.

He did as she asked, wishing…

He didn't know what he wished for. "Sorry," he said again softly, leaning toward her. She smelled like magnolias, and it was a scent that he really, really liked. "I told you. It's a habit."

"Let's go," she said.

He stepped in front of her one last time, tempted to tip her chin up and murmur the words that everything would be okay. He longed to do it so badly that his fingers actually tingled. But he didn't touch her and eventually she met his gaze.

"If you were jilted…the man was a fool," he said gently. It was all he dared to say.

Her breath caught. He could see her chest still for a moment, but when she started to breathe again, the expression on her face changed…and *not* for the better. Oh, no. There was a look in her eyes akin to crime-scene-barrier tape.

Do not cross.

"Yes," she said, "but you can't 'fool' me twice."

She slipped outside and he found himself in an empty room.

CHAPTER THREE

"DID YOU GET to speak to him privately? What was he like? Where you terrified up there? Ohmigosh! I can't *believe* you got to meet Braden James."

The words passed through Alysa's mouth with the rapidity of machine-gun fire, although the last had been uttered in envy.

"I should have filled out *ten* entry cards," she added, clutching Dana's hand so hard it made Dana wince. Alysa dragged her away from the souvenir hauler, although not without one last longing glance in Braden's direction. The sexy race car driver didn't even look their way. He was too busy signing autographs.

If you were jilted...the man was a fool.

Yeah, well, she'd been the bigger fool.

"Alysa, if you'd put our names down more than once, that would have been cheating. Besides, you're going to meet him in an hour."

"What?" Alysa cried, drawing the attention of anyone within hearing distance, which must have been about half the race track. "I get to meet him?" she cried, spinning and clutching Dana by the shoulders. Dana winced again. At this rate Alysa would leave her with more bruises than Stewart had. "How?"

"Calm down," Dana cried. "People are staring."

"Who cares? *What do you mean I get to meet him?*"

Dana winced again, because Alysa was still clutching her shoulders.

Braden had touched her.

Best not to think about *that.*

"I finagled some pit passes for you. In about an hour we're to go to the NASCAR credential office, whatever that is, and pick up some HotPasses… whatever those are, so we can go inside and meet up with Braden James."

Alysa looked like a parrot trying to form its first word. Her mouth open and closed, opened and closed. Not for the first time Dana found herself wondering if Alysa's body had been snatched by sense-stealing aliens because gone was the elegant, sophisticated genius who was one of the best CPAs in the firm. In her place stood a woman who could only be called, well, a *groupie.* It was kind of funny.

"You got us HotPasses," Alysa said in a low, dis-believing tone.

"Yes, I did. That's a good thing, right?" Because when it boiled right down to it, Dana wanted this for Alysa. Alysa had been kind to her, even more so after Dana told her what had happened with Stewart. Sure, she'd seemed a little bit jealous when Dana had won the date, but maybe Alysa didn't realize Dana wasn't interested in *any* man, much less a famous race car driver. Maybe once Alysa met Braden she'd realize Dana was no threat. Maybe once Braden locked eyes on Alysa, he'd quit asking questions. Alysa was very, *very* pretty. They'd be perfect for each other. Just because Stewart had put Dana off dating men didn't mean Alysa couldn't have a good time.

"Come on," Dana said, hooking her arm through Alysa's, something she had to do because Alysa looked as dazed as a patient waking up from a coma. "I assume you want to get all dolled up for Braden, which means a trip back to our car and that bag of tricks you call a purse. This credential office is about a mile away, out behind the race track, according to Mr. James's PR person, so we'll have to drive there."

"Drive there," Alysa repeated.

"We'll need photo IDs, too, when we check in. Or so I was told."

"Photo IDs." Alysa nodded.

And for the first time in *days,* Dana wanted to laugh. Alysa was well and truly gobsmacked. "Come on," she said. "Let's get you all fixed up for your handsome prince."

A prince who'd made Dana tremble when he touched her.

And *not* because she feared him.

IT TOOK THEM NEARLY an hour to find the credential office and by the time they arrived, Dana's mood had fizzled a bit, like a leaky tire. But Alysa had enough energy for the two of them. And as she watched her friend from work primp and preen, Dana found herself thinking it felt like high school all over again. She just couldn't believe the smart and stylish Alysa Anderson was acting like a fan-club president.

"Not to rain on your parade, Ms. Anderson, but isn't being in the pits dangerous?" Dana asked, pulling into a spot next to a dark green SUV. It was a question that'd been bugging her for the past hour, and even more now that they were finally in front of the credential office. Not that she was a coward or anything. She just didn't like loud noises and already she could hear cars racing around inside the track. Those cars were fast. Did they ever hit pedestrians?

"Are you kidding?" Alysa said. "It won't be dangerous. It'll be amazing. We'll be able to go right up to drivers like Lance Cooper and Adam Drake and Todd Peters."

"All people I've never heard of," Dana muttered, eyeing the predominately white tractor trailer that'd taken them forever to find, the words NASCAR Sprint Cup Series emblazoned on the side. Dana was convinced the thing's location was something only the President of the United States knew.

"We'll be able to take close-up shots of their cars," Alysa prattled on, slipping out of the rental car before the tires came to a complete stop.

"Alysa," Dana cried in dismay.

"Just wait until I tell everyone at the office," Dana heard Alysa say. "They're going to be soooo jealous of us."

Dana shut off the engine and joined Alysa near the front of the car. Dana was very nearly scalded by the heat radiating off the hood. She had to squint to avoid spots dancing before her eyes.

"I hope he wants to go out with me," Alysa said in a giddy voice.

Dana had told Alysa about her plan. Her friend had practically crowed in delight at the thought of going out on a date with Braden James.

"Heck," Alysa added. "Maybe I could turn one date into two. Maybe I could snag him as a boyfriend. Wouldn't that be cool? I could go to all his races, stand by him in Victory Lane…."

Have his children.

"Watch him race from pit road," Alysa added. "That'd be so great."

Whoo, boy.

Braden James had no idea what he was in for. In fact, she felt kind of sorry for the guy.

He'd seemed nice.

She hadn't expected that. Granted, everything she knew about celebrity athletes came from gossip columns and entertainment television, but she'd expected Braden to be arrogant and condescending. Instead he'd treated her with warmth and compassion. That perplexed her.

"Ohmigosh, ohmigosh," Alysa said, coming to a sudden stop and causing Dana to crash into her friend's back. "We're here!"

"It's great," Dana murmured distractedly, scanning the outside of the hauler for the forms she'd been told they'd need to fill out.

The credentialing process was tantamount to gaining access to the Pentagon—or so it felt. They were asked to provide the yellow form they'd filled out, along with a photo ID, and a blood sample. Okay, not really a blood sample, but their social security numbers were asked for. Fortunately, there was no line so they were in and out pretty quickly. Alysa—tucking the coveted green card into the plastic holder they'd both bought earlier—looked like someone who held a winning lottery ticket.

"Infield parking passes, too," Alysa muttered. "I can't believe it. I just *can't believe* it."

Yup. Alysa owed her big-time.

Now that they had their passes, Dana had to admit the whole thing felt sort of surreal to her, too. She'd caught a glimpse of a NASCAR race on television, but just a glimpse. A part of her had always wondered what it'd be like to watch a race live. If she were honest with herself, that's why she'd agreed to come with Alysa. Now they'd get to see that race from inside the track. By the sound of it, they were lucky to have been given the privilege.

"You ready?" Dana asked.

"Are you kidding?" Alysa asked. "My hands are shaking."

Dana's hands were shaking, too, but for a different reason. She would get to see Braden James again, a man who disturbed her in more ways than one. Just the thought of him had her trembling.

They found the tunnel entrance to the infield with relative ease. The car plunged into the darkness like a ride at a water park. A small dot of sunshine grew bigger as they approached the opposite end, and when they emerged a few seconds later, light enveloped them with warm, welcoming rays. Dana blinked a few times, then felt her brows lift.

From the inside, the place was *huge.*

Wow.

Like a high-school football stadium on steroids. Sure, they'd taken a peek when they'd first arrived, but being in the middle of the track gave her a whole new perspective. Grandstands tipped away like cupped hands. At first Dana thought those stands were already full, but then she realized track officials had merely painted the seats a multitude of colors to make it appear as if every seat was taken. Above the rows of colored bleachers, light poles stretched skyward at regular intervals—pole after pole after pole so that Dana knew the place would be lit up like a casino come nighttime.

"Keep going," Alysa said, waving her forward. "This is the NASCAR Nationwide Series garage."

"How do you know?"

"The cars are smaller. Plus, you can see them coming in and out of the garage. It's their practice time right now according to the schedule I picked up at the credential office."

"You scare me, you know that?" Dana said. But, honestly, she was grateful at least *one* of them knew what was going on.

"I pay attention. You'll start paying attention, too. Trust me, Dana, once you get close to these cars you'll be hooked for life."

Dana was starting to think that might be true.

They found a spot near the NASCAR Sprint Cup garage. They were so close that when Dana slipped out of the car, she could hear motors idling in the distance. She could *smell* what was to come, too. The acidic odor of cleanser. The unmistakable scent of rubber tires. The burnt scent of electrical equipment. Her rental car's engine tick-tick-ticked in time to the beat of her heart. Dana was suddenly overcome by the feeling that if she stepped away from the rental car, it might just change her life.

Forever.

"Come on," Alysa said. "I think we get in over there."

Her friend pointed toward a crowd of people huddled around some sort of opening. A security guard stood nearby, the shadow of a pedestrian overcrossing with colorful banners strewn across it blocked him from the heat of the day. Smart man.

"Alysa, maybe you should go in without me," Dana said suddenly. "This is more your thing. If you see Mr. James, tell him I'll talk to him about the date later. He has my contact information."

She turned back toward their rental car even as she called herself a coward.

Story of her life.

"Oh, no you don't!" Alysa cried, stepping in front of her. "I need *your* help to set up my date with Braden James. You're not going anywhere."

"Alysa, I don't need to go inside to do that. I can do it over the phone."

"Not the same," Alysa said, hooking their arms together. "They're more apt to do as you ask if you bat those big brown eyes."

"I doubt that," Dana said.

"Besides," Alysa went on, ignoring her. "You can't leave now. That's like getting tickets to the Super Bowl and sitting out in the parking lot. Jeesh. Do you realize what a once-in-a-lifetime opportunity this is? You might never get a chance to see the inside of a NASCAR garage again."

Yeah, but that wouldn't necessarily be a *bad* thing. She felt far better about watching the race from the safety of the stands. Still…her friend was right. When would something so completely unexpected happen to her again? And hadn't she just told herself she wanted to be more spontaneous?

"Come on," Alysa said, oblivious to Dana's inner turmoil. "We're going in."

"But, Alysa." Dana eyed the orange-colored garage. Inside she could see team members milling about. "I really don't feel up to it."

"You'll feel better once you get inside."

Alysa wasn't taking no for an answer. Dana should put her foot down. She really should. Instead, she followed Alysa inside.

Atop the garage, a second story had been erected, but it was really no more than a covered walkway or an observation deck. Alysa had told her earlier that windows were set into the walls so people could peer into the interior of the garage, or, failing that, they could congregate around the exterior railing

and watch what was going on down below, outside
the garage, something more than a few people were
doing at the moment.

"Look, the car numbers are hanging from the
second-story roof," Alysa said, pointing. "Let's go
find Braden."

As it turned out, the garage looked more like an in-
dustrial complex than a workshop for high-dollar race
cars. Haulers had been lined up alongside the perimeter fence, opposite the orange-and-blue building.
Crew members congregated around the backs of those
haulers, more than one man leaning against a giant
toolbox or sitting in a waist-high director's chair.

"Those trucks carry the race cars from race to
race," Alysa said, having taken on the role of tour
guide.

"So I gathered," Dana said.

"There it is," Alysa said, causing Dana to jump.
"And look, their hauler is parked right next to Todd
Peters's. How totally cool is that?"

"Way cool," Dana muttered, hoping she sounded
somewhat enthusiastic.

"Dana," someone called.

To her shock, Dana realized that was Braden standing near the back of the hauler, a tall man next to him.

"This must be Alysa," he said, moving forward,
the shadow he'd been standing beneath abruptly
dissolving.

He remembered her friend's name?

Alysa took the hand Braden extended and stared. She didn't say hi. She didn't clutch his hand back. She just put her hand into his own big palm and gawked.

Dana almost smiled. *Almost.* She would have, too, if she hadn't been so damn jittery.

"Nice to meet you," Braden said.

"Uh…yeah," Alysa mumbled.

"Look," Braden said, letting go of Alysa's hand and leaning toward Dana. "I'm sorry to do this to you on such short notice, but there's someone who wants to meet you—"

"Is this the girl?" a big-chested man said, his red-and-white shirt proclaiming him to be with Braden's sponsor.

"This is her," Braden said over his shoulder.

Dana looked between Braden and the heavyset man, growing edgier by the minute. They'd begun to attract quite a bit of attention. Alysa had explained earlier that it was a "cold" time, which meant race fans would be wandering about. Those fans had spotted Braden, a number of them hanging back so they could stare. More than a few started to encircle them. The sensation of being trapped made Dana's teeth clench together.

"Dana," Braden said, "this is Max Arnold, *My-Lovematch.com*'s CEO. Unfortunately, his flight was delayed and he couldn't make the draw this morning. He was thrilled to learn you'd be joining us in the garage."

"Oh," Dana said. "Nice to meet you, Mr. Arnold." She tried to smile, but she doubted it reached her eyes.

Alysa nudged her. Dana glanced in her direction. She mouthed the word *date,* and inclined her head in the CEO's direction as if she expected Dana to blurt out then and there that she wanted Alysa to go on the date with Braden instead of her.

"Wow," the CEO said. "You were right, Braden. She's really pretty. I think we got lucky. What are you? Hispanic or something?"

"Excuse me?" Dana said, forgetting about Alysa for a moment.

"Sorry," Mr. Arnold said. "No offense. It's just that your ethnicity makes you all the more marketable for our advertising campaign."

"Advertising campaign?" Dana asked. Alysa nudged her again, harder.

"Didn't Braden tell you?" the CEO asked.

Braden stepped between her and his boss, or sponsor...or whatever he was. "Alysa," he said, turning to her friend. "Would you mind giving us a moment alone?"

Alysa looked as if that was the last thing she wanted to do. But she muttered, "Sure. As long as you promise to spend some alone time with *me* later."

Dana saw Braden stiffen. "Ah, yeah. Sure."

"Why can't you just talk to me here?" Dana asked, because she wasn't going anywhere with Braden.

"Humor me for a moment," Braden said.

"What is it you need to tell me?" she asked.

"I'm sure he wants to go over the fine print of the contest," the big man said. "By entering, you agreed to—"

"I'll tell her," Braden interrupted, hooking her arm with his and drawing her away.

She tried to pull out of his grasp, but he wouldn't let her. Dana would have resisted with more force if the crowd hadn't gotten thicker. She refused to deal with a full-blown panic attack. Not in front of Braden…and a bunch of his fans.

"Do it quickly," the big man called. "The sooner we get this show on the road, the better."

Dana caught the look in Alysa's eyes. Her friend's gaze begged her to switch the date as soon as possible.

I'll do what I can, was the look Dana shot back.

"What show?" Dana asked as Braden led her toward a narrow space between his hauler and the next. The truck cast a huge shadow, one that swallowed them whole. With each step they took, the crowd receded, and Dana's panic eased, but only a little.

"Look, I hate to spring this on you," he said, once they were sheltered from the public's view. "But Max wants to—" He crooked his head to the side. "Hey." He leaned toward her. "What's wrong?"

"Huh?" she asked. "What do mean 'what's wrong'?"

"Did that crowd freak you out?"

"No," she lied.

"You *are* upset," he said. "I can see your pulse pounding." He touched a spot on the side of her neck, gently, but the stroke of his fingers caused a temporary paralysis in Dana's lungs.

Why did he keep touching her?

"That's nothing," she said again, because she wasn't about to tell him the truth—that ever since last week, when she'd left Stewart and he'd said those horrible words, accusing her of being frigid and cold and messed up, she'd felt as if she were falling... falling to a place that scared her to death.

Was she cold and frigid and messed up?

There *must* be something wrong with her to listen to Stewart's excuses not once, but twice.

"What's the matter?" he asked softly.

"Nothing," she said. "Except the heat. But I'm better now that I'm in the shade. What's up?"

Right then a breeze whistled up the aisle, blowing a lock of hair across her face. She pushed it away, her skin prickling beneath the wind's cold touch.

"You sure?" he asked, tipping his head a bit.

"What's this about fine print?" she asked. She didn't want him to pry any further. Not now. Not ever.

He remained silent for a moment, as if he were

contemplating her, but then he looked past her. She followed his gaze. The CEO of *My-Lovematch.com* glanced at his watch pointedly and Dana knew Braden wouldn't be asking her any more questions—well, not personal questions at least.

"Look," he said, "I'm sorry to spring this on you, but when you entered the contest, you signed your name, which means you agreed to the terms and conditions."

"Terms and conditions?" Dana repeated, knowing she wouldn't like what was coming next.

"Yes," Braden said. "And one of the most important terms is that you agreed to do media appearances."

"I did?"

"I know you probably didn't read the sweepstakes rules," he quickly added. "Most people don't. But now we're in a bind. One of the major networks is interested in doing a segment on our date. It's a major coup for *My-Lovematch.com,* and something they're really excited about. Frankly, it's exactly the type of publicity they hoped to generate by holding this contest. But, well…" He ran a hand through his hair. "We'll need your assistance to pull it off."

Dana could tell which way the wind was blowing. "Did you talk to them about switching the date around?"

He frowned. "Yeah. It's a no-go, Dana. Your name's already been announced to the media.

Switching things would only create confusion. You're the winner and there's nothing we can do about that."

She swallowed. Hard.

"Sorry to have to disappoint your friend."

It wasn't surprising that he'd picked up on the fact that Alysa would do just about anything to go out on a date with him given the way Alysa had stared up at him.

"What is it you need me to do?" It was about twenty degrees cooler in the shade, which was why she'd started shivering.

"Well," Braden said, looking up and down the aisle as if worried someone might overhear them. "It's not really a media appearance. It's more like a publicity stunt, although I'm sure the gal doing the interview will want to talk to you privately."

"Just spit it out, Braden."

He appeared startled by the use of his name, and then he smiled, as if he *liked* her using it. "You need to go for a little ride with me."

"A ride," she repeated.

"In a race car."

"Excuse me?"

"A *special* race car," he quickly added. "Part of the local racing school. They teach people how to drive stock cars here, and so they have vehicles that are outfitted with passenger seats. You can sit next to me while I'm driving."

"And *where* will we be driving?" she asked, concerned when he didn't immediately respond.

He scrubbed a hand over his chin, once…twice, then said, "The track."

She swayed on her feet. "I think I'm going to be sick."

CHAPTER FOUR

SHE DIDN'T LOOK SO GOOD. "You okay?"

"No," she moaned.

"Hey," he said. "I know it's a lot to ask. But it'll only be for a little while. I don't expect the race to last longer than a few laps."

"Race?" she asked, starting to look even more upset. "*What* race?"

"It's part of the publicity stunt," he said, marveling at the way her eyes had turned gold in the ambient light—like a phosphorescent piece of amber. "One of the local charities auctioned off a chance to race a few of us drivers in a mock competition. Todd Peters, Lance Cooper, Adam Drake and myself are the pros, and three wealthy business owners are the 'Joes.' I guess these guys paid nearly twenty-five-thousand dollars apiece for the privilege."

"And you want me to sit next to you while you *drive in a race.*"

"That's the plan. The network gal loved the idea,

so much so she promised to put the spot in prime time. *My-Lovematch* is thrilled, but obviously we need your cooperation."

She'd gone back to looking worried again, although not quite with the same intensity as before. "I don't know, Braden," she said. "I'm not a big fan of doing risky things."

Somehow he'd known she'd say that. What's more, he couldn't help but wonder why she didn't like taking risks. Was it something to do with the sadness he saw lingering in her eyes?

"It'd just be for a few laps," he said again.

She glanced toward the back of the hauler. Braden followed her gaze. Max had moved, his big body now visible from where they stood. He glanced at his watch, touched it, his meaning obvious. Braden looked away. The man was a jerk, always barking orders at everyone. He acted as if he was the team's owner, not the sponsor, and as far as Braden was concerned, Max could just cool his heels.

"Look," he said, "I know it's a lot to ask, but the publicity will be good for the charity that organized this. Their eight-hundred number will be visible on every car. I'll bet you dollars to doughnuts the segment will prompt more than a few people to call in. I don't blame you for being anxious, but if there's any way you could see past your fear, I promise I'll take good care of you."

"How many laps?" she asked, and he could see her inner battle in her eyes.

"Twenty-five."

"Will I be safe?"

He nodded, hearing footsteps behind him. A crew member from an opposing team walked up the narrow aisle. Braden stepped aside, and the man eyed Dana.

Back off, Braden thought.

Whoa!

Where had that come from?

But he knew. He couldn't deny that there was something about Dana that made him want to protect her. He didn't know what it was. God knows he'd never felt such an instant emotional connection with a woman before, but now that he'd admitted it, he knew it was true. He wanted to keep her safe. To put a smile on her face. To show her that everything would be all right. He knew all about feeling lost and lonely. He'd felt that way his whole childhood thanks, no doubt, to being in and out of foster homes.

"I promise, I won't let anything happen to you," he said. And he meant it.

"How fast will we be going?"

She was actually considering it. "Not too fast," he said, although his idea of fast and *her* idea of fast might be two different things.

Her shoulders straightened. Her chin tipped up

and Braden was shocked at how hard it was for him not to reach out for that chin, to touch it. She mouthed a word. He thought it might have been *spontaneous,* but he couldn't be sure.

"Okay," she said. "I'll do it."

Atta girl. "Good. Excellent."

"When will you need me?"

"Well, ah, *actually,* we have to be out on pit road in a couple hours."

"A couple *hours?*" she cried. "I thought this was something that would happen tomorrow or next week or something."

"Nope," he said. "Today." And a good thing, too, because he could tell from her reaction that she'd have chickened out if given a day to think about it.

"Oh, dear," she murmured.

"Hey," he said. "It'll be fun. Remember, I'm a pro, not a Joe."

A COUPLE HOURS.

"Are you sure they won't let me go on the date in your place?"

Dana shook her head. "I'm sure." Dana crossed her arms in front of her and stared blindly at the ground. She heard Alysa sigh, and although it wasn't a sigh of annoyance, it definitely sounded like a sigh of impatience.

"I'm sorry, Alysa, but I really did try."

Alysa didn't say anything for a moment. In the distance, some kind of hydraulic tool whirred. Dana looked up, trying to spot where the sound had come from, but all she saw was rows of open garage stalls, race cars tucked neatly inside like toddlers in a bed.

"I know you did," Alysa said, sounding resigned. "At least we get to be inside the garage. Look at all the people lined up on the fence over there. Bet they wish they were us, huh?"

Dana looked to the left. Sure enough, a row of people three feet thick stood outside, scraps of paper in hand. They must be hoping to spot their favorite driver and get an autograph. Honestly, she would happily trade places with any one of them. Being driven around a race track by a world-famous driver was *not* her idea of fun, but she honestly didn't see a way out of it. If she bailed on the race, she'd be in violation of the terms and conditions of her sweepstakes entry. That meant losing out on the prize money, too, and right now she could use the cash.

"You look like you're going to puke," Alysa said.

"I think I'm going to," Dana admitted.

They were walking around the garage, Braden having told them to take it easy for a bit while he finished up with Max Arnold. He said he'd find them as soon as he was done—whenever that might be.

"In a couple of hours you'll be out there," Alysa motioned toward the race track. "Being driven around the track by Braden James. You should be thrilled. This is a once-in-a-lifetime opportunity."

"Then *you* do it."

"I wish I could."

They both knew that wasn't an option. Through some weird quirk of fate, Dana's life was now entwined with Braden James, a man whose cardboard cutout was sold in novelty stores.

And he didn't act like a famous superstar *at all*.

He was kind, she admitted, remembering how concerned he'd been when she'd been on the verge of that damn panic attack. Thank goodness it'd passed, although she wasn't certain her irrational fear wouldn't return the moment she climbed into a race car.

"You're looking sick again," Alysa observed.

They were passing through an area not populated by haulers and pedestrians, an area that appeared to be some sort of inspection site. A long, rectangular room stood off the end of the garage. Windows allowed her a glimpse inside a shop where odd-shaped metal cutouts rested on the floor. Card tables and computers were set up, and a colorful car stood in the center of the room—like a four-wheeled patient on an operating table. Dana paused for a moment under the guise of watching the process, but in truth, she was hardly paying attention.

"I don't think I can do it," she admitted. Ever since she'd been a kid she'd been afraid of small, confined spaces. She knew it had to do with all those times her mom had locked her in a closet to keep her safe from her dad. And she knew it was irrational. She should just get over it, but she couldn't seem to shake the anxiety that *always* accompanied being trapped in a small space.

They were standing in the shadow of a two-story building, and because there was another two-story building next to them, the wind whistled by as if powered by giant fans. Dana crossed her arms in front of her again to ward off the sudden chill. Hot in the sun, *freezing* in the shade. Welcome to the desert.

"Dana, you *have* to, at least if you want that prize money."

Maybe, she could put up a fuss. Tell Braden's sponsor that she just couldn't stomach climbing into a race car. But she didn't want to chicken out, damn it. A lifetime of playing it safe had led to the moment when Stewart had knocked her to the ground. The irony was, Stewart was supposed to have been the *safe* choice. Smart. Handsome. Well respected. She'd learned the hard way that a cool facade could hide a terrible side, too.

"You're looking a little less pale," Alysa said.

"That's because I'm going to do this, by gum. I don't care if I have to use a throw-up bag. From here on out I'm going to put my fears aside and do whatever crazy, irrational thing might come my way."

Alysa stopped, tilted her head a bit. "Wow. I think you might actually mean that."

"I do—" But Dana cut her words off. Alysa had suddenly stiffened, and Dana didn't need to look behind her to know who approached. She could read it in Alysa's eyes, and her body language. Her co-worker suddenly thrust back her shoulders, positioning her knockout body to full advantage. She removed her ball cap, too, and fluffed out her long, blond hair. She did everything but put herself in front of a fan, tip her head back and stick her rear end out like a poster girl.

Jeesh.

"Braden," Alysa said with a warm, welcoming smile.

And then someone else said his name, a female someone.

"Braden," yet another woman yelled from above them. "Braden James. Up here."

"Win this weekend, Braden," another lady said from the balcony.

"Call me, Braden," a woman cried. "Please! I'm staying at the Sahara Hotel."

Dana shook her head. The man was like a walking pheromone. Get him around the ladies and they were all swooning with lust.

"Is it like this everywhere you go?" Dana asked him, giving Alysa a look that told her to please settle down. She was making Dana uncomfortable.

He glanced up, waving at the group of people that had gathered. "Pretty much," he said, having to raise his voice over sudden cheers. "You guys ready?"

"Are you kidding?" Alysa said. "I was *born* ready." And the look in her eyes told Braden and anyone who was looking that she was ready to do more than take a tour of the garage. That was okay, Dana told herself. She didn't mind if Alysa and Braden ended up together.

Did she?

"Where are you taking us?" Dana asked.

I promise I won't let anything happen to you.

She believed him. In his eyes she'd seen the rarest of human emotions: empathy. He seemed to genuinely care. She wasn't quite certain what to make of that. In her experience, most men only ever cared about themselves.

"I was thinking it might be fun to take you through the tech inspection line, since we're standing right next to it."

He wore the same red shirt as before, but she noticed now that he'd tucked it into jeans that emphasized a narrow waist. Not a spare inch of fat on him, his stomach trim and his shoulders wide. This was a man who took physical fitness seriously.

"Terrific," Alysa said. "I've always wanted to see that up close and personal."

That wasn't the *only* thing Alysa wanted to see up close and personal, Dana thought. Why did that bother her? If Braden was interested in Alysa, that was great…for Alysa. Her friend would be in seventh heaven.

But the thing was, he didn't appear interested. Most red-blooded males were openly flirtatious with her coworker. She'd seen it time and again. They'd get a new male client and when Alysa walked by—bam—their tongues fell out. With her curly blond hair and quick mind, she was hard to resist. But apparently, Braden James was immune. Or maybe he was so used to good-looking women that Alysa was just another pretty face in the crowd.

"Follow me," he said.

That was it, she thought, following him toward the entrance. The guy could pick from the cream of the crop. Alysa might be gorgeous, but this was a guy who had a million acres of produce to choose from.

"Hey, Mike," Braden said to one of the white-clad officials inside the rectangular room.

"Well, if it isn't the great Braden James," the gray-haired man said, his round glasses catching the ambient light from outside so that the lenses resembled miniature headlights. He looked past Braden, his gaze settling on Alysa and then on her. "You've brought company."

"Hey, Braden," someone else said, and Dana was surprised to realize it was a crew member wearing the colors of another team.

"Barry!" Braden's eyes lit up when he spotted the dark-haired man who'd greeted him. "Long time no see, buddy."

The two did the man-hug thing, that caveman *thump-thump-thump* of the shoulder blades. "How's the wife and little one?" Braden asked.

"They're good," Barry said, drawing back with a wide smile. "When you've got a moment, stop by our hauler. I've got pictures on my laptop."

"You come here to do some spying?" one of the other crew guys said, his purple-and-pink work shirt an exact match to the car that waited to be inspected.

"Nah," Braden said. "What do I need to spy on you guys for? Y'all know my car is faster than yours."

Dana felt her brows lift. She expected the other guy to say something rude or get mad. But he just laughed.

"You ain't seen the best of us yet," the blond-haired man said.

"Yeah, sure," Braden drawled, his accent making her think of Southern gentlemen or handsome card sharks. "Tell it to my momma."

Everyone laughed then. Dana was perplexed by the good-natured rivalry between the teams.

"What'd you need?" Mike asked.

Braden redirected his attention. "I thought you could show these two ladies how you do things around here. Dana, Alysa, this is Mike. He runs things."

"Hi, Mike," Alysa said with a wide smile, holding out her hand. "I'm Alysa."

Dana's mouth nearly dropped open. Her CPA friend sounded like a one-nine-hundred operator.

It blew her away. She'd never seen her friend act so…so…*forward* before. She was a femme fatale. An eyelash-batting, flirtatious, smiling, *how-you-doin', big boy,* Mae West. "Nice to meet you, Alysa." His gaze lingered for a moment before turning to Dana.

"Hi," Dana pulled her attention from her friend. "I'm Dana. Hope we're not intruding."

"Oh, no," Mike said. "We're always happy to show people around…if we've got the time."

"Dana won the *Win A Date* contest," Braden said.

"You did?" Mike crossed his arms before he chuckled, the short-sleeved shirt he wore bunching around his shoulders. "Lucky you." He smiled. "Or should I say, lucky Braden."

"Oh, well…" Dana said, trying, and then failing, to keep from blushing. "I think it's more like poor Braden."

"I doubt that," Mike said suggestively before turning away. Dana caught Braden's gaze, her embarrassment so acute, she immediately had to look away.

"So you want to know how we do things around here?" Mike asked.

"Yeah," Alysa said. "I've always been curious."

"Well," Mike said, "we do inspections before the first practice, before qualifying and before the race. If you happen to win the pole, we'll inspect you *after* qualifying, too."

"What do you inspect?" Alysa prompted.

"We measure the shape of the car, using templates. See over there." He pointed to the odd-shaped cutouts Dana had noticed before. They were hanging on a rack. "There's different-colored templates for different manufacturers, obviously, and they're all color coded so we know the difference. We put a mark on the car so we always measure the same place each time we do our inspection." He pointed to a little black dot on the rear end of the car. "We measure the length of the car from bumper to bumper. The roof. The front end across the bumper…"

Dana listened with half an ear. Braden stood, watching Mike show Alysa around, and he didn't appear to be the least bit bored even though this had to be old hat to him. It was yet one more sign of his patience and kindness.

He must have sensed her gaze because he turned, cocking his head a bit in curiosity. "Looks like this interests you about as much as watching paint dry."

"Oh, no," she said quickly. "I was just thinking about how nice everyone is. You're even nice to each other."

"What do you mean?"

"That guy, Barry," she said, looking in the man's direction. "Have you known him long?"

"About as long as I've been driving stock cars," Braden said. "He was a teammate of mine when I first started driving on the circuit."

"And you've stayed friends," she stated the obvious.

"It's a small world when you drive in the NASCAR Sprint Cup Series. One of your best friends could go to work for a competitor at the drop of a hat. But nobody holds it against each other. It's just the way things are. Crew guys are always moving around."

"You don't mind?"

"Nah," he said, his green eyes piercing her own. "Why should I mind someone trying to better themselves?"

Why indeed, she thought, turning back to Mike and trying to pick up on what he was saying. Something about inspecting windshields. But she couldn't focus. Here was a man who didn't appear to be fazed by his fame. A man who seemed just as down-to-earth and nice as he'd probably been before he'd become a household name.

"You look perplexed," he said. "If it's about this afternoon, you could always develop a sudden illness or something."

She shook her head. "No," she said firmly. "I'm going to do it." *I* need *to do it,* she quickly amended silently. She needed to do something bold and adventurous. Something that would remind her that life was meant to be lived, not shoved into a corner and covered with dust, which was what Stewart had wanted.

Once they'd gotten engaged, he'd insisted she spend every hour with him. She hadn't minded at first, but then, not long after the ripped-dress incident, she'd insisted on going out—to a movie with friends—and he'd come unglued. Really, truly unglued. She'd been shocked, horrified and deeply troubled. Then had come the dog incident. That should have been the end of things. But, oh no, she'd given him another chance. Ironic, really. She'd lived her whole life trying to avoid men like her father, only to end up with Stewart.

"Well, all right," he said. "But if you're feeling queasy, I think I have some medicine for motion sickness out in my motor home."

She needed something a lot stronger than that. "Thanks," she said, attempting a smile. "I think I should probably take you up on the offer."

"Cheer up," he said. "We've still got an hour until pole time."

An hour? "Oh, great."

He chuckled. "Come on. I'll keep you company until then."

Which didn't settle her nerves *at all*. The thought of hanging around Braden filled her with more trepidation than the thought of climbing inside a race car.

That wasn't good. Right now she needed to stay away from men. She'd just broken up with Stewart, for God's sake. Even if she was the type to date a superstar race car driver, it'd be foolish to jump right into another relationship. No. Not just foolish. Dumb beyond belief.

Only she didn't want to stay away from Braden James. And that wasn't good. Not *at all*.

CHAPTER FIVE

HE'S A PRO. He's a pro. He's a pro.

The words were an unremitting chant in Dana's head, her eyes fixed on the track that stretched out in front of them like an unfurled roll of black carpet. Well, not really the track. They were on the strip of asphalt alongside pit road. Braden had drawn the pole, which meant she had a clear view out the front window. That was great…just great. All she could see was race track and that didn't calm her nerves. Not even close.

"You ready?"

No, Dana wanted to cry. She was very definitely *not* ready, because it was at that moment—the moment when Braden started the car and four-hundred horses roared to life—that Dana realized *saying* one would ride around a track was *way* different than actually doing it.

"Dana?" he asked, his hand clutching her knee.

That knee was presently encased in fire-retardant fabric. She tilted her head toward him, feeling like an astronaut in a spaceship thanks to the helmet she'd been forced to don.

"Ready for liftoff, captain," she said into the open mic that allowed them to communicate with each other.

Why are you doing this?

Because she needed to do something crazy. She wanted to forget for a moment how cruel Stewart had been to her on those days leading up to their wedding. Wanted to forget their last, final fight. Wanted to escape all the pain and anguish she'd felt upon realizing the man she'd loved was just like the father who'd abandoned her when she was eight and that the real Stewart, the man she'd been about to marry, was a controlling, egotistical maniac with a cruel streak a mile wide. It was working, too, because now she felt consumed by another emotion.

Terror.

Although she'd certainly felt that the two times Stewart had hit her.

"Relax," he said. Dana realized he was still clutching her knee. "This will be a piece of cake."

His voice sounded muffled, no doubt because he wore a helmet, too. But whereas his suit was red and white, hers was blue…the color of the driving school that owned the cars they sat in. Those vehicles looked exactly like Braden's real race car, or so she'd been told, right down to the sheet metal dashboard and the roll cage. A miniature camera sat directly ahead of her, the thing poised to catch every moment of the panic attack she felt building.

They rolled forward. Dana's stomach lurched.

Stop being ridiculous, she told herself. She'd survived her childhood. She'd even survived Stewart's terrible fits of rage. She'd survive this, too.

"They're giving us a few laps to warm up."

"Okay," she said, but she sounded panicked even to her own ears.

Braden must have picked up on it, because he didn't just clutch her knee again, he patted it.

"Don't you need that to drive?" She stared down at his hand pointedly.

She couldn't see his whole face, but she thought he might have smiled. At least the corners of his eyes crinkled. They were pretty eyes, she thought again.

"Only for a second," he said. Then he demonstrated how quickly he could shift gears. Dana blinked at the speed with which he worked the foot pedals. "See," he said, putting his hand back on her leg. "Piece of cake."

The car tilted sideways.

Dana gasped. She looked forward, catching a glimpse of her pale and pasty face—well, the eye and cheek portion, actually—in the rearview mirror that stretched across the roofline of the car. They'd moved onto the track.

What have I done?

There was a time, right after that horrible night with Stewart, when Dana had wanted to die. She'd been horrified by the realization that she'd almost followed in her mother's footsteps. Then anger had replaced the heartbreak. Only now, as the chain-link fence that surrounded the race track began to speed by, did Dana realize that she didn't want to die.

She didn't want to die *at all.*

"How do you *do* this for a living?" She scrambled for a piece of the roll cage, the seat…anything that would stop her from sliding to the right. Not that she had much room to move. No, the harness held her down like the belts on an operating table.

She heard a rumble in her ears, one that had no relation to the motor. He laughed.

"Relax," he said again. "We're only going about ninety."

"Miles per hour?" She turned to look at him, then immediately wished she hadn't. Through the net that covered his window, she could see the cars and RVs parked in the infield. They were streaming by at a rate best not thought about. She faced forward again, only to close her eyes.

"No. Degrees," he said with a laugh. "Of course miles per hour."

Turn three was directly ahead.

"Oh, crap," she said, moaning. "Please don't wreck, please don't wreck, please don't wreck."

He chuckled again. *Chuckled.* She was about to tell him she was not so easily amused, but then they were turning and the belts were digging, grinding, into her flesh and she was clutching the edge of her seat as hard as she could. She wanted to scream, but she couldn't get a breath out because it was all she could do to keep from hyperventilating. Then gravity eased and her eyes opened. The frontstretch loomed ahead.

"See," he said. "Nothing to it. That's as bad as it's going to get. These cars don't go very fast."

Not very fast. Was he *nuts?* This was the fastest she'd ever driven in her life.

"I think I'm going to puke."

"Really?" he asked, his concern evident. "Medication not working? Do you want me to pull over? I can do that. The race hasn't started yet."

"Would you keep your eyes on the road," she cried, pointing forward.

"Don't need to," he said. "I could do this in my sleep." He demonstrated by swishing the car back and forth.

"Braden!"

"You really gonna be sick?"

"No," she said. "Maybe. I don't know." Because it'd be just her luck to get violently ill while being filmed by a major network.

He stopped the rocking motion. "Sorry. I'm just trying to warm up the tires."

"Do you *have* to?" she asked.

He smiled. She could see the twinkle in his eyes. Miraculously, that grin helped to allay her fears.

"I kind of do." He rested his hand on top of the foam-covered steering wheel and looked for all the world like he was out for a Sunday drive.

"Terrific."

"Just relax. This is like driving on the freeway for me. It's nothing compared to how fast I usually go."

They began another turn. Dana could feel her stomach tingle. Centrifugal forces pushed her to the right and caused her head to tip. This time, with her eyes open, it wasn't as bad. Maybe it had to do with seeing where they were going, and recognizing they weren't about to wreck, or hearing the confidence in Braden's voice. Her stomach slithered back into her abdomen.

"Okay, I'm gonna warm up the tires again. Tell me if you feel sick."

She nodded, but she doubted he saw it. His attention was finally focused on the road in front of him.

"Three to go," someone said in her ear.

Three to go? What did that mean? Three more laps of feeling like a human pendulum? Three more laps until they crashed? Three more hours of this hell?

She focused forward and tried to relax so her body swayed with the motion of the car. That seemed to help. Her stomach still sloshed beneath her ribs, but at least she didn't feel sick.

"You okay?" he asked as they began to enter yet another turn.

"Fine," she choked out. The medicine she'd taken, apparently, was working.

"Just a few more laps, and then we'll be on our way."

She swallowed, her throat as prickly as the cactus that dotted the mountains around them. "Is that, ah…" She swallowed again. "Is that what whoever spoke meant when he said three to go?"

"Yeah. And it's my spotter you're hearing, Rod. He's on top of the roof, above the announcer's stand."

"Oh." She tried to focus on the conversation. "I've heard of spotters."

"Have you?" He seemed to want to keep the conversation going, too. He continued to rock the car, but gently now, and Dana was almost lulled by the motion. "What else do you know about stock car racing?"

"Well, I know that the templates used to measure the cars are color coded and that you inspect them at least three times, sometimes more if a car wins the pole."

He chuckled again. "In other words, everything you know about NASCAR you've learned today?"

"Well, no." She resisted the urge to close her eyes

as they rounded yet another curve. "I took a peek at a NASCAR guidebook while in the airport book-store."

"But you're not a fan."

She risked a glance at him. He was staring straight ahead, the bridge of his nose in profile. Even that tiny portion of his face was handsome. The man could wear a plastic sack over his head and *still* look good.

"No," she admitted. "I'm not really. Alysa is the fan. She's seen every race for the past few years."

"You've known Alysa long?"

"Nearly two years. She started working for Steele & Steele after I did—"

"One to go." The spotter's words cut her off. "They're giving the signal for one to go."

Oh, dear God.

"Roger that," Braden said, after opening the mic button on his steering wheel.

I can't do this. I. Can't. Do. This.

"And what do you do at Steele & Steele?"

"I'm a CPA."

"Really?" he asked.

"Yeah."

"So you're good with numbers?"

He was trying to keep her talking. She would have kissed him in gratitude if she wasn't strapped down like a mental patient.

"I am, yes," she said, swallowing what felt like Mount Everest. "Ever since I was a kid in school."

"That's great. I suck at math."

"Oh, yeah? That's too bad. I love crunching numbers."

Dana's heart rate started to escalate. They were entering turn three. That meant—

"You ready?" he asked.

"No," she moaned.

He glanced over at her.

"Keep your eyes on the road," she cried.

That deep rumble sounded in her ear again. "Dana, trust me, you're going to love this."

"I'm sure that's what plastic surgeons say to their patients just before they stab them with long needles."

Laughter sounded once again. "Trust me. There won't be any needles involved in today's race."

"Unless you wreck," she said, her voice sounding high and panicked again. They were coming out of turn four.

"I'm not going to wreck, and even if I did, you're surrounded by the best safety features NASCAR has to offer. You'll be fine."

They were speeding up. The sound of the engine grew louder. Things started to vibrate that hadn't vibrated before. She resisted the urge to close her eyes.

"Okay," he said as they exited four. "Just sit tight. This'll be over before you know it."

Yes, especially if they wrecked.

Dana gave up, closed her eyes. She knew that wasn't smart. Closing her eyes meant she became aware of every sound: the whine of the transmission, the chatter of the sheet metal; the hum of the tires, a hum that grew louder, and then louder still.

"Green, green, green," echoed in her ears.

Her eyes sprang open.

"Hang on."

To what? she wanted to ask. She wore gloves—fire retardant. To be honest she'd been looking for a solid handhold since the moment she'd climbed into the frickin' car.

Sunlight arched off something to her right. She could actually feel a beam of heat against her cheek. She glanced toward the source.

Mistake.

A car tried to pass them. "Jay-suz," she cried.

"Relax," Braden said again. "He's not *that* close."

"Yes, he is. And aren't you worried that…" She tried to swallow again. "I don't know, that maybe one of the Joes you're racing might do something stupid?"

"Actually," he said, sounding as calm and collected as a college professor at a lecture. "The only people allowed to bid on this deal own vintage stock cars. They race on a regular basis. They're seasoned veterans."

"Vintage stock cars?"

"Yeah," he said, beginning another turn. "It's not uncommon for teams to sell off some of their older race cars once they're no longer competitive." Dana could not believe he sounded so matter of fact.

"They fetch big dollars on the open market. There's a big group of men who buy the cars, race them, restore them, even show them. Frankly, I've always thought it was a way for wealthy businessmen to pretend they were race car drivers for a few minutes, but, heck, if it raises money for a worthy cause, I'm all for it."

"Well, I think one of those businessmen might be about to run you off the road."

"No worries. I was just letting him think he could catch me."

Their car lurched forward suddenly, and Dana was unable to hold back a gasp.

"It's the guy behind me I'm worried about," Braden said. "Lance Cooper is on my ass."

What? She looked back, or *tried*. The headrest wasn't really a headrest at all. More like a vise. Dana was unable to do more than glance left and right.

Bam.

"Aggh," she cried as the car lurched forward. But the funny thing was, she didn't get nervous…she got *angry*.

"Putz," Braden said nonchalantly.

"Doesn't he know this is an exhibition race? For charity," she added, trying to spot the idiot in the mirror.

"Sure he does. But it's still a race. He also knows I'm not going to get out of his way."

Bam.

"He did it again," Dana said, outraged.

"Yeah. I'm really getting tired of it."

She tried to look behind her again, which was silly because she knew she couldn't. But then her gaze caught on the rearview mirror. "Holy…" She straightened up so she could see better. "He's right on your—"

"I know, and I think it's time to do something about that."

"What?" Her heart beat so hard she could feel it rattle her ribs. But she wasn't as panicked as she had been before. It was the anger she felt, and something else, something like…

Excitement.

"Watch," Braden said.

"Watch what?"

He checked up. Her seat belt dug into her shoulder. She yipped in surprise.

"Ha," she heard Braden say, which made her look in the rearview mirror.

Lance was gone.

She stretched her neck left and right, trying to figure out where he'd disappeared to, asking, "Where's he at?" a moment later, not because she was worried, but because—

Could it be?

She had started to enjoy herself.

"In the wall."

"What?" She attempted once again to turn around. She would have liked to have seen Lance Cooper wreck.

"Well, not really in the wall," Braden said, meeting her gaze in the rearview mirror. He smiled at her, eyes crinkling, and that smile made her feel so…so…weird inside. "He just lost it a little bit. Ended up in the marbles. It'll take him a while to catch back up."

"You mean, we're out in front all by ourselves?"

"We are. For now."

"What do you mean?"

He met her gaze, but only for a split second because he was busy keeping his focus ahead of him, or behind them, or to the left and right of them. She noticed then that his pupils were constricted, adrenaline reducing the black irises to twin pencil points. He was on a natural high, his body stretched taut, hands no longer clutching the steering wheel carelessly.

Like a warrior in battle.

Hubba hubba.

Dana!

"I'm going to have to slow down pretty soon."

"Slow down? Why?" she asked. "Don't slow down."

Did you just tell this guy not *to slow down?*

Yes, she admitted. To her complete and utter shock she realized she'd begun to *enjoy* this. Or maybe it was just that out in front seemed safer.

"You sure you want me to keep going?"

She blinked. "I, ah... Yeah, I guess so."

He released the steering wheel and, for a split second, rested his hand on her leg. "That's the spirit."

Then she received her second shock of the day. When he touched her she felt... She looked out the window, trying to put a name to it.

Turned-on.

"This isn't good," she mumbled to herself. Because it was crazy, absolutely crazy to feel any type of attraction to anyone after everything she'd just been through.

"Sure it's good," he said. "It's great, but unfortunately, I'll have to slow down sooner or later. Wouldn't want someone to pay twenty-five thousand dollars only to lose."

"Huh?"

He smiled, she could see it in his eyes. "Yup. That way, they'll want to do this again. I'll lose a thousand races if that means raising money for my favorite charity."

Braden would never hurt her, she realized in that instant. He was so different from Stewart that she wondered how she could have ever thought Stewart was right for her. Braden was not the type of man to hit a woman. Not the type to be verbally abusive. He was a genuinely nice guy.

For some reason, that scared her more than anything else.

CHAPTER SIX

SHE'D GROWN QUIET.

He wondered what he could say to keep her mind off the race. He hated to see her upset.

He liked her, he thought, checking his mirrors.

She'd been through hell. A blind man could see that. Yet here she was, doing something brave. He admired that.

He checked his mirrors once again.

Time to slow down.

The race would end in less than ten laps and the nearest competitor was six car-lengths away. He would need to do some serious backpedaling to allow the guy to catch up.

"You're slowing down, aren't you?" she said the minute his foot came off the accelerator.

Aha, so she hadn't lost the ability to speak. "Yup. We'll be done pretty soon."

She nodded, and Braden noticed she no longer gripped the edge of her seat like a teenager on an amusement-park ride.

She had gumption.

Earlier, when she'd come out of his hauler in her blue-and-white fire suit, she'd been as frightened as a lost child. Clearly, she'd have been happier not to have to climb inside a race car, and yet she'd done it. When they'd started out, she hadn't succumbed to full-on panic. That told him a lot about her personality. She was a fighter. He respected that. He was a fighter, too. His childhood had ensured that. He'd been raised in foster homes, and he'd seen more than his fair share of physical violence. Perhaps that's what attracted him to her. He recognized a kindred soul.

"What are you doing after this?" he found himself asking.

"Huh?"

He glanced in his mirrors yet again, reducing his speed even further. After practicing at one-hundred-and-fifty miles per hour in his NASCAR Sprint Cup car, going ninety felt like driving through a school zone.

"After we're through here, what are you and Alysa doing tonight?"

"Ah, well..." He saw her glance in the side mirror, saw her brows lift as the nearest car began to catch up. "We'll probably go back to the hotel. Have dinner." He saw her frown. "If I recover my appetite, that is." But her words stemmed from sarcasm, not fear. He could hear the difference now.

He found himself smiling again. Yeah, he liked her, and it surprised him how much he wanted to see her again, contest or not. Usually he wasn't quite so overt in his pursuit of a woman, and yet he found himself saying, "I was just sort of wondering if I could take you to dinner."

"Excuse me?" Her pretty gold eyes met his own. Granted, she stared at him through the mirror, but he could still see shock and dismay in their shimmery depths. They were the most amazingly expressive eyes.

"I just thought it might be good, you know, for the two of us to get to know each other a little better before our big date."

That sounded lame even to his own ears. He very nearly winced, would have, too, except one of the Joes was now on his rear. He tried to spot Cooper or Peters, but they were hanging back, too. They knew how the game was played.

"You mean, like a predate?" She spotted the driver on his tail, too. Her gloved hands dropped to the edge of the seat again, gripping the sides, but her knuckles weren't white this time.

"Yeah," he said, slowing down even more. At this rate he'd have to go backward to let the guy catch him. *Come on. Hurry up.* "Exactly."

"Outside high," his spotter said.

Finally. "Roger that," Braden said.

"Is, ah…" his spotter hesitated. "Is your setup going away?"

"Um, yeah." Braden was tempted to wave at fans as he drove by. "That's right. My tires appear to be worn."

"Uh-huh," Rod answered drolly. "That's what I thought."

"Your foot's off the accelerator," Dana said.

"Is it?" he asked, the catch fence around the grandstands turning into less of a blur with each drop of the tachometer. "So is it a date?"

"Huh?" She frowned. The skin above her brows bunched up right where it met the edge of the helmet.

"Me taking you out."

"Not a good idea."

"Why not?"

She glanced in the mirror again, her body edging up the back of the seat when the blue car began to duck down in front of him.

"Clear," his spotter said.

And that's the way you pass a famous race car driver, Braden thought. 'Course, you have to pay twenty-five thousand for the privilege. But Braden didn't mind losing. He was having fun. It was nice to ride around the blacktop without the pressure of winning or getting the pole. It gave him the chance to scope out the race track, too. He might not be in his normal race car, but he could still feel minor ripples in the track's surface. Get a sense of which lines were the smoothest to drive. How badly the marbles felt up high. All of that information might help tomorrow.

"Dana?" he prompted.

"Do you mind asking me that question again when the race is over?"

He studied her almond-shaped eyes in the mirror. She wouldn't meet his gaze. "Actually," he said, throwing caution to the wind. "I do mind. I like you, Dana. I like you a lot. But if you want me to wait until the race is over…"

He popped the clutch; his car immediately stumbled.

"Braden!"

He ducked to the inside of the track.

"What's the matter?" his spotter asked.

"Tranny," Braden immediately answered. "Think I blew it." He glanced over at Dana. "Happy now?"

THE WORLD BEGAN TO slow. Or maybe not. Maybe it was still spinning. Dana couldn't tell. She was finding it hard to breathe.

So, is it a date?

His words repeated in her head, over and over and over again.

"You just threw the race," she said.

"Yup," he said, shutting off the engine as the other cars roared by in rhythmic order. *Zoom. Zoom. Zoom, zoom, zoom.* "But I was going to do that anyway."

"Yeah, but—" She didn't know what to say. He couldn't seriously be asking her out, could he? And he really hadn't just blown his transmission just so he could hear her answer.

Had he?

"Well?" he prompted. "Won't you go out with me?"

They'd come to a stop, which, since they were sitting at the bottom of a race track, meant the car felt jacked up on the right side. The other drivers zoomed by, making their car rock with each passage. Braden's hands moved, and Velcro ripped as he pulled off his gloves then tossed them onto the dash. Next he touched his helmet, lifting his head a bit as he undid the strap beneath his chin. In a practiced move, he pulled the thing off, his cheeks creased like crumpled paper from the pressure of the foam inserts.

"That feels better," he said, tugging the tape off his ear, tiny earphones adhering to the sticky surface. He brushed a hand through his dark hair. "You should take yours off, too. We might be here awhile."

She didn't want to take her helmet off. She wanted to keep her armor on.

She found him attractive.

After everything she'd been through, she'd turned into a Braden James fan-girl.

What the heck was wrong *with her?*

"If it's all the same to you, I'd like to keep mine on," she said.

"Huh?" He cupped his ear and tipped his head toward her.

With the helmet on, her words were muffled. "I said I want to keep my helmet on," she all but yelled.

"Huh?" he asked again, leaning even closer.

She jerked her gloves off, then the helmet. "There," she said at the same time she pulled her own earpieces out.

"Why don't you want to go out with me?" he quickly retorted with a twinkle in his eyes.

"Personal reasons," she snapped back.

"You look cute with your hair all messy, by the way."

"Do I?" she asked sarcastically.

"Your face is red, too," he added. "But I'm not sure if that's because you're mad at me, or because you're hot."

"I need to get out of here." She eyed the net to his left. Her side didn't have a door, just a space for her to crawl out of, but she wasn't about to shimmy out of a window and onto a race track.

Trapped. Nowhere to go. She should be close to panic.

But she wasn't.

Oh, her heart was racing, all right, but not because she feared being confined in a small space.

"I don't know any woman who'd look as pretty as you after tugging off a helmet."

She looked away, her ponytail slinking over one shoulder.

"Was he jealous when other men looked at you?" Braden asked softly. "Is that why he hit you?"

Dana gasped, faced him.

His eyes were soft and full of compassion. "You have a bruise beneath your jawline. You've done a good job hiding it, but when you pulled off your helmet, I could tell right away what it was. Don't worry," he said with a gentle look in his eyes. "Your secret's safe with me."

She sat there, unable to speak, unable to form a single thought, because sluicing through her brain were the words *he knows*.

"I just hope you hit him back."

She found her voice hiding in a frightened corner of her mind. "Oh, *that* bruise," she said with a false note of bravado. "That's nothing. When I was getting in my car, I bumped my chin on the corner of the door."

He didn't say anything, at least not right away. "Uh-huh."

She held his gaze, determined to brazen it out. "I can really be a klutz sometimes."

"Dana," he said softly. "I've seen that kind of bruise before. And it didn't come from a car door."

Run. That's all she wanted to do. Get out of the car and run. But she couldn't. She looked away out the front windshield, anywhere but at him.

And spotted the tiny camera.

She stiffened. "I don't want to talk about it," she said with what she hoped was a firm voice. "I bruise easily, that's all. It was my own fault. How long will we be sitting here?"

Ignore his words. Deny the problem. How many times in her life had she watched her mom do the same thing? What the hell was wrong with her that she would so closely follow in her mother's footsteps? Granted, Dana didn't deny that Stewart had hit her. Not to herself, at least. And she wasn't about to give Stewart another chance. She'd warned him after the dog incident that if he hit her again, she'd leave him. Well, he'd hit her again and she'd left him. She still hadn't recovered, and yet for some crazy reason she was *attracted* to Braden. Had she lost her mind?

"Not long," he said softly. "Here comes the wrecker."

She glanced in the rearview mirror, saw a yellow truck pull up behind them.

He knows.

And you *denied it.*

Actually, she'd denied it because of the camera

pointed in their direction. And, really, she thought, he only *suspected*. That was a long way from knowing.

He knows.

But as long as she kept denying it, she'd be safe. Wouldn't she? Because even though she was a long way from Stewart now, she couldn't forget his words.

Tell anyone and you're dead.

God help her, she believed him.

CHAPTER SEVEN

"DANA, WHAT HAPPENED?" Alysa asked, brought up short by the sight of her friend all but jumping out of the tow truck that pulled Braden's broken race car behind it. "Are you hurt—"

"Be right back," Dana said, brushing past Alysa so fast her ponytail looked like it belonged on an angry horse.

"Where are you going?" Alysa called.

But Dana ignored her. Alysa watched as she jumped over the concrete barrier that stood between the track and pit road.

"Wow. What happened to her?" she asked no one in particular.

"She's running away."

Alysa stiffened, recognizing that voice. What NASCAR fan *wouldn't* recognize that voice? Braden James. Damn. She got goose bumps just knowing he stood nearby.

She steeled herself to turn and face him. Wouldn't do for him to see—again—what a starstruck fool she was. "Running away from what?" Alysa asked, trying hard to sound nonchalant. "She looked upset."

They were on pit road, something Alysa didn't think she could ever get used to. The grandstands had started to fill, the NASCAR Nationwide Series due to race in a few short hours. They weren't scheduled to attend that race, but they seemed to be in the minority. Already, she could hear the steady drum of media helicopters flying overhead, could see people staring down at her from across the blacktop, many of them no doubt wondering who the blonde was talking to Braden James.

That would be me, she silently told them. *Alysa Anderson. Me!*

"I saw the bruise," Braden said.

Every lustful thought vanished from her mind.

"The bruise?" she asked, her mind whirling.

"I've seen that kind of mark before," he said, switching his helmet to his other hand. "Plus, Dana has bruises on her arms that I noticed earlier. One of my foster moms would get the same kind of marks when she went toe-to-toe with my foster dad."

Alysa couldn't speak. But, really, what could she say? She'd been sworn to secrecy, and since she happened to work with both Stewart and Dana, she didn't want to rock the boat.

"Did she press charges?"

Braden James—*the* Braden James—stared down

at her with concern in his eyes and she wanted to melt, just melt.

But the concern was for Dana. Damn it, it wasn't fair. Dana didn't even know anything about NASCAR. Well, okay, maybe that wasn't true. She knew a few things. Still, Dana and Braden seemed far from a perfect match, especially since Dana had just broken up with Stewart.

"I don't know what you're talking about," she said.

She covered for Dana because she'd promised and because of her job, and because she worried what Stewart might do. If Stewart was brought up on charges, he might lose his mind. Plus, the publicity might look bad for the firm, maybe even cost Alysa her job if she were embroiled in the whole mess.

Braden James stared down at her for three heart-pounding seconds. "I think you do, Alysa."

"Do you think I might be able to peek inside one of your race cars?" Alysa asked, trying to change the subject.

"Tell her she should go to the police," he said, "if she hasn't already. If she doesn't, it'll just happen to someone else. Assuming she dumped the bastard. That is what she did, isn't it?"

He sounded like he really cared. Maybe he did. Everyone knew he'd grown up a ward of the State. His journey from foster homes to NASCAR was the stuff of Sunday-night movies.

"Look, Braden," Alysa said carefully. "I'd really like to stand here and chat with you about... things." She looked hard into his eyes. "But I... can't."

Their eyes locked—and, oh Lord—Alysa forgot to breathe for a moment. She watched as he pulled on the front of his driving suit, the Velcro tearing apart with a crackling rip. He wore a white tank beneath—she could see it—that and a sprinkling of chest hair.

"Can we go look at your race car?"

His lips pressed together. He looked about to reply when someone called out, "Braden. They're ready to interview you in the media center."

Alysa looked over at the woman who'd spoken, her red shirt proclaiming her a part of Braden's race team, her pretty green eyes curious as she stared at them.

"I'll be there in a second," he called, his gaze never leaving Alysa's. "I want to go out with Dana."

Alysa had to work to keep her mouth from falling open.

He really *was* interested in Dana.

"Not like that," he said, his gaze flicking between her and the woman in the red shirt. "I just want to talk to her some more. Maybe see if I can help her."

So maybe there was hope. But on the heels of that thought came the realization that she would have to talk fast to turn his attention away from Dana.

She would do it, but not for her own benefit. No. Dana was in no way, shape or form ready to start dating someone new. Alysa would be doing Braden a big favor by trying to distract him. "She doesn't need any help."

"You're covering for her."

"Braden," the other woman called. "We really need to get going."

"Don't make excuses for her," he said, edging away. "Not if you consider yourself a friend. I'm going to call you later, to talk about this." He began to walk backward. "Give your cell-phone number to Elizabeth here."

"Braden," she said, the word barely audible. But he was already gone, rushing toward his next task like a man on his way to fight a fire.

"You can give me your number now," Elizabeth said, amusement shining in her eyes. "I have a pen and paper right here."

"Great," Alysa said. When she talked to Braden, it wouldn't be about Dana. "He sure is persistent."

"That he is," the petite blonde said. "One thing I've learned about Braden, once he gets an idea in his head, he's like a dog with a bone."

"That's what I'm afraid of," Alysa muttered, because she couldn't deny one thing.

Deep down inside, she was afraid of Stewart, too.

"I DON'T WANT TO TALK about it," Dana said the moment Alysa opened their rental car door. She'd thought she'd be alone out here for a little while, at least.

"Well, tough." Alysa slid into the driver's seat next to her. "We have to talk."

Dana had removed her fire suit, but she still felt warm in her T-shirt and pants. "Do you know what he asked me?" Dana said, leaning forward in agitation. "He asked me where I got the bruise."

"I know," her friend said, her blue eyes full of concern. "He asked me the same thing."

"He did?"

Alysa nodded.

Dana leaned back and closed her eyes, groaning. "I can't *believe* this. What the heck kind of famous person asks a perfect stranger about a bruise?"

"Someone who's a really nice guy," Alysa said breathily.

Dana groaned. "What if someone from the network reviews that tape? What if they get curious about my bruises, too. What then?"

"It might get messy for Stewart," Alysa said. "And you don't want that."

Alysa didn't know the half of it. She hadn't been on the receiving end of Stewart's threats. She hadn't read the text messages Stewart had sent.

If you turn on me, I'll turn on you.

Dana shivered.

"I'm going to talk to him. Tell him to leave me alone."

"And then what?"

"I'm going to fly home, tonight if possible, and forget this ever happened."

"Dana," Alysa said. "You can't do that. It'd look suspicious. Plus, what are you going to do about the *My-Lovematch* date in a few weeks?"

"They can't force me to go on that date, Alysa. Not if I walk away from the prize money and everything else, and at this point, I'm willing to do that."

"Dana—"

"I'm not going," she interrupted her friend. "And I'm not doing that interview with the reporter, either. I'm going back to the hotel where I hope to forget this entire day."

"You can't do that," Alysa said. "Not without first telling Braden's sponsors."

"*You* tell them. I can't face him again."

"Yes, you can. And honestly, if you don't, I have a feeling he'll track you down. He seems hell-bent on ensuring you're all right." Alysa almost sounded disappointed by that. "Best to talk to him face-to-face. Get it over with. Reassure him that you're okay and that you're not running scared. The last thing you need is for Braden to drag Stewart's name into all this."

"You don't think Braden would really come after me, do you?" Dana asked.

"He might. He seemed concerned enough."

"Damn."

"Just go find him. I'll go check out the souvenir haulers. It'll take two seconds for you to talk to him."

Dana shook her head in resignation. "Fine. I'll talk to him, tell him how I feel, ask him to take care of things with *My-Lovematch*. But after that, the closest I hope to get to the man is watching him on TV."

FINDING BRADEN JAMES PROVED to be a lot more difficult than it had earlier in the day. He wasn't in the hauler that carried his race car, at least not according to one of his red-clad crew members. Frankly, the garage seemed pretty devoid of activity. *None* of the drivers were around. Yeah, there were race fans—she had a feeling there would always be race fans—but the cars were tucked in, many of them covered, a few still being dutifully worked on by their crews.

Frustrated, she was about to go back to the car when her cell phone rang. Her brows shot up when she noted the caller ID. An out-of-state area code.

Could it be… "Braden?"

"A little birdie told me you're trying to track me down."

The breath seemed to leave her. Funny how that always happened around him. "I've been trying," she said, attempting to sound nonchalant. "But you're MIA."

"I'm in the NASCAR Nationwide Series garage. They're getting ready to race over here. Did you do your interview with that reporter yet?"

"Ah, no." She was supposed to meet the woman in about an hour, but not if she convinced Braden to let her out of the deal. "Can I meet you over there? Is that okay?"

"Of course," he said. "The race isn't due to start for a couple hours. I'm just hanging out until I have another appearance. Come on over."

He gave her directions. Dana's anxiety tripled with every step she took. The two garages were connected, and it was an easy task to make her way over. But whereas the NASCAR Sprint Cup Series garage was a study in architectural elegance, the NASCAR Nationwide Series garage seemed more low-key. Single-story white building. Gray-and-white paint scheme. But the simplicity of design was really the only difference. The crew members dashing around looked just as tense as their NASCAR Sprint Cup brethren. Dana would have known there was a race in the works just by the expression on everyone's face.

"Excuse me," she said, turning sideways to slip through the crowd outside the garage. "I need to get through."

The crowd parted. Someone said, "And there she is."

Braden.

"Sorry," Dana muttered, nearly stepping on someone's toe.

"Come on in." He motioned her into the building. It just took a moment for her eyes to adjust. She eyed the car Braden stood in front of, it's light blue-and-white paint scheme matching the colors of a nationally recognized brand of long-lasting fireplace logs.

"Dana, this is Ryan," Braden said, nodding at a dark-haired kid who stood next to him. "He's our NASCAR Nationwide Series driver. I was just giving him a pep talk."

Dana attempted a smile, though it had probably come out looking sickly. She was as nervous as a cat at a vet clinic. "Hi, there," she said.

"Ryan's going to be the next big thing. You should stick around and watch him drive. You'll be blown away."

The kid smiled bashfully, but Dana could tell he was thrilled with Braden's generous praise. "Hi, Dana," he said. "Nice to meet you."

He was so young, Dana thought. Or maybe it was only the light blue ball cap that made him appear to be in eighth grade. Clearly he idolized Braden, whose red ball cap did not in any way make him look like a boy.

"They're about to push his car off for tech inspection. You want to walk with them or do you want to stay here?"

"I'd, ah…I'd really rather stay here. I need to talk to you. In private."

Or as private as was possible with what seemed like a million people peering at them. She had a feeling they'd stay put while she and Braden talked, most of them no doubt hoping for an autograph.

"Well, okay then," Braden said with a smile. "Ryan, I'll talk to you on the radio tonight if I don't see you beforehand."

"Hey, thanks for all the tips," Ryan said. "Seriously, Mr. James, I really appreciate the time you've spent with me."

"Anytime," Braden said.

"Can we clear a path?" asked one of Ryan's crew members, the crowd outside the garage instantly parting to let the car through. Braden gently clasped her elbow, turning her away from the crowd that called his name when they realized he was about to leave.

"Come on," he said. "They won't follow us once they realize I want some privacy."

"How do you deal with it?" she found herself asking. "It's nonstop."

"It's part of the job." He guided her around multicolored toolboxes utilized by various race teams. "But we can slip out the side door here and no one will see us."

They did exactly that, and Dana blinked against the sudden blast of sunshine that hit them like a heated breath.

"Where are we going?" she asked.

"This way," he said, moving her toward the parking area.

She felt her stomach bunch up, found herself swallowing to alleviate the unpleasant sensation. "Look, Braden, about what happened earlier—"

"You hungry?" he asked. "Did you have any lunch today?"

"Well, I…" No, now that she thought about it. She'd lost her appetite once she'd learned she was going to ride in a race car. "Not yet," she admitted. "But I really don't think I could eat."

"No? I'm starved." He tugged his ball cap down low as they passed a group of fans. "Come on. Let's grab some munchies."

Did she really have a choice? Apparently not, because he was moving forward again at a speed that made talking nearly impossible.

"Why are you going so fast?" she asked.

"Because if I slow down, we'll be ambushed by race fans. Come on." He dashed toward an opening in the chain-link fence that kept people out of the garage. "I have a friend that I give parking passes to. She keeps a supply of food handy. Watch it," he said, pulling her toward him and away from an approaching golf cart.

Now that they'd left the garage they were on an area of blacktop that served as the main road from the garage to the infield tunnel, and a stream of motorized vehicles trekked in and out of the track. To their left, row after row of cars glistened beneath the sun. Beyond that lay a multitude of motor homes, each of them flying the colors of their favorite driver, the standards snapping to attention thanks to the ever-present wind. Up ahead and to her right, she could see an area where more motor homes were parked. That appeared to be where they were headed.

"Don't you have a fancy motor home here or something?" she asked, curious despite herself. "I could have sworn Alysa told me that."

"Yeah, usually I do." He said, letting go of her elbow. "But not here. It's not cost effective to have someone drive it out to the West Coast, so I end up giving my passes away most of the time. That way I have a place to escape. And to eat."

Like now, she thought, wondering if he worried someone might recognize him.

"You'll like Belinda," he said. "I call her the Martha Stewart of NASCAR. She always puts out the most amazing spread. Stacks a whole table with food. It's great."

They quickly made their way toward a more private entrance, one with a security guard out front.

"She's with me," Braden said, flashing a card he'd

tucked beneath his red polo shirt. He didn't even give the guy time to respond, just walked right past as if he owned the place.

The security guy must have recognized him because all he did was lift a hand. Her escort didn't seem to notice.

"Normally," Braden said, "this type of parking area is packed wall-to-wall, but it always looks deserted here."

"Deserted" meant two absolutely massive bus-type things and a few normal looking motor homes. "Wow." She eyed one vehicle in particular, its black paint scheme turned silver by sunlight. "Do you have one of those?"

"Yup," he said, his attention fixed on something to his right. "That's Belinda's place." He pointed toward a motor home that was more low-key than its fancy cousins. Its two-tone brown-and-white exterior was similar to a million others she'd seen on the road. "She keeps things simple."

"Simple is good," Dana said, thinking she'd never be comfortable in one of those rolling mansions. She might not be wealthy, but she was a CPA. She knew what they cost—nearly two million dollars.

"Hallelujua," Braden said when they reached the bug-spattered grill of the motor home. "I smell food."

"So do I," Dana said.

They rounded the front of the diesel pusher. Beneath a canopy stood a table, and just as Braden had promised, it sagged beneath the weight of several bowls, a couple metal pots, foil trays and one massive cooler.

"It looks great." Strangely enough, she was suddenly hungry. She hadn't had a healthy appetite in weeks, ever since she'd realized she couldn't go through with her wedding to Stewart. Too bad it'd taken her so long to work up the courage to tell the man. Maybe he wouldn't have hit her a second time if she hadn't waited until the day before their wedding to break things off.

And maybe she should stop making excuses for him... Mom. You should have broken up with him after the first time.

"Braden?" someone cried, the door to her right opening. "Braden James, is that you?"

"It's me," Braden sang back, a silly grin coming to his face as he set down a lid that he'd just pulled off a pot, the scent of oregano filling the air. Good thing he set it down, too, because a heavyset woman just about knocked him over when she rushed into his arms.

"You big geek," she said. "Where the heck you been?"

"Whoa," Braden said, rocking back. But he hugged her, too. It was a coming-home-type embrace, the kind exchanged by extremely good friends. The woman's plump arms flexed with the force of her welcome. Dana found herself looking away.

"I thought for sure we'd see you for breakfast this morning," the woman said.

"Couldn't. You know how it is. They have me going twenty different directions. This is the first break I've gotten so, of course, I came right to you."

"Well, good," Belinda said, nodding so sharply the knot she'd twisted her brown hair into slipped sideways. Dana worried it might come undone. "I'm glad you made it."

Braden picked up a spoon and dove into the pot. He didn't use a plate. He scooped up a big mouthful of noodles and sauce, which he quickly shoveled into his mouth. "Mmm," he said. "Just as I remember."

"And who's this?" the woman asked, turning to Dana with wispy tendrils of loose brown hair floating around her face. Dana noticed then that Belinda wore a Braden James shirt, one stretched taut across her generous chest.

"This is Dana," Braden explained between chewing. "She's the contest winner."

Belinda's smile grew. "Really? What a lucky girl you are, then. Braden is the kindest, sweetest man I know. You'll have a great time on your date."

"Yeah, but she doesn't want to go out with me," Braden said, scooping another mouthful.

"Braden, get yourself a plate." Belinda turned to

Dana. "What does he mean you don't want to go out with him?" The skin on her forehead bunched up, she lifted her eyebrows so high. "You crazy?"

Braden grabbed a plate, but not before a grin stretched from earlobe to earlobe. "I know," he said. "Can you believe it?"

"Girl," Belinda said. "What's wrong with you?"

I've got a broken heart, horrible taste in men and I certainly can't trust a good-looking race car driver, no matter how kind he appears to be.

"Actually," Dana said to Braden, "I wanted to talk to you about our date."

"Uh-oh," Braden said. "I had a feeling this was coming. It's why I brought you to Belinda. I'm hoping she can talk some sense into you."

"Huh?" Dana asked.

"You got any garlic bread?" he asked after serving himself some spaghetti.

"It's over there."

Braden's smile grew before he turned back to Dana. "I scared you earlier when I asked you out, didn't I?"

"You asked her out?" Belinda asked. "As in out-out? Not the contest thing?"

"Yup," Braden said. "But she turned me down flat."

Dana looked between Belinda and him, wondering if she should deny it, maybe get Braden away from a woman who so clearly adored him and who was so very obviously on his side. But she had a feeling whatever she said to Braden would be repeated to Belinda later anyway. Might as well spill it now.

"I just think this whole thing is a bad idea, and I'm not talking about the date-date. I'm talking about the *Win a Date* thing, too. I'm not…I'm not…" *Ready.* "A good contest winner. I worry that I'll mess this up for you, especially if I have to give that interview."

And what happened to turning over a new leaf? a little voice asked. *What happened to doing something bold and adventurous?*

She *was* turning over a new leaf, she thought. She just didn't think going out with a man so soon after her breakup with Stewart was a good idea.

"Dana," Braden said. "You're not going to mess things up. I just want to go out to dinner with you. That's all."

And when he did he'd ask her about her bruise again, Dana would bet, and *that* she didn't want to talk about, not with Stewart's ominous threats ringing in her ears. "I'm sorry, Braden," she said with a shake of her head. "I just think I should bow out of the whole thing."

Belinda's eyes narrowed, her focus darting between the two of them as if she could see right into their minds. Dana couldn't be sure, but she thought Belinda's gaze snagged on her bruise, too. Terrific. More questions.

"You know what?" Belinda said. "I've got an

idea. Why don't I take Dana inside while you finish eating, Braden."

"Inside?" Dana said. "Oh, no—"

"That sounds like an excellent idea," Braden said. "I'd love to absorb some rays."

Bologne, Dana wanted to say.

"Perfect." Belinda preempted Dana's protest. "You sit out here and enjoy yourself while I give Dana a little pep talk."

"What," Dana cried. "A pep—"

"You can talk to him about the contest *after* Braden has a full stomach." Belinda tugged her toward the trailer. "He has to keep up his strength. I bet this is the only thing he'll eat all day."

"You're probably right," Braden agreed, snatching up some salad.

"But—"

"No ifs, ands or buts," Belinda said. "Let him eat. Trust me, you'll get a lot farther with him if he has a full stomach."

Dana could tell Belinda wasn't going to take no for an answer.

"Come on," she said, tugging harder. "It's a lot cooler inside. I can't believe how hot it is when you're out of the wind."

Dana followed in the woman's wake despite herself. Of course, Belinda had taken her hand and so it was impossible to pull away without being out-and-out rude.

"You sit over there," Belinda said, pointing toward a bench seat beneath a tiny kitchen table. "You want a soda or something?"

Dana sank onto the seat and when she glanced out the window to her left, she saw Braden outside, his head intersected by vertical blinds. He was helping himself to more spaghetti.

"No, thanks," Dana said. "I'm fine."

"Scotch and whiskey?"

"I don't drink."

"Honey," Belinda said a few seconds later, plopping a can of pop down in front of her. When Dana looked up, a pair of knowing brown eyes stared down at her. "Anyone with a bruise like yours is *entitled* to drink. Hell, it's what got me through the tough times."

CHAPTER EIGHT

DANA IGNORED the soda can.

"Don't look so surprised." Belinda took the bench seat opposite her and snapped open the lid of her own can with a loud *pop*. "Braden told me about it."

"Told you what?"

"About the mark on your neck. And the ones on your arm."

"It's from a car door," Dana said. "I accidentally hit myself."

Belinda eyed Dana for a long moment, one of her fingers stroking the side of her drink. "Did Braden tell you how we met?" she asked.

"No," Dana choked out, wishing she'd thought to wear long sleeves. But she hadn't thought anyone, especially someone like Braden James, might recognize how she'd gotten her bruises.

"I came through his autograph line two years ago, in Fontana. I'd driven all night to meet him, slept in my car, waited for hours before the event so I'd get a good spot. I was too sleep-deprived to care if he noticed the black eye my ex-husband gave me when I refused to stay home and cook for his friends. Most of it was covered by my sunglasses, anyway, or so I thought. Braden was a big star. All he'd do was sign the autograph book I put in front of him. I was wrong."

I once had a woman come through my line with a black eye...

Dana knew in that instant *this* was the woman.

"He took me aside. Boy, that was a big surprise, let me tell you. One minute I was plopping down an open book and the next he was asking his fans if they'd mind waiting a minute. I had no idea what he was talking about until he asked me to come around the back of the souvenir hauler. I thought maybe I'd won a special prize. You know—fan of the day or something. But when he got me alone he removed my glasses and asked me who the hell had hit me." Belinda shook her head, her eyes losing focus for a moment. "I will never forget how I felt when he asked me that question, nor the instant denial that rose to my lips."

Dana looked away, she *had* to look away. This woman could be her mother.

This woman could be her.

But it wasn't the same thing, she reminded herself again. Her reasons for denying Stewart's abuse were entirely different.

Weren't they?

"He *knew*," Belinda said after taking a sip of her drink. "And still, probably much like you, I brushed it off, told him it was no big deal. I'd bumped my head on the coffee table, I'd told him. But Braden wouldn't let the matter drop. He's like that. When he asked me if I had kids, I said yes, not knowing where he was going with the question. But then he asked me what I would do when my husband started hitting them, too. I don't know why his words struck me like they did, but suddenly, I wanted to cry. Ralph hadn't hit our kids...yet, but I suppose in hindsight it was my secret fear. I'd left them with my sister that weekend because I'd been concerned he'd take his anger out on them, and the realization that this man, this perfect stranger who'd I'd idolized for years, *knew* the truth..." She leaned back. "Well, it was just too much. But Braden..." she smiled at the memory "...he just patted my back, told me it'd be all right."

Belinda's gaze sharpened again, and Dana had to resist the urge to look away.

"That man has the biggest heart of any person I know. He helped me get my life back. I don't know what man in your life did that to you—" she pointed to Dana's chin, then to her arms "—but I know Braden well enough to recognize that he's found another wounded bird. What *you* don't know are his reasons for wanting to help you."

But in that, Belinda was wrong. Dana knew. Of

course she knew. She might not know much about NASCAR, but she'd heard the story from Alysa.

"He was abused himself," Dana said.

"He was. And if you've figured that out then you've probably reasoned out why he's so obstinate about these things."

Dana didn't say anything. What could she say? That Belinda was right? Her ex *had* hit her. Not once, but twice. And that she'd been a fool to let him back into her life after the first time? It was true. She had been a fool.

"I won't let him near me again," Dana said. "He's out of my life now." Well, sort of. But she was quitting on Monday, so he was almost out of her life for good.

Dana expected triumph to light Belinda's eyes after that confession. Instead all she saw was incredible sadness. "Yes, but the next woman he hits might not be so lucky."

Dana looked away, out beyond Braden to the grandstands. How many women who would sit there tonight were like her? Frightened, too scared to tell the truth?

"I'm afraid to press charges," she admitted, and it felt good to do so.

"Did he threaten you?"

"He did," she said, her stomach tightening to the point that it bound up inside her like a broken motor.

"But don't they always?" It was more than she meant to say, and she bit her lips to stop from saying anything else.

Belinda didn't miss a thing. Her eyes narrowed. "He really did a number on you, didn't he?" she asked.

The things she knew about him. The things he'd said. Hands grabbing her arms. Her head jerked back. Sudden, blinding pain when she'd been knocked to the floor. Memories she fought so hard to keep barred from her mind.

"I think Braden is done eating." Dana started to rise.

Belinda's hand stopped her. "Don't go. I don't mean to pry. Honestly, I don't. It's just that since I left my ex-husband, I've done what I can to help others who're in trouble."

"He wasn't my husband."

"Fine. Terrific. That makes things easier. My point is that I don't want to scare you away. I want to help. Just like Braden helped me two years ago. He's like a son to me now. I'm almost ashamed to admit that I used to think of him in romantic terms." She rolled her eyes. "But he's a friend now. A *good* friend. I would do anything for that man, and like he said, he brought you here in the hopes that I could talk some sense into you."

Dana shook her head, her heart starting to pound all over again. What would life have been like for

Dana if her mother had had someone like Belinda to guide her? Would she have continued to drift in and out of one bad relationship after another? Would Dana's life have been a little more stable? Would her mother have married someone like Roger earlier in life?

It was hard not to wonder.

Belinda stared at her questioningly.

"It's not like that, really," Dana said. "I already took care of the matter and now it's over. There's no need to worry about me, although I appreciate your concern."

This time, she didn't let Belinda stop her from standing. Only when her hand touched the door did her breathing begin to ease.

"Is he dating someone else?" Belinda asked.

Dana froze.

"That's usually what happens, you know. You break up with the bastard and he moves right on to the next victim."

Dana didn't say anything.

"If you'd been through this before you'd know that it's true."

That was the problem. Dana did know it was true. Damn it all. But if she were honest with herself, she was also wishing the problem would just go away.

How noble of you, Dana.

"He'll do it again," Belinda added. "To another woman…unless you stop him."

Dana felt ill. "I better go. My friend Alysa's probably wondering what happened to me." She straightened her shoulders, forced herself to look Belinda in the eyes. "Tell Braden I really think it's best he tell his sponsor I can't do what they've asked, including the interview today. Tell him I'm sorry."

Coward!

She stepped outside.

But was she really a coward? Or was she being sensible? Stewart frightened her. Look what had happened when she had pushed him into a corner. How much worse might things get if she pushed him again?

"Where you going?" Braden asked when her feet touched the ground.

"It was nice meeting you, Braden," she said. "I had a great day."

"Hey, wait," he said, setting down his plate.

She kept walking. She needed to clear her head, to think.

"Wait," he cried out again.

Was she doing the right thing not reporting Stewart? Or was she being like her mom?

"Dana!"

"Please." She turned back to Braden and held out her hand. "I need some space." She was horrified to realize she was on the verge of crying.

He drew up short, his expression one of concern. But then his gaze softened and she realized he truly was a remarkable man. "Yeah," he said softly. "I suppose you do."

She sucked in a breath.

"I'll call you later?"

Would he? she wondered, listening for his footfalls as she walked away.

God help her, she *wanted* him to call her.

And *that,* she realized, was the most troubling thing of all.

CHAPTER NINE

"Sooner or later you'll need to tell me what happened with Braden," Alysa said as they drove back to their hotel.

Dana nodded. Sooner or later. Just not right now. Right now all she wanted to do was study the Las Vegas skyline through the windshield.

"Are you worried Braden will cause trouble for Stewart?"

Dana shook her head. "He doesn't even know who Stewart is."

"No, but with his money, he could find out."

"He wouldn't do that." Dana leaned against the seat. Would he? She scanned the clear blue sky, as if hoping to pull the answer out of thin air, but all she spotted was a tall skyscraper with a saucer-shaped hotel on top.

"Look," Alysa said. "I know you don't want to hear this, but you should be careful about what you say. Braden is a celebrity. You don't want to drag him into your private life."

That was true, and something she hadn't considered.

"I promise not to drag him into anything."

"Good." They'd stopped at a traffic light and Alysa turned toward her. "Look, I know Stewart's an ass, but this could get really ugly if Braden gets involved."

"I know." Dana took in a deep gulp of new-car-scented air, and her fingers clenched the leg of her pants. Funny that just hours before she'd been doing the same thing while taking the ride of her life in a race car.

They drove on in silence until the next light, when Alysa asked, "How are you going to cope with Stewart at work? It's bound to be awkward. People will take sides. It won't be easy."

"I'm going to give notice."

"Really?" Alysa asked, sounding surprised.

"Do I have any other choice?"

"No. I suppose not."

The situation was unfair. *She* hadn't done anything wrong.

Sure, there was a part of her that worried she'd come too close to following in her mother's footsteps. But Stewart had been the one who'd flirted with her. Stewart was the one who couldn't control his temper. Stewart was the bad guy. Yet *she* was the one who had to quit. The one who would have to face discomfort if she decided to press charges.

Alysa must have sensed that Dana needed peace and quiet. The only sound to reach her ears was the low-edged murmur of the radio until they reached the Las Vegas Strip. The amusement-park-like sounds ebbed and flowed from most of the casinos. Their own hotel had a theme of pirates, complete with a giant ship, booming guns and a wannabe Captain Jack Sparrow. The sound of cannons firing had driven Dana nuts last night.

"We're still going out tonight," Alysa pronounced.

"I don't think—"

"No ifs, ands or buts," she said, sounding just like Belinda. "You need to get out. Hell, *I* need to get out. I didn't bring you here so we could lock ourselves in a hotel room. Let's enjoy the rest of the weekend. You know, we never did have lunch and I'm starving. Let's get an early dinner right now—that way we won't have to eat at the track."

Dana didn't have the heart to tell Alysa she wasn't really hungry. "Sure. That sounds great."

But two hours later, they left the restaurant. Dana had eaten very little. Even sitting in front of tortilla chips and salsa hadn't stirred her appetite.

"You really have to perk up," Alysa said in dismay as they pulled into a multilevel garage, the kind with tiny parking spots and a narrow access road. "Especially before tomorrow."

"Speaking of that," Dana said, relieved when they

finally found a spot, since they'd nearly been hit while circling for a place to park. "I'm not going to the race tomorrow."

"What!" Alysa jerked her keys out of the ignition. "Are you *nuts?* I mean, I can understand not wanting to go into the garage. That's fine. I'll go into the garage by myself. But not go to the race? Don't be ridiculous."

Dana shook her head and slipped out of the car, saying across the rooftop, "I might try and catch an early flight out. That way you can enjoy yourself without me bringing you down."

Alysa frowned and held her gaze. "You're not bringing me down. I just think you should go tomorrow. You paid a lot of money for your ticket. Don't let it go to waste. Stare at Braden from a distance. Surely that won't be so bad, especially if you're looking at him from the rear," she said with a wiggle of her eyebrows.

Dana knew Alysa was right. There was no reason to go back home when all that waited for her was an empty apartment. She was just longing for peace and quiet…and to be where she wasn't reminded of Braden James everywhere she looked.

Reminded of something she couldn't have.

"Look," Alysa said, apparently unable to stand the silence any longer. "Let's enjoy ourselves tonight. Go to a bar. Maybe see a show. Live it up a little. It'll be fun."

"All right," Dana said.

They'd reached the pedestrian bridge that stretched from the parking garage to the back of the hotel. Casinos, Dana had decided, were like giant mazes, with numerous slot machines acting as giant balls of cheese designed to lure clueless mice into tossing away their money. She'd come to the conclusion that management didn't really want guests to find the main elevators, either. They made it difficult in the hopes that customers might get bored and play a few slot machines. The darn thing was hidden in the farthest corner of the hotel. Her feet were killing her by the time they reached the security desk stationed near the bank of elevators.

"Room cards," a burly man said.

"Do you have yours handy?" she asked Alysa.

"No," she answered. "Do you?"

Dana smiled as they both started fishing about. Other guests were being asked to do the same thing and they were soon in a small crowd of people rooting around in purses and pockets. That must have been why Dana didn't hear that rich baritone voice. It blended with the ding-ding-ding of electronic machines and the cries of big winners.

"What's the matter?" it asked again. "Lose something?"

Her hand froze, the colorful piece of plastic she'd been searching for forgotten.

"Oh. My. God," she heard Alysa say.

Dana finally looked up…and into the eyes of her ex-fiancé.

CHAPTER TEN

"WHAT THE *HELL* are you doing here?" Dana cried.

"What do you *think* I'm doing here." Stewart's dark eyes honed in on Alysa. "I'm here to bring you home, which I wouldn't have to do if *Alysa* hadn't kidnapped you."

"Excuse me?" Alysa asked. "I didn't kidnap her. I had an extra ticket. She took it. End of story."

Dana had known this would happen—that they'd be face-to-face again one day soon. She'd even convinced herself that when it finally *did* happen, she'd be so full of self-confidence there wouldn't be room for fear.

She was wrong.

The man standing in front of her wasn't the Stewart she'd fallen in love with. This was someone different. Someone mean and ugly who now inhabited Stewart's tall, fit body. Someone who wore his tailored, black silk suit with a white dress shirt beneath—open at the collar, of course—and had a strong jaw, masculine lips, stylishly messy black hair. It was all Stewart...and yet, not.

"Is there a problem here?"

Dana glanced at the security guard who'd spoken. "No," she said, clutching her fear and stuffing it into a mental garbage can. "Nope. No problem. My *ex*-fiancé was just about to leave."

The security guard whose name badge said "Ben" stared at the three of them. "Sir," he asked. "Are you a guest here?"

Stewart narrowed his eyes. "I'm with her," he said, nodding in Dana's direction.

"Ha." It felt good to speak out. So good, in fact, that she faced him confidently.

When Stewart spotted her bravado, she saw the same flash that had always scared her before and that had culminated in his violence. The darkening of his irises that made her mouth dry. The brackets that framed his mouth and made her heart pump double-time. The tension in his face as he stared down at her.

Dear old dad had looked at her mother in the exact same way, she suddenly realized.

The security guard wasn't stupid. He must have picked up on what was going on. "Step away from her, sir. I'm armed."

Dana's eyes never left Stewart's. She would not let him intimidate her. Not again. Frankly, after braving Braden's race car, nothing seemed frightening anymore. "Alysa, maybe you should go on up to our room."

"No problem," Alysa said.

"I'll be up in a second," Dana called, somewhat disappointed by Alysa's easy acquiescence. But this was, after all, between her and Stewart. "What I have to say won't take more than a couple minutes."

"Hanging out with the office slut now, are we?" Stewart asked, trying to turn her away from the security guard.

Dana jerked back. "She's not a slut," she hissed. The security guard rushed forward, but she stayed him with a hand. "And you're hardly in a position to cast aspersions on someone else's character."

"Now, honey," he said in a soft, soothing voice, glancing at Ben. "No need to be rude. I've gone to a lot of trouble to meet with you here. I've been waiting on that damn uncomfortable chair over there for nearly four hours."

"Well, you can go on sitting there. I've got nothing to say to you."

"C'mon," he said, stepping in front of her. "Aren't you curious as to how I found you?"

"No." They'd switched positions and now she was facing Ben. She shot the security guard a look, one that reassured him she was okay…for now.

"It wasn't hard," he continued as if she hadn't spoken, his lips curling into a smile. "All I had to do was shed a few tears and every woman in our office was willing to tell me where you were. They practically bought me a plane ticket."

That's the way it would be, she admitted, because people didn't know the truth. Well, except for Alysa. But everyone else thought she and Stewart had quarreled. They had prewedding jitters. They hadn't seen the ugly bruise that had sprouted on her jaw, the same bruise she'd tried to cover up all weekend. Nor had they seen the other bruises—the ones he'd left behind the first time he'd hit her.

"Go home, Stewart," she said. "I have nothing to say to you." She tried to step around him.

"Wait." He blocked her path. "I need to talk to you."

"Get out of my way."

"Not before we talk." She could tell he was losing patience. Well, good. She'd lost patience the moment she'd seen him standing there.

"Talk? About what? You must think I'm crazy if you expect me to listen to anything you have to say." It took every ounce of courage she possessed, but she took a tiny step toward him. "After what you did, and what you said afterward. Forget it. You're the one who's crazy."

She briefly glimpsed surprise in his eyes, followed by confusion, but it was quickly masked by what could only be called rage. "Don't tell me you really believe that I'm some kind of wife beater or something?"

Dana felt her jaw sag for a moment, the same jaw he'd hit seven days ago. The same jaw he'd struck one time before. Worse, the words exactly echoed ones she'd heard before—from her father's mouth. That angered her all the more. "Why, yes, Stewart," she said, "that's exactly what I believe."

He let out a snort of disbelief. "Don't be ridiculous."

She stood there for a few moments, stunned speechless by his denial. "Whatever." She shook her head. "I'm wasting my time." She knew that from experience. "You're wasting your time, too. Goodbye, Stewart."

"Dana," he said in warning.

"Have a nice life, Stewart. I'll have someone come by and pick up my stuff. I know you'll let them in, you being such a nice guy and all."

"Dana, don't do this," he said quickly. "Do you know how poorly it'll reflect on us if we call the whole thing off? I have clients that were invited to our wedding. Do you know how humiliated I felt when I had to call them last weekend and tell them you were nowhere to be found?"

"Probably about as humiliated as I felt when you nearly knocked me out. Again. After everything I told you about my childhood. After crying on your shoulder when you kicked that dog. After admitting to you what it'd been like to grow up watching my mom get beat up by my dad. And then to go and hit me. *Again*—" She lost the ability to speak. She was too torn apart to do anything other than try not to cry in front of him.

The pain.

Lord help her, it hurt so bad to think that he could do that to her.

"Damn it, Dana." He bent toward her. She stopped herself from leaning away just in time. "I'm not playing anymore. I want to marry you and I'm prepared to forgive you for running away from me like you did."

Prepared to forgive...

Once again, he'd rendered her speechless.

"I mean, sure, we have some issues, but it's nothing we can't work out. I'll even admit that I have a bit of a temper, but I can control that."

With or without the use of physical force? Dana wanted to ask. "We're finished, Stewart. I'm not coming back. If you're worried about what people will say, I suggest you take a leave of absence. Or move out of state."

"Dana—"

"I'm through with you. Now leave me alone."

She didn't expect him to grab her.

"Hey!" called Ben, the security guard. "Unhand her."

"Let me go," she growled with a glare that'd do a tigress proud. But inside she was falling apart. It all came back to her—her childhood, the memory of the time he'd struck her before. The raised fists—both his and her father's. The pain that'd blossomed along her jaw started to ache all over again. It took everything she had to stand there and face him.

"I'm not done talking to you," he growled.

"Oh, yes, you are." Someone wedged himself between them.

Only it wasn't the security guard.

Dana gasped, but not because Stewart's grip had tightened, which it had. She gasped because her rescuer finally came into focus.

Braden had stepped between the two of them.

"You've said everything you need to say." He lowered his voice. "And you are *never* going to touch her again."

BRADEN STARED INTO THE eyes of the man who'd hit Dana and had to fight—had to literally clench his fists—not to lift one of his hands and punch the asshole right between the eyes. He looked at Dana. She might have assumed a brave stance, but he recognized the terror in her eyes.

"Who the hell are you?" the ex-boyfriend asked.

"Someone who knows what a loser you are." Braden squared off with the man.

"Do you know him?" asked the security guard.

"Yes," she said. "He's my friend."

"Well, you and your friend need to take this outside."

"Braden," Dana implored. "Just ignore him. I'm okay now."

He shook his head. He knew what to do. God knows, he'd been in this position before…too many times before.

"Leave her alone," Braden said. "It's over."

"Who the hell are you?" the man asked.

"Like she said," Braden said, "I'm a friend."

"Hey, you two," the security guard said. "I'm asking you guys nicely. *Take it outside.*"

"Wow, Dana," her ex said. "You didn't waste any time, did you?"

"It's not like that," Braden said.

"Yeah, right."

"Stewart, just go away," Dana said.

"Not until I talk to you."

"We've already talked," she said. "Braden, let's go."

"Is he your boyfriend?" Stewart called. "If so, you must have really bad taste, *Braden.*"

"That does it." Braden turned back.

"Braden, no—"

"Apologize," Braden said.

"Or what?" Stewart taunted.

"Or I'll make you."

"Yeah, right."

"And unlike Dana here, you won't get a chance to knock me to the ground."

"I didn't knock her down," Stewart said.

"Uh-huh. That bruise just sprouted itself on her chin all on its own. And the ones on her arms, too."

"I didn't hit her."

"Then where'd the bruises come from, asshole?"

"She fell."

"Yeah, into your fist. I'm going to see to it that the police know. And your friends, and your family. *Everyone.*"

"You wouldn't dare."

"Try me." Braden stepped toward him.

"Back off."

"What's the matter? Afraid of being hit *first* this time?"

Stewart's fist came out of nowhere. Braden almost ducked left, remembered Dana stood behind him, and ducked right instead. Stewart's knuckles connected with the side of his head, but it was a glancing blow. No big deal. And now it was his turn to knock the guy's teeth into the next building.

He never got a chance.

Faster than Braden would have thought possible, security was on him. More than one gray-and-black-clad officer surrounded the two of them. One moved in front of him, and Braden's balled up fist dropped back to his side.

Braden stepped back and turned to Dana. She looked stunned.

"You okay?" he asked, surprised to note his hands shook. His heart pounded, too, the adrenaline rushing through him the same as on race day.

"Fine," she said, watching as they contained her ex.

"Hey," someone cried. "You're Braden James."

Braden glanced at the person who'd spoken.

Oh, crap.

Not here. Not now.

There would be no escaping it. The hotel was packed with race fans. After his name was said, he saw more than one person turn his way. Damn it. He might have been able to deny it, except he hadn't even bothered to change out of his *My-Lovematch.com* corporate shirt.

"Hey," he said with a nod, then turned back to Dana.

"He hit you," Dana said.

"Yeah, but it didn't hurt."

"You okay?" the security officer asked.

"Fine," Braden said.

"Mr. James," said a woman who didn't look much older than him. "Can I have your autograph?"

"Look, guys," he said to a gathering group of fans. "I'm kind of in the middle of something. Can I have a moment or two?"

"You somebody famous?" the security guard asked.

And that was why he never took himself too seriously, Braden admitted. Not everybody knew his name, and that was fine with him.

"Sort of."

"Are you kidding?" said a fan. "This is Braden James. He's a famous race car driver."

Oh, brother.

"Then let's get you guys out of here," the security guy said, pointing toward the elevators.

"Can I have my autograph?" the same woman asked.

"In a minute," Braden said, not looking up from Dana's ex. Their eyes connected. Stewart glared. His eyes caught on Dana like a grappling hook. He looked ready to hit her.

Try it, Braden told the man with his gaze.

You're next, the man's eyes projected.

Yeah, right, Braden went to Dana and placed an arm around her back. She stiffened but didn't pull away.

Stewart snickered.

Braden wanted to smash his fists into the man's face. If he hadn't been surrounded by security he probably would have, too. Bad enough the guy had hit her before, but to come after Dana like this.... Braden shook his head, knowing the emotional fallout from the incident would be felt for weeks to come.

Damn it.

"Come on," he gently urged. "Let's get out of the way."

"Your friend is right," the security guard said. "Mr. James is attracting a crowd."

"Mr. James, will you sign my T-shirt?"

"Can I get a picture?"

"You think you're going to win tomorrow?"

"Not now," the security guard announced to the growing crowd. "I'm taking Mr. James upstairs."

Thank God, Braden thought. He'd been in this type of situation before. Once word got out that NASCAR driver Braden James was in the house, people would go nuts. Didn't matter if they were a Braden James fan or not. A NASCAR driver was a NASCAR driver, and in their eyes, he was a prize. They'd be asking for his T-shirt next.

"Let's go." He gently clasped Dana's hand this time.

She looked up at him, and he was glad to see some of the color had returned to her high cheekbones. She squeezed his hand.

"It's okay," he said soothingly. "We'll deal with this upstairs."

She nodded, and it shocked Braden how much he wanted to pull her into his arms, to tell her everything would be fine. But he knew better. In her present frame of mind, touching her was out of the question.

"What are they going to do with him?" she asked the security guard.

"They'll take him outside. Suggest to him that it's in his best interest to leave. It's up to Mr. James here what happens after that. If he presses charges—"

"I'm pressing charges."

"Braden, no," she said. "If you do that it'll only cause a fuss."

To hell with it. He cupped her face with his hands. "I don't care." He leaned toward her, wanting to kiss her so badly. It shocked him just how much. "I'm not afraid of your ex-boyfriend. All I care about is you."

CHAPTER ELEVEN

ALL I CARE ABOUT IS YOU.

Dana blinked up at him, shocked into speechlessness. "Braden, I—"

Really wish you'd hold me.

The words popped into her head from nowhere. "I don't want to embroil you in my affairs."

"Too late." He smiled down at her gently. "If pressing charges is what it takes to keep that bum away from you, I'll do it." His right thumb stroked her cheek and Dana had to fight the urge not to close her eyes and lean into him.

You just met him.

But that didn't seem to matter.

"What if the media finds out?"

He glanced around them at the crowd with a wry expression. "Chances are, that's already out of our hands."

When the press got wind of what'd happened, they'd crucify Braden. He'd be just another reckless celebrity brawling in public. Unless he pressed charges. If he did that, it might take the wind out of everyone's sails, especially when combined with eyewitness accounts of Stewart hitting him first.

The security guard rushed them up to the casino's third floor suite. The offices looked more like they belonged to a metropolitan police department than a Las Vegas casino.

"You can expect LVPD to take over once we're done here, Mr. James. Since you're filing charges."

"Braden, you really don't have to do that," Dana said again.

"Yes," he said with a reassuring smile, "I do."

She supposed he did.

From that point forward, they were put through the reporting process with a speed and efficiency that told Dana just how commonplace such occurrences were.

"We'll call you if we need anything else," Ben said when they were done.

Dana nodded, then couldn't help but ask, "Braden, are you absolutely certain you want to—"

"I'm certain."

"Well, I think it's the right thing to do," Alysa said, all but batting her lashes. Dana had called her to tell her they'd been delayed, and once Alysa had learned Braden James was with her, there'd been no stopping her from coming downstairs. Not that Dana expected anything less. It'd become apparent during the past half hour that Alysa was gunning for Braden's attention. Good for her. She *should* make a play for him. That's what Dana wanted for her friend.

Wasn't it?

"Don't you have your NASCAR Nationwide Series race to go to?" Dana asked.

"I do," he said, glancing at his watch. "It'll be starting in a little while."

"Aw, you mean you aren't going to join us for dinner?" asked the woman who'd just stuffed herself with a burrito an hour before.

"No, I'm afraid not."

"Too bad," Alysa said.

"Actually," he said, "I was hoping to speak to Dana alone."

"Oh." Alysa glanced between the two of them, her eyebrows slowly lifting. "Well, um, maybe tomorrow, then."

"Maybe," he said.

Dana felt the oddest sensation as she stared into his eyes.

Alysa smiled and waved goodbye. "I'll see you upstairs."

Dana nodded, but she couldn't meet Alysa's gaze. A few seconds later, the private elevator at the end of the long hall binged open, and Alysa gave Braden a wave before she left.

"I have a feeling I'm going to get a lecture from her later on," Dana announced.

"Why?"

"I don't think she likes that I've dragged you into this mess."

"Well, it's too late now. I'm dragged."

"Just why *have* you embroiled yourself?"

She could see a mark, one near his ear. Not a bruise. Not yet, but it would become one. Damn that Stewart.

"Actually, I didn't come here to save you from would-be attackers."

"No," she said with an almost-smile. "I suppose not."

"I actually have some bad news."

Uh-oh. "What?"

It was his turn to look uncomfortable. "The reporter, she, ah, she reviewed the in-car footage while putting her story together. *All* of the footage, and I'm afraid she's put two and two together about you and your ex. She called my PR rep and asked all kinds of questions. Now, with what just happened downstairs, I'm even more worried. If word gets out I was involved in a fistfight, things are likely to get hairy. I mean," he said quickly, "I don't care what anybody says, don't get me wrong. I'm used to the media spinning things into headlines. But I figured you might not be and so I thought I should tell you. You know, face-to-face…you know, in case you change your mind about doing the interview."

The elevator binged once more, and Dana looked down the hall in time to see the doors open again. Someone in a suit nodded, but when the man's attention moved to Braden, his eyes widened. Damn. Did everyone know who Braden was?

"What kind of spin do you think they'll put on it?"

"Well, the woman asked my PR rep if I'd ever championed abused women before."

Abused women...

Oh, crap.

"I'm not a victim of abuse. Stewart hit me. A couple times. But that was it. It's why I left him. Why I'll never go back to him."

"Good for you," he said gently.

She'd never met a man with such kind eyes.

"Why would she care?" Dana found herself asking. "What difference is it to her if I have ghosts in my past?"

"Who knows? It might be a slow news week. She might be a champion of abused women herself. I've stopped trying to understand reporters and their hidden agendas. Just be prepared. I think she really wants to talk to you."

Dana shook her head. "This is nuts." After what had just happened downstairs, their troubles were far from over. But it wasn't really *her* the press would be interested in. They'd sling their arrows in Braden's direction. Misbehaving sports celebrities were big news, and she would bet some enterprising reporter would spin what'd happened earlier into something it wasn't.

"I don't want to talk to her," she said. She didn't want *any* of this. How had winning a contest turned into something so complicated?

"I understand," he said.

And he did. She could see it in his eyes.

"I'll do what I can from my end," he said. "But I can't promise she won't track you down for a comment or two."

Dana nodded, knowing he would do his best for her. He was that kind of guy.

"But there's another, more important reason I needed to talk to you. I know by the way you rushed away from the track this afternoon that you're really hesitant to go on any sort of public date with me, but I talked to my sponsor today and they asked me to ask you." He shook his head wryly. "Actually, they told me to *beg* you. Please reconsider."

Instantly, "no" came to mind. But, really, after what had just happened, bailing out on their date would only make things look worse.

Celebrity Date Winner Cancels Night Out After Brawl With Fiancé.

It wouldn't matter that Stewart was her *ex*-fiancé. Someone would get that wrong, maybe even intentionally, and turn their confrontation into something tawdry and lewd.

"Let me think about it," she said. "I'm not promising anything right now. But let me think about it."

"Okay," he said with a smile. "Good. I'll take it. You can let me know tomorrow."

She nodded. He glanced at his watch. "Guess I better get going. Thanks, Dana, for being such a good sport."

He was the one who had been a good sport. "Thank you, Braden," she said. "I hope what happened earlier doesn't cause you too much trouble."

He chuckled softly. She liked his laughter. Soft and friendly and completely natural.

"Oh, it probably will," he said. "But it's nothing I haven't dealt with before."

BRADEN JAMES INVOLVED In Casino Brawl.

Dana groaned.

Someone had, indeed, tipped the press. A quick scan of the newspapers in front of the casino's main gift shop revealed that almost every major headline was the same sort. Most merely teased it, the bulk of the story in the Sports section. A few actually gave it space on the front page. She scanned one of those articles, her legs feeling heavier and heavier the more she read. They didn't mention Stewart's name—probably because no one had put it together that the man Braden had hit was connected to her—but they didn't need to ID Stewart to make Braden look bad.

"Damn it." She stepped back so fast she nearly bumped into someone else perusing the rack of papers. "Sorry," she murmured, keeping her head down as if she might be recognized as the woman involved in the brawl. Ridiculous. The article she'd just read had made no mention of her. Rather, the sports reporter had chosen to focus on the deplorable lack of morals that seemed to plague most major sports celebrities these days.

They'd gotten it all wrong.

She turned away, blindly blending in with a crowd of merrymakers on their way to an early breakfast. They were race fans. She could tell by their colorful shirts and high spirits, and for a moment Dana wished she could be as lighthearted and trouble free. But life had never been that way for her.

She'd clawed her way to the top of the corporate ladder. Putting herself through school on her own dime. Working two, sometimes three jobs. Getting ahead a little bit at a time. But just when things began to look up, she'd met Stewart.

Right after they'd gotten engaged, she'd watched him hurl his neighbor's dog through the air. His actions had filled her with so much horror she'd gotten physically ill. Then, later, when she'd tried to explain to Stewart that an animal sniffing one's lawn was no reason to send it sailing through the air—*with one's foot*—Stewart had descended into a rage that had left her bruised and battered for the first time. She should have left him right then and there; she'd known it was over. Instead she'd stayed with him, tried to forgive him. Looking back on it, she'd probably been scared to break things off, scared of what he might do to her, which was why she'd waited until the last minute to end it.

Now look at the mess she was in.

Her cell phone rang, the tone blending in with the bings and bleeps of the slot machines. By the time she realized it was ringing, she had to dive to get it, not even looking at the display as she answered.

"Tell your boyfriend he better not press charges."

Her stomach turned.

"He's not my *boyfriend*. And Braden is free to do whatever he likes."

Where was Stewart? Was he watching her? What if he was right behind her?

She turned suddenly, somehow convinced that's exactly what was going on. But there were only more race fans, this time a husband and wife.

"Tell him if he doesn't do as I ask, I'll go to the press. After reading today's headlines, I'm certain they'll want to hear all about the man who stole my fiancée from me."

Dana's stomach flipped. She stopped walking.

"Don't be ridiculous, Stewart. I hadn't even met Braden James until this weekend."

"The press doesn't know that."

"I won a date with him. Hundreds of people saw it happen."

"Rigged."

"It was not," she all but yelled, catching the eye of a young couple walking by. She forced a smile in their direction.

"Maybe it was. Maybe it wasn't. But I'm looking at a headline right now, one with your friend's picture, and I'm thinking he's probably hoping this whole thing will go away."

"A thing *you* started."

"Tell him to leave me alone, or it *won't* go away."

She shook her head, thinking about everything she now knew about Stewart, all the secrets she would never tell. "I don't know what I ever saw in you."

In that moment she finally understood how it was that her mom had stuck it out with her dad for so long. It wasn't out of love. It wasn't out of loyalty. It was out of fear and sadness and a blind hope that maybe, just maybe, he might change.

"I'm only trying to protect my reputation," he said a moment later.

She understood that now. "You should have thought about that before you took a swing at him." *And at me.*

"This is our *life* he's messing with, Dana. *Our* life and *our* future."

"*We* don't have a future."

"Once you get your head on straight you'll see that's not true."

She couldn't believe he'd say such a thing, not after everything that'd happened, and especially not after yesterday.

Thank God she'd been stronger than her mother and had broken it off with him before it was too late.

"It's over, Stewart," she said as patiently as she could. "As far as Braden is concerned, you'll have to talk to him yourself."

Preferably in court, she thought, slamming closed her phone. Her hands shook. Truth be told, she was worried. First Stewart had followed her to Las Vegas and now he was making more threats.

Tell him to leave me alone.

She would have to tell Braden.

Her phone rang again. She glanced at the caller ID this time.

Stewart.

She flinched, entered a code to permanently block the number, then promptly shut off her phone. But she couldn't block him on Monday when they both went back to work. She'd be forced to deal with him face-to-face again.

Unless she quit over the phone.

No, she couldn't do that. She *refused* to do that. Stewart would not disrupt her life any more than he already had. She would be brave.

But practical. She'd install new locks on her doors. Maybe change her phone number, too, and the sooner she did it, the better. A restless night had convinced her of that fact. Stewart was here. In Vegas. If she left now, before *he* did, she could do all the stuff that needed to be done before he returned to town. She didn't want to believe that he would hurt her again, but she didn't want to be foolish, either. That meant missing the race.

She couldn't believe how much that disappointed her.

Just yesterday she'd been talking about skipping out, but now, if she were honest with herself, she wanted to see Braden.

Even though that wasn't a good idea.

Better to say goodbye now before this thing between them spun even further out of control.

Unfortunately, she didn't have his number. When she checked the received calls on her cell phone, his name came up restricted. But Alysa knew how to reach him. She'd told Dana last night that he'd given Alysa his information in case she ever needed it. It looked like that time was now.

"Are you kidding?" Alysa said when Dana confronted her on her way to breakfast. "I'm not going to let you call him this morning. He's got a race to run this afternoon."

Dana had gone back to her hotel room, and her suitcase was now packed and standing by the door. Dana might not be going to the race, but Alysa was. Her friend would watch Braden make his laps from pit road while Dana left to go back home.

"What's the race got to do with Stewart's threats?" Dana asked, genuinely baffled.

"Dana," Alysa said, hands on her hips. "A driver is like a finely tuned instrument. If you give them bad news just before a race, you might ruin the symphony."

Dana felt her brow scrunch together. "You think Stewart's threats are a bad note?"

Alysa nodded, and whereas before her expression had been concerned, now it turned serious. "You need to control the situation, Dana. By dragging Braden into this you might damage his career. Sponsors are weird about the reputations of their drivers. You can't let this thing get out of hand."

Too late, Dana almost chirped. But she didn't feel up to telling Alysa about today's headlines.

"Believe me," Dana said. "I know how serious the situation is, which is why I should tell him about Stewart's threats."

"I'll tell him," Alysa said. "And it won't matter if I give Braden your message after the race."

Maybe. Maybe not. Dana wasn't going to argue

the point. But as she glanced at her suitcase sitting by the door, she suddenly felt consumed by guilt. The situation was all her fault, and she was skipping out on her duties as the contest winner. Now she was giving Alysa the job of delivering her bad news. That didn't seem right.

But there was something else that concerned her, something unexpected.

She didn't like Alysa interacting with Braden.

Unbelievable. And silly, she told herself. She had no business feeling possessive about a man she'd just met, especially with Stewart still in the picture.

Stewart. The man who was trying to control her life. Still.

"You don't have to deliver the message."

"I don't?"

"I'm going to the race." She wouldn't let Stewart scare her away. Maybe it was foolishness on her part to think there might be something between her and Braden. Maybe she really had lost her mind. But she couldn't deny that whenever she was near him she felt attraction. And something else, too, something more important.

She felt safe and sheltered and cared for.

"I've changed my mind," Dana said. "I'm going." *Time to be brave.*

"Dana, are you sure that's a good idea?"

Dana found herself wondering if Alysa's concern was genuine.

"I'm going," Dana said again. "And I'm going on that date with Braden, too."

Something flittered through Alysa's eyes, something like dismay followed quickly by shock.

"I just hope it's not too late to tell Braden I've changed my mind."

"SHE'S HERE," ELIZABETH SAID, entering the lounge without so much as a knock.

"Hey." Braden jerked up his fire suit so his PR rep wouldn't see him half-naked.

"I almost fell over in shock when I saw her walk up to the hauler," Elizabeth said, ignoring his protest. "She's here and she wants to talk to you."

"Who's here?" he asked, pressing the Velcro opening closed.

"Dana Johnson."

"What?" Braden asked, fire suit forgotten. "Are you sure?"

"Sure I'm sure. I recognized her from yesterday. And, boy, am I ever glad to have her here. We need to do some damage control and we could sure use her help."

Dana was here. In the garage. Braden couldn't believe it.

"Does she want to talk to me now?"

Elizabeth nodded. "She does. If you have time. Do you?"

"You know I do." Had she seen the headlines? They'd be impossible to miss. But he'd told her yesterday he'd deal with the fallout. He'd been doing exactly that all morning. Things would die down eventually. But she didn't know that.

"Tell her to come on in."

"You've got five minutes before you have to start on morning interviews," Elizabeth said. "After that you're booked solid."

"I know, I know," Braden said. "Same old, same old." It was like this every race morning. Interviews first. A sponsor appearance or two later. Meetings after that. Driver intros just before the race. Although with the weather being what it was, things might not happen that way. They were predicting rain by the start of the race.

He checked his reflection in the mirrors that hung on the room's back wall. Not out of vanity, just to make sure his driver's suit was sealed straight, and that he didn't have any smudges on his face, and that his hair wasn't sticking out.

And why did he care about his appearance, anyway?

He had no time to analyze the thought because suddenly Dana was there, standing behind him. He could see her framed in the doorway, her eyes scanning the leather couch to her right and the cabinets and desktop to her left. Braden turned toward her, feeling sheepish about being caught staring at his own reflection.

"Hi," he said.

"Hi," she said right back.

Braden had to admit, she was every bit as pretty as he remembered. Prettier. She wasn't wearing anything fancy. Just jeans and a white T-shirt. But her brown hair had been left long and loose around her back. The wind must have kicked it into curls because it framed her heart-shaped face and golden-brown eyes. Damn. If she hadn't ended up winning his contest, he would have very definitely done his best to secure a date with her once she'd come through his line.

But she wouldn't have come through his line.

He knew that now. Just as he knew her well enough after less than twenty-four hours to know that she was nervous about being alone with him.

"I was going to go home," she said, looking away from him, her long lashes concealing her gaze. "But something happened."

"What?" he asked, surprised at how instantly concerned he felt. "Was it Stewart?"

She met his gaze again and Braden felt the same surge of protectiveness that he always felt when he looked into her eyes.

"No. Well, yes. In a way," she said, looking uneasy. "I saw what they're saying in the papers."

He shrugged. "No big deal. I had a feeling something like this might happen. It'll blow over soon enough."

"Yeah, but you'll end up looking like a bad guy in the process."

"So I'm this week's celebrity villain. No big deal."

"Maybe not to you, but it is to me." She looked uneasy again. "I've decided to go on our date."

If he'd been in denial about his interest in her before, her words would have forced him to see the truth. He felt such a surge of pleasure, it was all he could do not to break into a silly smile.

"I hope it's not too late to change my mind. Again."

"Are you kidding? *My-Lovematch* will be thrilled."

They'd been none too thrilled with him last night after he'd confessed what had happened at the hotel. It didn't matter that it hadn't been his fault. Bad press was bad press and *My-Lovematch,* like any sponsor, didn't like it. Dana's participation in the date might go a long way toward assuaging their concerns.

"I can't imagine they're too happy with the headlines this morning, either."

"Uh, yeah," he said with a reassuring smile. "You could say that."

"I'm so sorry, Braden."

"Hey, it's okay," he said, wanting so badly to go to her, to pull her into his arms. "Have you heard from the putz this morning?"

She looked away.

"Dana?"

She kept her gaze on the floor.

"What'd he say?"

"Nothing," she murmured.

"Dana."

"So he called me," she said. "I told him to buzz off."

She gave him a brave smile. Damn, but he admired her courage.

"Something tells me more was said than that."

She shook her head. "No. That was about it."

"What'd he say?"

"Nothing," she said quickly. Too quickly.

"Did he threaten you?"

He could tell she wasn't certain how much to say. "No."

Braden crossed his arms, not liking the sound of this. "Wait. Let me guess. He threatened me."

She looked away again.

"He *did* threaten me, didn't he?"

She must have recognized the futility of being evasive, because she looked him in the eye again. "He told me if you decide to press charges, you'd better watch out. He's going to tell the media a bunch of lies."

"So?" Braden said. "I'll just deny his allegations. In a few weeks, maybe even a few days, this will all blow over."

"But he's going to tell lies."

She was outraged on his behalf. "Dana," he said softly, moving toward her against his better judgment. "People tell lies about me all the time. It's part of being in the public eye. I'm used to it."

She held his gaze and he saw she was nervous about his sudden proximity. Was she afraid to be alone with him? After what she'd been through, he wouldn't blame her.

"Why didn't you want to tell me?" he asked.

She licked her lips, and suddenly Braden's thoughts went in a whole new direction. His body began to do things it shouldn't be doing. Not now. Not with this woman.

"Alysa told me not to mention it. Something about a symphony and being off-key." Her eyes locked with his own. "To be honest, I didn't really understand."

He smiled. He felt his hand begin to lift. He almost forced it back to his side, but something made him take a chance. "I'm glad you came," he said, touching her bare arm. Just like before, his fingers seemed to vibrate, a connection passing between them that was as startling as it was pleasant. He saw her lashes part in surprise, knew she felt it, too.

"I'm not afraid of your ex." And he wasn't afraid to pursue her, either, he suddenly realized, despite her recent breakup. "But I am afraid of what he might do to you."

"What do you mean?"

He took an even bigger chance, closing the distance between them slowly, as if he approached a fractious horse. "He's come after you once before, Dana. What if he does it again?"

"He won't."

"What if he does?"

"Then I'll file a restraining order."

"Those don't always work."

"I know." She looked away.

"You'll need to be careful."

"I will," she said softly.

He was right next to her now and, God, it was killing him not to pull her closer, not to tip up her face and bend down and kiss her lips. He wanted to reassure her without words that not all men were bad. That he could be trusted. That some men might actually cherish and protect a woman as warm and brave as Dana.

His hand lifted to her face. She didn't move away, the tension between them escalating to the point that his blood rushed through his veins and roared in his ears.

"If he's as big an ass as I think he is, I wouldn't put it past him to try and humiliate you right along with me."

"I know," she said. "That's why I was thinking I should talk to that reporter. The one who was asking questions last night. Maybe if I go on record first, it'll minimize the effect of what he's going to say. Because I assume you're not going to bow down to his threats."

"No." His fingers gently stroked her cheek. She didn't pull away, didn't tell him not to touch her. Just stared up at him as he said, "It's too late, anyway. I've already talked to the police."

She didn't say anything and Braden knew she felt every bit as blown away by what stirred between them as he did. Growing bolder, he dared to touch her hair, the incredibly soft strands tickling his palm like strands of a web. He tugged on one curl near her shoulder, watched as it popped back into place. Almost...almost he slipped his hand behind her head, wanting to pull her toward him. But he knew better. She was too fragile for bold moves.

He stepped back.

"I need to get going."

She nodded, her eyes glittering with—what was that?—tears? "Good luck today."

Why would she be crying? "I think I'll need it," he said. "Especially if it rains."

"Do they make you race in the rain?"

He almost laughed, but he didn't want to embarrass her. Obviously, she knew nothing about NASCAR. "No," he said. "They'll run the race as long as it's safe to do so and then they'll red flag us."

"Red flag?" she asked, her chest expanding as

she inhaled sharply. Her breath sounded jagged, as if she truly *had* been holding back tears.

"It means stop racing."

"And then what? The race is over?"

"Sometimes. Sometimes not. Depends on how badly it's raining."

"I see."

Someone knocked on the door. Elizabeth, no doubt. "Braden," she said, staying outside as if afraid he might have Dana in his arms. "We've got to go."

"You going to watch the race from pit road?"

"No. I'm planning on leaving early."

"Don't do that," he said. "Stay."

"I don't want to bump into Stewart at the airport. But I'll watch you for a few laps."

"You going to let that jerk ruin your race day?"

"Well, I—"

"Stay," he said again.

"I'll be in the way."

He shook his head, his smile growing bigger. "You won't be in the way."

Another deep breath and when she exhaled, she'd begun to look more like herself. "I don't know…"

"Braden," Elizabeth called, louder.

He glanced at the door. "My PR rep. She's persistent."

"Yeah, well, I suppose she'd have to be to keep you on schedule."

"Come on," he said, holding out an arm toward the door. "I'll walk you outside."

"Are you sure?"

"We have guests in our pits all the time. You'll be perfectly fine."

He wanted to touch her again. To make her promise to be there for him after the race, but he hated to push her. It was too soon. The timing was horrible.

"Be careful out there, Braden."

"I always am."

It was her turn to smile and Braden felt his spirits lift. "You forget, I've driven in a car with you."

"Ah, that was nothing," he said. "You should be in the car with me when I'm really hauling ass."

"That's what I'm worried about," she said wryly.

He couldn't help himself. Before he could think better of it, he bent and kissed her lightly on the lips. "Don't worry about me," he said softly.

He wanted to kiss her again. Instead he said, "See you after the race."

CHAPTER TWELVE

THE SKIES ABOVE the Las Vegas track looked as ominous and dark as a portent of biblical doom.

He'd kissed her.

Cold wind whipped across Dana's face as she headed toward pit road where she was supposed to meet Alysa. Her arms were crossed in front of her, the hair she'd left long and loose around her shoulders blinding her upon occasion.

He'd kissed her.

She wished he'd done so much more.

She couldn't deny it anymore. Hell, he was why she was sticking around when she should be flying home. Why she'd been on the verge of tears when he'd touched her cheek earlier. The feelings he aroused in her were so completely foreign, so frightening and exhilarating, especially in light of all that she'd been through, all she'd wanted to do was turn tail and run.

"Watch out," someone called. Dana looked up just in time to stop herself from running into a camera crew filming the interior of an empty garage.

"Sorry." She stepped around them and nearly bumped into the spectators busy taking pictures of the camera crew.

Strange.

But it was *all* strange. Her feelings for Braden. Being in a NASCAR garage. Being kissed by one of racing's biggest stars.

What did it all mean? Was he interested in her? Did he truly want to date her? Not an impersonal getting-to-know-you dinner, like he'd suggested, but actually *date-date* her? More importantly, was it too soon to start seeing someone?

"Dana, wait up."

Alysa.

She wasn't certain she wanted Alysa to know that something had happened between her and Braden.

Dana hoped she'd had enough time to collect herself.

"How'd it go?" Alysa asked, all but sliding to a stop in front of Dana.

"Fine." Dana took a deep breath and hoped she'd cleared any emotional residue from her eyes. Alysa knew her well enough that she'd be able to spot a problem. That's what'd led to Vegas. She'd used Alysa as a shoulder to cry on. One confession had led to another....

"Did you tell him about Stewart?"

Dana squared her shoulders because she knew Alysa wouldn't like her answer. "I did."

"How'd he take it?" Alysa narrowed her eyes. Dana knew instantly that if Braden didn't finish well, Alysa would hold Dana personally responsible.

"He was fine with it, Alysa. Really. It's no big deal. I guess he's used to people saying bad things about him."

Alysa's face cleared as she swiped a strand of hair away from her face. "Oh, well…I suppose that's true."

"He said he hoped to see us after the race." Dana didn't add that he'd made it clear how much he hoped to see her after the race. Or that he'd kissed her before he'd left her side.

"After? I thought you were leaving."

"I've changed my mind."

Alysa's eyebrows swung upward. "What about Stewart?"

"I'm not worried about Stewart anymore."

"No?"

Dana shook her head, but she knew it was a lie. Stewart's behavior worried her a great deal. And she knew Alysa knew that, too.

Alysa looked out over pit road and said, "I was hoping to walk with Braden to his car."

"They let people do that?"

Alysa shrugged, her eyes strangely evasive. What was up? She'd been acting strange all morning.

"Sure they do," Alysa said. "I see girls walking with drivers all the time."

Yeah, but something told Dana those women were probably girlfriends or wives. "Well, maybe we'll see him before the race starts." Although she doubted it. She was pretty certain Braden would have offered to be with them if he'd thought he'd have the time. Then again, he'd left the hauler so quickly, she wasn't certain what to think.

He'd kissed her. And she'd wanted to kiss him back. How could she want to kiss a man back so soon after Stewart?

"Braden was insistent we watch the race from pit road."

"Well, duh," Alysa said. "Of course that's where we'll watch it."

Dana frowned, not liking Alysa's sarcasm. "Do you know where it is?" Dana asked, about to tell her she'd lead them there.

But Alysa's, "Dana, we were on pit road yesterday," preempted her words.

Something was wrong. While she and Alysa weren't exactly best friends, it wasn't like her to be so sharp-tongued. "I meant do you know which pit place he has, because if you don't, I do."

"Pit *stall*," Alysa corrected. "And how do you know where it is?"

"I passed it while I was looking for you."

"Oh. Then lead the way," Alysa said with a brusque motion of her hands.

Dana resisted the urge to shake her head. What was Alysa's problem? She was acting like a brat.

There were tons of people out on pit road, more than a few of them wearing team uniforms covered by jackets. Dana glanced skyward. It really did look like it might rain, the clouds having picked up since they'd arrived.

"Alysa," Dana asked as they made their way to Braden's pit stall, "are you upset with me for changing my mind about going on that date with Braden?"

"Upset?" she asked. "Why would I be upset?"

But Alysa's response was too glib, the tone too sharp for Dana to believe her.

"I don't know," Dana said, shrugging. "I thought you might still have been hoping I could give the date to you. But I tried to switch, Alysa. I really did. And now you just seem…different."

"That's because my lips are frozen," Alysa said briskly. "I can't believe I didn't think to bring a jacket."

"You could always change," Dana said. "Our suitcases are in our car." They'd packed up their belongings already so they wouldn't miss the hotel's checkout time.

"Are you kidding? I love this shirt. I've been fantasizing about wearing it to a race since the moment

I spotted it. I'm not covering it up with a jacket, especially now that we're in the pits."

So she'd freeze to death instead. Dana shook her head. "Well, I'm going to go back and grab my jacket. Braden's pit is just up ahead. I'll meet you back here in a minute."

"Fine, sure," Alysa said, brushing her off. Dana saw why in a moment. The ever flirtatious Alysa had caught the eye of a particularly handsome crew member. The man's gaze followed Alysa's progress down pit road. But then his focus shifted, coming to rest on Dana. She saw Alysa glance in her direction and stiffen.

"I'll see you later," Alysa said, stepping in front of her and blocking her from the view of the interested crew member. But that was okay with Dana. Anything to get away from Alysa. She'd grown claws, and Dana knew the reason why. Competition. Alysa didn't like the fact that guys were interested in Dana. Or one man in particular.

It felt good to don the jacket she'd brought in case of a weather emergency. Made out of suede, it was almost too big for her. Dana could hunker down inside it, shielded from the weather and other people's gazes. She'd brought a matching leather hat, one with sheepskin lining. She pulled the thing on low, making sure it covered as much of her face as possible. She probably looked like an undercover agent, she thought, her only splash of color was the red-hot pass Elizabeth had given her.

What Dana didn't realize—what she couldn't have known—was that far from blending in, the hat and jacket made her stand out. She looked like a fashion model, something that would have made Dana laugh given how completely she underestimated her own good looks. Eyes continued to follow her, but she didn't notice. She was too busy keeping her gaze down as she made her way through the crowds in the garage.

Or at least that's what Elizabeth assumed when she spotted Dana's tall frame. Braden had told her Dana was oblivious to how pretty she was, something Elizabeth had doubted until that moment. The woman seemed oblivious to the heads she was turning.

"Dana," Elizabeth called. "Wait up."

As if surprised to hear her name, Dana came to a sudden halt. Golden-brown eyes filled with warmth when they spied her. She could like this woman, Elizabeth thought.

"Braden told me you're willing to talk to that reporter now. The one who wanted to interview you. I need to talk to you about that so I'm glad I found you."

"Willing, yes. Looking forward to it, no."

Elizabeth's smile turned wry. "You're smart to be cautious. My phone's been ringing off the hook thanks to Braden's little run-in with your ex. That's part of what I wanted to talk to you about. Someone dropped your name to the media and now the reporter has questions about you and Braden. I'm fairly certain she'll change the slant of her interview. I'm almost half tempted to call the whole thing off."

They'd made it to the opening in the fence that led to the race track, Elizabeth slowed down when they caught up to a car being pushed onto pit road.

"So, you think I shouldn't do it?" Dana asked.

"No," Elizabeth replied. "I think it's important you talk to her, especially since she's seen the in-car footage. She knows Braden questioned you about the mark on your face. Whether it's bruised from an accident or no, she's going to ask questions…especially after yesterday's altercation at the hotel."

"I know," Dana said.

"It probably won't be easy. I mean, there's no way to know for sure, but I suspect the slant of the story has changed from winning a date with one of America's favorite sports celebrities to a hard-hitting report on violent behavior. I don't think she'll go after you, personally, but she'll probably dig for information on Braden. Are you prepared for that?"

Elizabeth watched as emotions flitted across Dana's face. She saw trepidation, and fear, but in the end steely determination won out. "I'm prepared."

"All right," she said. "I'll set it up. And look—" she pointed at Braden's pit stall "—there's your friend." Flirting with one of the crew members, Elizabeth noticed, and probably freezing cold in that outfit. "I'll catch up with you later."

"Thanks, Elizabeth. I appreciate your patience with me, and this whole date thing."

"Not a problem. Braden filled me in on what's been going on in your life. You've got a lot on your plate right now, so I totally understand."

"Still," Dana said. "I'm grateful for everything you've done, especially since Braden got in trouble last night because of me."

"Hey, you weren't the one who hit him."

"No, my ex did, but I feel bad about it."

"Don't worry. Braden is used to the media. I'm more worried about how this will affect you."

"I'll be okay."

She sure hoped so, Elizabeth thought. It wasn't easy to have the media sniffing after you. A lot of drivers had a tough time dealing with that. "I'll call the newscaster once the race starts. Right now I've got to go grab Braden for the driver introductions." She stopped just outside the pit stall. "I don't know if Braden introduced you to Pat or not, you know, the man with sideburns standing near the pit wall. He's Braden's crew chief. He'll fill you in on where you should stand during the race and what to do during pit stops."

"Braden said we wouldn't be in the way, but I think he was only being nice."

"Nah. Just stand back when Braden comes in. Pat will tell you what to do. It's easy."

Dana hoped the woman was right. Her heart beat a little faster as Elizabeth walked away. Despite the incoming weather, the number of people out on pit road surprised Dana, although to be honest, she wasn't certain just *what* she'd expected. Crew members zinged and zoomed between the spectators that crowded the narrow aisle. The men were busy filling their patches of asphalt with the equipment they'd need during the race: red hoses, giant cans of fuel and—most of all—tires. Lots and lots of tires. Dana had to step over a few to get to Alysa.

"There you are!" Alysa said with false brightness, her blond hair looking a little worse for wear thanks to the weather. "I was starting to get worried."

Yeah, right. "I was talking to Elizabeth, Braden's PR rep."

"Oh," Alysa said, obviously not really interested. "Have you met Zach?" She turned toward her handsome new friend. Dark hair, dark eyes and a muscular build that was noticeable even beneath his red team jacket.

"No," Dana said.

"He's the tire changer," Alysa said with a wide

grin. "Isn't that neat? He's been filling me in on what he does on race day."

That's not all he wanted to fill her in on, Dana thought, at least judging by the flirtatious way Zach smiled in Alysa's direction. Obviously, she hadn't spotted the wedding band the guy wore. Or if she had, she didn't care. She smiled at the guy as if she was one step away from giving him her phone number.

What the heck was she doing here? Dana felt so out of place. People eyed her up and down. Not just crew members, but race fans, too. Some were the interested stares of men, and some of the stares came from women, who obviously wondered who she was.

Who was she?

A nobody. Someone who, through an odd twist of fate, found herself in a NASCAR garage and who, crazily enough, had just been kissed by a famous driver.

Tucking her hands beneath her arms, Dana crossed to the white wall that separated the pit stalls from the race track. People milled about, talking in excited voices. All the people were glad to be in Las Vegas at a NASCAR race. She told herself she should be excited, too. But her mind kept going back to one thing:

Braden had kissed her.

And she'd *liked* it.

Stop thinking about it!

She tried. She really did. She even forced herself to look around even though all she wanted to do was keep her head down. There was a stage off to her right, one that partially blocked her view of the grandstands. The dark clouds overhead dimmed the daylight so that whenever someone took a picture, the flash was activated. The bleachers twinkled like a constellation of stars. Despite the incoming weather, an airplane buzzed overhead, a huge banner trailing behind it, kicking violently in the wind. Speakers blared a constant stream of sound. Dana caught a word here and there. They were saying something about driver introductions. That, she knew, meant Braden would be out on the track soon, driven around in the back of a pickup truck or in a fancy car so his fans could see him before the race.

Famous.

She'd known he was. But nothing had prepared her for the sound of the crowd when Braden's name was announced. She leaned forward, trying to figure out where he was. To her surprise he stood near the stage to her right, not less than fifty yards away. He was one of the first drivers to be introduced. He climbed the steps in a single bound and lifted his hands. A deafening roar erupted when the crowd saw him. It made Dana jump. He waved and smiled as if the crowd's reaction was no big deal. And to

Braden, she realized, it *wasn't* a big deal. He stood atop a similar stage every weekend.

"Braden," someone screamed. "Braden James."

Dana turned. Three feet away a woman cried his name, arms lifted as she tried to catch Braden's attention. As if that were possible. He was too far away to hear her. Plus, he was busy being interviewed. A reporter held a microphone to his mouth, and Dana suddenly caught the sound of Braden's voice over the PA.

"Glad...to...here."

She looked at the speaker as if that might enable her to hear better. But the wind snatched the words away, toying with them so that she only caught bits and pieces. Dana clutched at her hat to keep it from blowing off her head.

"Braden," the middle-aged woman screamed even louder.

The reporter on stage clapped Braden on the back. The crowd cheered again as Braden moved away, toward some stairs at the end of the dais.

"Braden!" the woman screamed even louder.

Suddenly, he looked in their direction. Dana thought he wouldn't recognize her in her hat and jacket, and yet he *did*. The smile that splashed onto his face was as warm as summer rain.

"Oh my gosh," the woman next to her said. "Did you see that? He waved at me."

Had he? Or had he spotted Dana?

Braden was darting down the stage stairs, arms holding on to the rail, legs swinging. Elizabeth met him at the bottom. Dana lost sight of him momentarily because a crowd enveloped him, but a second or two later, he was through, security keeping his fans at bay. A few followed him, but his speed and direction was a deterrent and they gave up. Dana thought he'd head to the vehicle waiting to drive him around the track. Instead he kept coming toward them.

"Oh my gosh. He's headed our way," the woman said, bouncing up and down. Dana's cheeks burned bright because it quickly became apparent that the only reason he was headed that way was because of her.

"I found you," he said to Dana, his hand lifting to her hat. "Despite your disguise."

"Oh my gosh, do you know him?" the woman asked, turning toward her.

"Braden," Dana heard Elizabeth say. His PR rep tugged at his arm. "You need to get in the truck." She pointed toward the red vehicle that would carry Braden around the track. "Hi, Dana." Elizabeth shot Dana a smile.

"I'm coming, I'm coming," he said with a wink at Dana, but his smile included the woman next to her, too. "Hi."

"Hi," the woman gushed in a breathy voice. Honestly, she acted like a teenager rather than the fifty-something-year-old she must have been.

"You want me to sign an autograph?" Braden asked her.

"Braden," Elizabeth said, her hand lifting to the tiny speaker embedded in her ear. "I'm getting yelled at by the event coordinator."

"Tell them to hold their horses." Braden took the woman's pen. "It's going to start raining soon, anyway."

As if God himself heard his words, Dana felt a drop hit her nose.

"See," Braden said, popping the lid off a black pen.

"He signed my hand," the woman cried in excitement.

"Better get that hand under cover," Braden said.

Just then the heavens opened up. Dana glanced skyward and got a faceful of rain.

"Come on." Braden lightly clutched her elbow to help her over the wall.

"Hey," someone yelled. "I want an autograph, too."

But Braden was turning away, as he helped Dana over.

"They're delaying the race," Elizabeth said.

"Told you."

"Yeah, yeah, yeah," Elizabeth muttered with a long-suffering smile.

Braden didn't let go of her arm and Dana felt a thousand pairs of eyes staring at them.

"But they still want you to drive around the track. Sorry, Dana, you can't ride with him."

"That's fine with me," Dana said. A small crowd had formed and Dana's heart started to beat harder.

Because Braden is touching you, whispered a little voice.

And that was true, but she also didn't do well in crowds.

"Why can't she go?" Braden asked.

"You know they won't allow that. Besides, there's no room," Elizabeth said. "Listen, when you're done, you're to remain on standby, so don't go far."

"Like I'm going to make a run for fast food or something."

"I wouldn't put it past you."

He gave Dana a wide grin. "I love hamburgers."

"The rain actually works in our favor," Elizabeth said. "Melanie Murray wanted to talk to Dana once the race got underway, but with this rain, you can *both* do the interview."

"You already talked to her?" Dana asked.

Elizabeth nodded. "She returned my call practically the moment I hung up. We're green-lighted for an interview. Provided you're ready, and I want to prep you on some potential questions if that's okay."

Dana glanced at Braden, wishing she'd stayed out

of sight. She'd been hoping to put off the interview for as long as possible, but it appeared as if that wasn't to be.

"Fine," Dana said.

"I'll feel better knowing you're prepared," Elizabeth said. "It should help you to relax, as well. Nothing like knowing the answers to questions before they're asked."

She'd never feel adequately prepared though. Never. Nor would she ever feel comfortable in front of a camera. That was Braden's job.

Yet somehow it'd suddenly become hers.

THE INTERVIEW DIDN'T start well.

"So tell me," the sharp-nosed brunette reporter asked, her light blue eyes so intensely focused that Dana had to force herself to make eye contact. "How long were you abused by your fiancé?"

They had her in a room at the Media Center, one with soundproof walls to shield them from the noise of the track—not that there was any racing going on what with rain pouring down outside—and yet Dana could have sworn it became quieter inside the tiny ten-by-ten area with that question.

"Excuse me?"

The woman who'd introduced herself as Melanie Murray recrossed her legs. "I've seen the in-car footage," the woman said, her tone slightly accusatory.

"After what happened at your hotel last night, combined with your reaction to Braden's questions, it's pretty obvious there's something going on."

Dana glanced at the camera, trying to see beyond the bright lights to the man operating the controls. Braden was outside, waiting for his turn. Melanie had wanted to interview them separately, but Dana would have given anything to have him in the room with her.

"Not necessarily," Dana said.

"Would you like to watch the tape yourself?"

No, she wouldn't. What she wanted to do was hop out of the green director's chair and walk away. But she couldn't do that.

"Look, I fail to see what this has to do with my winning a date with Braden James. I thought that's what this interview was about."

"It is," the woman said, the black business suit she wore bunching around her shoulders as she leaned forward. "In part. But as a reporter, it's my job to get background information, as well."

Dana did her own leaning forward. "Well, this background information is none of your business."

Melanie stared at her for a long moment. She held a clipboard in her hand and Dana watched her flip through a few pages before leaning back in her own green chair. "You were engaged prior to entering the contest, were you not?"

Wow. The woman had done her homework, and

fast. But did she know Braden's altercation had been with Stewart? Somehow Dana doubted it.

"I was," Dana said.

"Did you break up because that boyfriend was abusing you?"

Elizabeth had prepared her for this question. "I broke up with my fiancé for personal reasons," Dana said. "None of which have to do with my date with Braden James. Please focus on that."

"So you're saying your breakup had nothing to do with the mark on your jaw?"

Jeez. The woman wouldn't give up. "I thought I was clear," Dana said. "I don't want to talk about my personal life. If you want to ask me about how I feel about my date with Braden, that's fine, but nothing more."

Again, the long stare, then a tip of the woman's head. "I understand your reluctance to divulge personal information. But if there's something in your past that might, perhaps, shed some light on what happened yesterday, I recommend you tell me. It might take some of the heat off Braden."

Had Melanie reasoned that Braden had been protecting Dana from her ex-fiancé yesterday? Dana couldn't be sure. One thing was certain—the woman was as persistent as a hungry mosquito. It was a nice attempt at shaming her into a confession.

"Sorry," Dana said. "All I'm here to talk about is

my date with Braden." It was the line Elizabeth had coached her to say. Dana used it unflinchingly.

"Uh-huh," Melanie said, her mouth pinching together. "Okay, fine. Then let's talk about that date for a moment. You win a date with a famous race car driver, then the next thing you know, he's proposing a *real* date. How'd *that* come about?"

She'd been expecting this question, too, thanks to that in-car camera. "He didn't really ask me out," Dana said. "He explained to me later that he just wanted to get to know me a little better before our time together in Napa, before the cameras started rolling. Kind of a break-the-ice sort of thing."

"Oh, really," Melanie said. "That's interesting because I watched that tape at least six times and believe me, he didn't sound impersonal."

"Then I suggest you watch the tape again."

Melanie didn't look happy with Dana. "I *might* be mistaken," the woman said, riffling through some pages on her clipboard. "But what if I'm not? What if Braden James turns out to be the Prince Charming you've always been looking for?"

Dana shook her head. "There is no such thing as a Prince Charming."

The words slipped out before Dana could stop them.

Melanie pounced. "I don't blame you for saying that. Especially after all the trouble you've had with your fiancé."

"Huh?"

Melanie tipped her head to the right. "Let's talk about March sixteenth of last year."

March sixteenth? Why did she want to talk about—

Then Dana knew what the woman had uncovered.

It took every ounce of Dana's strength not to bolt from the chair.

CHAPTER THIRTEEN

HOW COULD MELANIE KNOW? Dana wondered. She'd never pressed charges.

"I have no idea what you're talking about. And frankly," she said, "if you refuse to keep the focus of this interview on my date with Braden, the date that I *won,* then I think we're through here."

That was another line Elizabeth had taught her in the short time they'd had to practice, and Dana was grateful.

The reporter tipped her head, as if needing another angle from which to study her. "Leave us alone for a second," she said to the guy operating the camera.

Dana sat there, fighting the urge to flee. She could feel anxiety rushing in to claim her. She tried to keep it at bay, but her heart had started to pound, her palms to sweat and she didn't know how much longer she could sit in that chair with a white, hot light shining down on her.

"Look," Melanie said the moment they were alone, "I've read some of the headlines about

Braden, and if I don't miss my guess, the guy Braden hit was your ex-boyfriend. I don't know that for sure because the LVPD and the casino are keeping quiet. But if it was your ex-boyfriend…if there is another side of the story, wouldn't you like to get that on tape? It'd put an end to the negative headlines about Braden."

It would, but Dana felt ill at the thought of revealing the dirty details of her past. Plus, there was no telling what Stewart would do if she started naming names. He might go off the deep end and do more than hit someone.

"Why?" she asked, hoping to distract the woman. "Why do you care? Surely there are other, more important stories you could pursue? Like famine in Africa. Or war in the Middle East." Something far more important than Braden James and Dana Johnson.

At first Dana didn't think the woman planned to respond, but she quickly realized Melanie was just taking time to frame her words. "You're right," she said with a slow nod. "I could keep this a human interest story. Small-town girl wins date with superstar driver. I doubt my network would air it now, not after what happened between Braden and your ex. His image has been tarnished too much.

"But I did the research this afternoon. Don't ask me how I know about your past, Dana, I can't reveal my sources, but I know there's more to your story than meets the eye. So we have two choices. I can ask you fluff questions about your date with Braden James. Keep it simple. The interview will be over in less than five minutes. Or we can turn up the heat. We can use this as a platform to discuss something real and important. We could set the record straight, too. Talk about Braden and how he was trying to protect you from your ex, or so I suspect. He'll end up looking like a hero, not like a spoiled celebrity, which is how other media outlets are spinning it."

By now Dana's heart beat so fast she was surprised the woman couldn't hear it. She took a deep breath, forced herself to stay calm. "How do I know you won't take what I say and twist it around?"

Melanie slipped out of her chair. "You have my word as a broadcaster and, more importantly, as a woman who's been in your shoes."

Dana straightened in surprise.

Another nod. "When I was in college, one of my boyfriends thought he could get me drunk and have a little fun. I fought him off, but not without getting hurt in the process. I nearly stopped going to college because of it. More than a few of his friends called me a tease and a tart, tried to smear my name. But I knew what had happened. So did the jerk that tried to force himself on me. I pressed charges, made sure the guy didn't get away with it. It wasn't easy, but I did it. You could do the same."

If you turn on me, I'll turn on you.

Melanie was right.

Belinda and Braden were right.

To hell with Stewart. She was tired of him pushing her around.

"I won't name names. If I do, I'm afraid of what he'll do to me next," Dana said. "And I'd rather you keep Braden out of it."

"No names is fine. But I can't keep Braden out of it. I need him to sell the story. As much as I hate to admit it, nobody will care about you and your problems. But if you add Braden into the mix, if we talk about how he's tried to help you and, I suspect, how he's helped others, my bosses might go for it. Especially if we scoop other media outlets on what *really* happened at that casino."

"What makes you think Braden has tried to help others?"

Melanie smirked. "The garage is full of talk. I've heard rumors. A few questions here and there and I figured out pretty quickly Braden does a lot of stuff for people, stuff nobody's ever heard of. I even know about—" she riffled through some notes on her clipboard "—Belinda."

She knew about Belinda?

"I want to talk about Braden and how he helped

you out with someone from your past. We don't have to name your fiancé specifically, although people might put two and two together."

Dana swallowed. She felt, for a moment, as if she stood at the edge of a cliff. This was the moment. The moment when she either kept quiet for the rest of her life, or exposed Stewart for the jerk he was.

To hell with it.

"Fine."

Melanie broke into a smile—a *real* smile, one that made Dana think she might have sold her soul to the devil. "Let's get the cameraman back in here."

When the door opened, she could hear Braden talking to someone. She wished again that he was in here with her.

"Okay," Melanie said. "Let's start with winning the date. We can work our way toward the other stuff gradually. Will you be okay talking about your ex sending you to the hospital?"

No. She hated thinking about that day. March sixteenth. The day Stewart had sent her to the hospital for daring to tell him not to kick the neighbor's dog.

"If you think it's necessary," she said.

"We might not have to. Let's see how it goes."

But they ended up talking about that and more. The interview lasted no longer than a half hour, but it felt like an eternity to Dana. She skated around some issues, such as where she lived, or where she worked and what she did for a living. But Melanie forced her to talk about her painful relationship with Stewart, and in the end Dana felt as raw and exposed as a broken tooth.

"Thanks," Melanie said when they were done. "That was great."

Dana's throat was dry. She had to swallow a few times before she could choke out, "You're welcome."

Her hands shook as she tried to disengage the mic from her shirt collar. She ended up dropping the thing and had to fish it out from beneath her white shirt. When she slipped the battery off a moment later, she knew she was on the verge of another panic attack.

"Dana," the reporter said, touching her hand, the woman's fingers cold. "I promise, Braden will come out looking like a hero."

"I hope so," Dana said, because he didn't deserve to be vilified. Now maybe he wouldn't be, Dana thought. Maybe she'd done some damage control.

If you turn on me, I'll turn on you.

That's what Dana was afraid of. Stewart. He'd sent her to the hospital once, and very nearly a second time, too.

"Could you tell Braden to come on in here?"

Dana nodded, grabbing her coat and her hat on the way out. The moment she passed through the door, Braden was there, leaving a crowd of reporters and coming to her side. It was a busy room, and more

than a few drivers stood around or sat being interviewed by various members of the press. Journalists
sat at tables, laptops open or cell phones to their
ears. It might be raining outside, but work was still
going on, and everywhere, *everyone* wanted to talk
to Braden about what had happened yesterday.

"You okay?" he asked, his uniform like a red
beacon in a sea of unfamiliarity.

"Fine," she said, not looking him in the eye. "She
wants to see you now."

"You look like you could use some fresh air."

She was upset, she admitted. She'd outted
Stewart. Oh, she hadn't mentioned him by name,
but people would figure it out, especially those who
knew her well. But maybe outing him was a good
thing. He wouldn't dare act on his threats now…
would he?

She felt her stomach turn.

"Braden, wait," one of the reporters called. "We
still have a few questions."

"Braden, my network wants to know—"

"Braden, is this the woman who was with you
yesterday?"

"Let's go," Braden said.

She shook her head. "Melanie needs you."

"She can wait."

Dana hesitated. He must have felt that hesitation
because suddenly he was looking down at her, and

just as quickly, he stilled. Her heart raced, each staccato beat getting louder and louder.

"Poor thing," he said. "You've had a rough weekend."

It amazed her how quickly tears rose in her eyes. She tried to hide them, but there was no way she could conceal her fear and uncertainty and the terror she felt at betraying a man who'd already hurt her twice before.

"I just want to go home," she admitted, knowing she sounded like a little girl but unable to stop herself.

She hugged her jacket close, wishing she could crawl into a corner and hide.

"Come on," he said, grabbing her hand.

"Braden," one of the journalists called out again.

"Not now, guys," Braden said. "Elizabeth is over there." He pointed to a corner of the room where his PR representative spoke into a cell phone. "Talk to her about scheduling some time with me."

He turned toward the exit, and used his body to herd her out the door. Dana didn't protest. She needed air, even if that air was as cold as her insides.

When they were out from beneath the shelter of the building, the rain hit her hard. She crammed her hat on. "I need to find Alysa," she mumbled halfheartedly.

"The guys are taking care of her."

"Yeah, but I should probably make sure she's okay," she said, knowing it was an excuse. She wanted to be alone.

"The only place you're going is with me," he said, clasping her hand, his fingers warm compared to her own.

She let him lead her away. She knew he couldn't go far. He had a race to run and Melanie to talk to.

She glanced toward the grandstands. People sat on the glistening, aluminum bleachers, umbrellas raised. The devotion of NASCAR fans amazed her.

"Braden," someone called. And then another person cried his name. And another and another. Fans up on the catwalk, she realized. They'd spotted him walking toward the garage. He ignored them, and headed toward the area where they were working on his car. He tugged her inside the nearly vacant building, her wet shoes squeaking on the concrete floor. Other people were huddled inside the work space, too. Fat drops of rain fell to the ground outside, so much water covering the asphalt that when the droplets landed, tiny waterfalls erupted.

"Come on," he said, stopping opposite the hauler that carried his car from race track to race track. "Let's make a run for it."

He was taking her back to the lounge, she realized, ducking her head against the rain. Back to where he'd kissed her. That wasn't a good idea. It was all too much. The interview. Stewart's threats. Her feelings for Braden. But he wouldn't let her hang back, he just pulled her forward. Only when they reached the shelter of the hauler did he stop.

"Stay here for a second," Braden said.

Okay, so maybe he wasn't taking her into the lounge. That reassured her. But if not there, where? She glanced around. With the sun obscured by clouds, the tinted glass doors at the back of the hauler had turned opaque. Inside, her back turned to the door, she could see Alysa talking to a group of men, the bunch of them laughing. Dana lifted a hand, waved. But her friend spared her hardly a glance. She was too busy smiling at Braden. A come-hither smile.

Dana's own smile faded. Braden's reply must have been short. He went to a cabinet, opened it, took something out, then nodded at Alysa before turning back to Dana. Alysa's gaze slipped past Braden and met Dana. Dana waited for her friend to follow Braden out, but she didn't, she just turned back to the group of men.

Obviously, Alysa was jealous. But Dana was tired of bending her life to suit other people. She wasn't going to bend where Braden was concerned.

"Come on," Braden said. He turned, taking her down the narrow aisle that ran between the haulers. Dana hardly noticed Braden's face plastered across the metal side. Or the face of the other guy on the hauler next to them. Even the noise of the generator hardly penetrated. She was too busy thinking how good it felt to hold Braden's hand, and that it was too soon for her to feel good about being with another man.

"Here we are." Something jiggled in his hand. Keys, she realized. That's what he'd retrieved from the cabinet.

"What are you doing?"

"We're going inside." He unlocked the door. "It's about the only place where we can have privacy. No prying eyes. No roving reporters. No race fans."

"Braden, no," she said. "That's not a good idea."

"You need to be alone. I can see that." He opened the door and began to climb inside.

"Braden, no. I can't…I mean, I don't—"

Want to be alone with you.

He'd paused with his hand on the driver's side door, searching her face. "Don't look at me like that," he said softly.

She swallowed. "Like what?"

"Like you're about to crumple."

She took a deep breath, looked him straight in the eyes. "I am not about to crumple. I'm just…I'm just—"

Frightened of the way I feel for you.

"Aw, honey," he said gently. "I'm here for you."

He misunderstood. He thought she was upset about the interview. But that wasn't it. That wasn't it at all.

He opened the door, put his hands on her waist and lifted her inside. She should have protested. She should have told him not to touch her.

She was helpless to stop him.

"I want to hold you," he said, staring up at her. "To comfort you. To prove to you that I can be trusted."

She felt her eyes burn.

"Will you let me do that?"

She had to blink against the rain that still drizzled into the cab despite the roof's partial protection. Or maybe those were tears in her eyes. She didn't know. The burning beneath her lashes matched a burning inside her heart.

She'd finally met a worthy man, and the timing was all wrong.

But God help her, she said, "Yes," anyway.

CHAPTER FOURTEEN

IT WASN'T THE MOST romantic place to bring a woman, Braden admitted. But he wasn't trying to seduce her. All he wanted to do was offer her comfort. Reassure her. God willing, to help restore some of her shattered faith.

He scooted in next to her.

Normally, he wouldn't dare intrude on someone else's private space, and that's exactly what the car was—a sort of private residence for the hauler's device. But they were between drivers right now and the space was deserted.

No one would think to look for them here. Not even Elizabeth. Of course, his PR rep could still reach him via the walkie-talkie feature on his phone, but he didn't expect to be in touch with her anytime soon. She'd offer Melanie Murray a convenient excuse and then leave him alone for a while. Elizabeth knew the drill. And the rain would last for hours, or so he'd been told. He wouldn't be surprised if they didn't end up racing tomorrow.

"Braden, are you sure this is okay?" She slid as far away from him as possible on the passenger seat. Braden tried not to feel offended.

"It's okay." He slipped the keys into the ignition. It'd been a while since he'd started up one of the haulers. "There we go," he said once the engine roared to life. "Let's see if I can figure out how to turn the heat on."

When he glanced right, he caught the expression on her face in the reflection of the passenger-side mirror. She looked so close to tears, his heart ached for her—actually *ached*—like a physical pain.

"Hey, it's okay," he said, patting her hand. "Everthing's going to be okay."

"I'm not so sure," she murmured.

"Was it the interview? Did she say something in there to upset you?"

"No," she said. "Not really. Everything I told her, I could have kept to myself."

And Braden knew then that the focus of the interview had been her ex. That's what had her looking so upset. And scared. It had nothing to do with being alone with him.

"Are you afraid he'll come after you?"

She looked at him in surprise.

"I assume you discussed what happened between you and Stewart."

"We did," she said, looking away. He couldn't help

but think her profile was truly lovely. She had a face any actress would envy. Not that it was perfect. Her nose had a tiny bump near the bridge. Her chin was perhaps a little too sharp, but all her features blended together to form a face that was truly extraordinary.

"I won't let him hurt you."

"I know," she said.

He wanted to touch her, but didn't dare. If he did, he was afraid she'd fly away like a startled butterfly.

"Honestly, Dana. I'll hire you round-the-clock security if I have to. I won't let him harm a hair on your head."

She sniffed. Braden realized then that she was crying.

"I just want to run away." She tipped her head back with a moan. "And that's so silly because I'm a grown woman and I have no reason to be afraid. Not anymore. But I *am* afraid. Deep down inside, I'm terrified. The last time I was with him, he would have killed me if I hadn't bought a baseball bat before I confronted him. I didn't think I'd need it. God, I feel like such a fool for thinking he'd changed. But he hadn't changed, and when I told him I didn't think I could marry him, one minute I was sitting on the couch and the next I was on the floor."

"I'm sorry." He couldn't keep himself from sliding next to her, reaching out and placing a hand on her leg. It was meant to be innocent, but the moment he touched her, he felt a spark of arousal that shocked him.

He started to pull back, but before he could, she'd turned to him, burying her face in his chest.

"Shh," he soothed, touching her again, biting back a groan at the sharp stab of desire that sluiced through him.

"He would have killed me," she said, her voice so devoid of emotion it alarmed him.

"Shh." His hands moved to her back. God, what was wrong with him? He shouldn't want to kiss her. Not now. But that's exactly what he wanted to do.

"I'm such an idiot for thinking I could fix him."

"No," he instantly contradicted, tipping her chin up. "That's what's so special about you." She met his gaze and Braden was a lost man. "You have a loving heart." And even though he'd told himself to stop touching her, he couldn't resist moving his hand up her back, slowly, gently.

"Braden?"

"Dana." He tried to tell her without words that he wouldn't hurt her. Ever.

Her eyes widened.

"I want to kiss you," he said gently.

"I don't think that would be a good idea."

"I know," he said, lowering his head, "but I can't seem to stop myself."

She didn't say anything. Braden was afraid to

move without her consent. "Dana." His gaze darted around her face—catching on her pert little nose, pausing for a second on her lips—until his gaze was drawn inexorably upward. "You're so beautiful."

"Braden, please—"

He moved away. It was hard, but he did it.

She clutched his hand.

"No," she said softly.

He dared to hope.

"I meant, yes. Please…kiss me."

"Dana," he said partly in relief, partly in surprise. "Are you certain?"

She nodded.

He took it slow. He didn't want to scare her. He gave her plenty of time to pull away, too. But she didn't. No. What she did was take control. She pulled his head down the rest of the way and opened her mouth. The shock of her tongue stroking his lips pushed Braden over the edge.

He lost it.

He didn't mean to. He'd truly meant to give her plenty of time to pull away. They were in the cab of his hauler, for God's sake. But the realization that he'd broken through her barrier of fear, that not only had she kissed him back, but she'd instigated the kiss, was a turn-on like none he'd ever felt before. He slipped his hands beneath her jacket, pressed his hands against the small of her back, pulled her toward him. He wanted to feel her against him.

"Braden, no."

The word was softly uttered, but he immediately pulled back. He heard Dana's jagged breaths, knowing he sounded just the same.

"Damn," he said, wiping his palms on the front of his uniform. If not for the red fabric, if not for the fact that when he looked up he could see the tops of the grandstands, he might have forgotten where he was, or even what he was doing. She'd driven him that close to the edge.

"I'm sorry," he said. "I didn't bring you in here to kiss you. I was just going to hold you. Try and get to the bottom of why you looked so upset earlier. I swear, I never would have—"

"Stop." She lightly touched his arm, even smiled a little bit. "I know you didn't mean for this to happen."

He heard her take another breath.

"I'm just as much to blame as you are. But as much as I want to forget…things, it would be wrong of me to use you like this."

"You wouldn't be using me." God, no. She'd be relieving him of an impossible ache, one that grew worse the longer he stayed in her company.

"Yes, I would, Braden. I'm not ready for anything more than a fling. But even a fling would be incredibly foolish right now."

"But what if it wasn't a fling? What if there's something between us?"

She stared into his eyes, appearing to consider his words. But then she shook her head. "It would never work out." She lifted a hand as if about to touch him, then obviously thought better of it. "I'm too raw from what I just went through. Too messed up."

"Dana—"

"I'm not saying I won't do the *Win A Date* thing. I know that's important to you and your sponsor. But anything more than that…not now. Not ever."

"Dana—"

"No." She cut him off, fumbling around for the door handle. "I'm not jumping from the fat into the fire, no matter how tempted I might be. That would be stupid. For once, Braden, I'm not going to let my heart rule my mind. This thing between us… whatever it is, wherever it might have taken us, it ends now. I'm sorry." She finally found the handle and pulled on it, her other hand blindly reaching for her hat. "That's how it's got to be."

She was out of the truck before he could stop her.

CHAPTER FIFTEEN

IT WAS STILL POURING BUCKETS when, nearly an hour later, Dana calmed down enough to seek out Alysa.

She wanted to go home.

Where R U?

That was the text message she sent Alysa from the safety of their rental car, the view out the front windshield blurred into a syrupy mess by the rain. She waited for a reply. Didn't get one.

Dana tried calling Alysa next, but she'd either turned off her phone or decided to ignore her messages. Dana'd begun to suspect it was the latter. That meant finding her own way to the airport. But she couldn't leave town without telling Alysa she was going, she had Alysa's suitcases in the car.

Dana hated the thought of going back into the garage or, even worse, back to pit road. That would mean running into Braden.

Or maybe not. With the rain, he was more than likely indoors.

Go, she told herself, leaving the shelter of the car, but only after she'd pulled her hat down low to shield her face from the rain. She needed to find Alysa...*and she would.* No more hiding from trouble.

By now the garage was nearly deserted. Vinyl covers protected the toolboxes from the rain. Stacks of tires had been moved to the shelter of the garage. Generators still hummed, spectators and news crews still walked around, but the activity had the feel of a circus about to leave town. Amidst it all she had to try to find Alysa, which turned out not to be that hard to do. She was exactly where Dana had left her—talking to Braden's pit crew in the hauler. Dana could see Alysa through the tinted glass windows.

Damn.

That meant approaching the transport and maybe running into Braden.

Dana opened her cell phone and dialed.

Inside, she saw Alysa stiffen then reach for her back pocket. Her travel partner checked the display, frowned, pressed a button, then slipped the phone back into her jeans.

Dana watched the whole thing with a sense of disbelief. Why that—

She almost charged inside, but she didn't feel

capable of dealing with Braden if she happened to run into him. So she sent her friend yet another text message.

I C U. Why R U ignoring me?

Alysa's reaction was immediate. She looked outside, shielding her eyes with her hand. Dana stepped out of the shelter of the garage. For a moment Dana thought Alysa might ignore her, again. But then Alysa said something to the group at large, smiled and slipped outside.

Her smile had disappeared by the time she crossed to the garage. Of course, that might be because her gauzy sleeves afforded little protection from the rain and she must have been freezing by the time she darted inside.

"Have you seen Braden?" Dana asked immediately.

"Humph," Alysa snorted. "I thought for sure you'd be the one to have seen him recently. A *lot* of him," Alysa added, crossing her arms.

"What makes you say that?"

Alysa shrugged. "Everyone inside that hauler— me included—knew what you were up to. It was totally obvious, especially when he started up the engine. Jeez, Dana, couldn't you have at least waited until the dust settled with Stewart?"

"You think we went there to…that he and I planned to…"

She couldn't finish the sentence.

"What do you think Stewart will do when he finds out? Do you really think it's smart to antagonize a man like that? One with *his* temper?"

Dana's body jerked at the words. "You've got it all wrong," Dana said. "That's not what happened. We're not... Braden didn't...*you know.*"

"Didn't he?"

"All right, he kissed me," Dana admitted. "And despite everything that's happened with Stewart, I'm attracted to Braden. But that's all he did—kiss me. And I put a stop to it because, you're right, it's too soon."

Alysa's gaze softened a little, but not for long. "Honestly, Dana, I don't know what to think of you anymore. I thought I knew what type of woman you were, but now I'm not so sure. The woman I knew wouldn't go running off with a man less than twenty-four hours after she met him, especially when she'd just ditched her fiancé. At this point, I'm not even certain Stewart's the evil ogre you've said he is."

Dana's breath caught as she fought back emotions. "If you were a true friend, you'd know I'm not lying to you about that."

"Where are you going?" Alysa asked as Dana turned away.

"Home," Dana called over her shoulder. She spun around, fished the keys from her pocket and tossed them in Alysa's direction. "You can take the rental. I'll find another way to the airport."

Something must have clicked in Alysa's brain then, some inner sense of guilt made her feel bad. "No. Wait. Don't do that. I'll drive you."

Dana just shook her head. "I saw a shuttle bus earlier. I'll take one of those."

"Dana, you don't have to do that."

"Goodbye, Alysa. I hope you get to watch a race today. If you bump into Braden, tell him I said goodbye, and that I'm sorry things didn't work out, and that I'll see him in Napa."

Dana turned her back on her friend…just as Alysa had turned her back on her.

SHE'D BAILED ON HIM.

"What do you mean she's gone?" Braden all but yelled.

Elizabeth's eyes widened, no doubt because he never, ever shouted at her. "I don't know why she's gone," she shouted right back. "I'm just relaying a message from her friend. Alicia or Carissa or whatever her name is."

Braden turned away from Elizabeth. They were inside the hauler, the race having been officially canceled—finally. When Dana had left him earlier he'd figured he'd find her later, after he was officially off the hook, maybe spend some more time alone with her.

"I'm sorry," he said, turning back to his PR rep. "I'm just surprised to hear she's gone, is all."

"Her friend said Dana asked her to tell you goodbye. And to tell you that she was sorry things didn't work out," Elizabeth said.

"Who left?" Pat asked, having entered the hauler during Braden's outburst. Braden and Elizabeth stood alone near the front, right outside the lounge, the rest of his team having scattered once they'd heard the race had been postponed. His crew chief opened up a cabinet, the black door obscuring Braden's view of him for a moment.

"That woman," Elizabeth said once Pat hung up the headset he'd been carrying, the cabinet's magnetic latch clicking closed. "The one that won the date."

"Oh," Pat said. "The pretty one. Caught yourself some luck there, bud. She could have been a toothless old hag."

"If it's any consolation," Jerry, one of the tire specialists said, coming in behind Pat. "The blonde one looked delighted to be staying behind. We made plans to hook up later."

"It's not the blonde I'm interested in," Braden muttered.

"She said to call her," Jerry said.

Braden perked up. "Who? Dana?"

"If Dana's the blonde then, yes," Jerry said with a smirk, the white cracks in his suntanned face growing more pronounced as he did so. "But if you don't want to call her, and I can tell by your face that you don't, then I will."

Help yourself, Braden wanted to say.

He didn't want things with Dana to end just yet. Especially not like this. He'd see her again…in a few weeks, but after her reaction to their kiss, he was pretty certain Dana would put a freeze on any budding relationship.

"Damn," he muttered.

"Don't forget," Elizabeth said. "Melanie Murray still wants to talk to you."

"I know." Braden turned toward the lounge, where he'd change into his street clothes. "I thought I'd head over to the Media Center after I'm done here." He pulled the front of his fire suit open, the Velcro coming apart with a satisfying crackle. Maybe he should leave her alone. She seemed really frightened that Stewart might come after her, and he couldn't imagine a guy like that being happy about Dana moving on, especially so soon after they'd broken up.

"The sooner she can file her story, the better," Elizabeth reminded him. "So when you're finished we can walk over together. There's a whole slew of people who want to talk to you. I'm thinking that rather than losing steam, the story of you and that guy at the casino will gain it."

"Well, that's the whole point of talking to Melanie Murray," Braden said. "To set the record straight."

Yeah…he should probably leave Dana alone. Let things chill out a little between her and Stewart. He just wished he believed that leaving her alone was the right thing to do. He had a feeling once the Melanie Murray story aired that shit might hit the fan. He should be there for her when it did.

Or maybe he'd only make things worse.

"C'mon. I'll walk over there with you," Elizabeth said again.

But as Braden followed her out, he couldn't help wondering if he was kidding himself about the spark between him and Dana. Maybe he should try to forget her, find someone else to date.

Unfortunately, the only person he wanted to get to know was Dana.

HER JET LANDED AT LAX beneath clear and sunny skies. Funny how you could leave one state on a cold and rainy day, and arrive in another state experiencing completely different conditions.

Dana headed down the Jetway amongst a slew of disappointed race fans, most of them vowing to call in sick the next day so they could watch the race from the comfort of their own homes.

Dana wouldn't be watching.

Now that she was back home, she planned to

put as much distance between her and Braden James as possible.

Until Napa.

She had no idea how she'd get through Napa. Or the next couple of weeks. Because, quite honestly, returning home meant dealing with Stewart, and her job and her botched wedding plans. In some respects, it would have been simpler to have stayed in Las Vegas. At least then she could have delayed the inevitable for a little while longer. Alas, her life had never been simple.

She hadn't been born to one of those families with lots of aunts and uncles. Her mom had been single for nearly all of Dana's childhood. Well, aside from the men she'd brought home. In high school, Dana had focused on getting good grades just so she could get a scholarship and go to college. But even that hadn't worked out exactly as planned. The scholarship she'd received was good, but not good enough to cover everything and so she'd worked two jobs, sometimes three. Only after she'd graduated had things gotten a little easier, but only a little. The cost of living in Los Angeles was so high she sometimes wondered why she stuck it out.

Probably because you refuse to quit.

That, she realized, was half her problem. Sometimes a person needed to know when to throw in the towel.

Nothing demonstrated that better than when she woke up in her own bed the next morning, the world of NASCAR and sexy race car drivers seeming far, far away. She toyed with the idea of calling in sick, but she refused to be a coward. She'd been on "vacation" the week prior to her wedding, supposedly to give her more time to prepare for her big day. Nobody knew the truth behind her cancelled marriage. Now, she needed to speak to her boss face-to-face, to explain why she was giving notice and why she felt it unwise to spend even one more hour at Steele & Steele. It meant leaving her boss in the lurch, but she really didn't have a choice. God willing, she wouldn't run into Stewart on the way in or out.

And if she did?

She would just be brave, she thought, the words of her newfound mantra. A *good* mantra, she told herself, dressing in her best battle armor: a black suit that fit her like a glove and always made her feel polished and poised. She even pulled her hair back in a bun, something she rarely did, preferring to sweep the curling masses into a ponytail or up on her head. A part of her thought it seemed silly to go to such extremes to arm herself against Stewart. He'd never do anything to her in public. That wasn't his M.O.

Get in, get out. That's all she needed to do.

At least…that's all she *thought* she'd have to do,

right up until she walked into the posh high-rise suite and ran straight into the devil incarnate.

"Well, well, well," Stewart said. "Look what the cat dragged in."

"And look what fell out of the garbage bin," she volleyed right back, her heart pounding despite her show of bravado.

They'd come face-to-face just inside the front entrance. That meant Pauline, the receptionist, had the best seat in the house. The twentysomething college student had a tendency to wear too much makeup and her blackened eyes looked even wider as she stared at the two of them.

"Word to the wise," Stewart said, leaning toward Dana, the glass windows behind Pauline's desk reflected in his eyes. "Jilting me so you could run off to Vegas to be with your famous, race car driving boyfriend didn't exactly win you any brownie points around here."

"Jilting you—" Dana's eyes narrowed. "Why you lying piece of—"

"Uh-uh-uh," Stewart admonished, and he actually had the audacity to place a finger against her lips. "Don't bother denying it. Front-page news, remember? And I didn't end up looking like the bad guy."

"Not yet," she muttered.

Stewart stepped closer, and in a voice meant for her ears only he said, "I warned your boyfriend not to mess with me, Dana. It's just too bad you'll be the one to pay the price."

"I highly doubt that." Dana was tempted to tell him about Melanie Murray. But let the bastard find out *after* the piece aired on prime-time news. "But I really don't care what anyone thinks about me, Stewart, especially since I plan to quit."

She'd taken him by surprise. She could tell by the way he drew back, by the way his handsome, arrogant face slackened. But like most sociopaths, he worked quickly to get himself back under control. "That's funny, because rumor has it, you're about to be let go."

"Yeah, right," Dana said. "Where'd you hear that?"

Stewart shrugged. "Not from your friend, Alysa. She called in sick today." His eyes growing even more malicious, he said, "Ellington wants to see you ASAP."

Dana wondered how she could have ever loved such a man. She should have ditched him the first time he'd hit her.

Ellington Steele, one of the company's founding partners and Stewart's golfing buddy. She should have expected as much.

"What kind of nonsense did you tell him?"

"Nothing that he can't read about in the paper."

She thought of all the things she knew about Stewart, all the secrets she could reveal. Almost, *almost,* Dana let the Melanie Murray thing slip. Oh, how she wanted to tell the bastard what was about to come. But she didn't.

"Someday," she said instead, "people will see you as you truly are, Stewart. I'm only grateful I spotted it before we walked down the aisle."

She spun on her heel, waiting for him to say something snide. He didn't. For that she was grateful, although her stomach burned at the thought of facing Ellington Steele. Dana would bet the new high heels she wore that he wanted to see her about her job— just as Stewart had warned.

If the top-floor offices of Steele & Steele were meant to impress with their wall-to-wall windows and swanky chrome decor, Ellington Steele's office was meant to intimidate. It overlooked the Los Angeles basin, and Dana often wondered if Ellington stared out his window and contemplated the vast amount of money he made off the populace. He was a small man, and she'd long suspected he liked things done in a big way to compensate for his height.

"You wanted to see me?" she asked, after gently knocking on his partially open door.

With a head of thinning brown hair and watery blue eyes, Ellington was not an attractive man. If he hadn't been one of the city's most successful CPAs, she doubted women would find him attractive at all. Two weeks after going to work for him, he'd hit on her. She'd refused. They'd been on shaky ground ever since.

"Dana," he said, not even bothering to move from behind his colossally big desk, which was cut from a slab of marble that reminded Dana of the Bible. He looked up from the magazine he'd been studying with the unspoken attitude that she'd interrupted something important. Yeah, right.

"I see we managed to make it in this morning," he said.

"Um, yeah." Had he expected her to call in sick? Like Alysa? She felt her eyes narrow. Stewart. Obviously her ex had told Ellington that he expected her to stay in Las Vegas and watch Braden race. How nice of him.

"Stewart—" the total dip-wad, überjerk, horrible asshole "—told me you wanted to see me."

Her boss steepled his hands, like a politician about to deliver some heavy, world-shattering news. "Before we begin, I'd like to tell you how disappointed I was to hear that you and Stewart had called things off."

Somehow Dana doubted it. After she'd brushed him off, Ellington had not endorsed Stewart dating her. They were cut from the same cloth, her ex and her boss. But Stewart had been born with the looks to match his brains, and Ellington would forever be in his shadow. She had a feeling the two shared a symbiotic relationship. Stewart had charisma. Ellington liked basking in his glory.

"Thank you," Dana said. *I think,* she silently added.

"I hear you're already seeing somebody new?" His eyes gently rebuked her.

She'd come into work too late. Stewart had been spreading his falsehoods.

"Actually, no. I'm not certain where you might have heard that, but it's not true."

"Oh," he said, adjusting the flaps of his dark gray suit jacket. "I see."

Dana's feeling of dread increased with each passing second.

"Dana, I'm afraid I have some bad news," he said with a false look of sympathy.

"Oh?" she asked, her pulse like a sledgehammer.

"I'm afraid we haven't had a very good year at Steele & Steele, financially I mean."

Bull! She was a CPA. She could do the math. Times might be tough for America, but taxes never went away. They were as busy as ever.

"We've had to make some difficult choices. Choices directly related to our financial crisis."

She knew what was coming, had suspected as much from the evil little grin on Stewart's face when he'd told her Ellington wanted to talk to her.

"You're firing me."

CHAPTER SIXTEEN

"WELL, NOW," HER BOSS SAID. "Not firing, precisely. Laying you off. If things change, you would most certainly be eligible for rehire."

If things change. What did that mean? Was she being blackmailed?

"Is this because of Stewart?" She realized in that instant that she'd changed over the past week. Maybe getting to know someone like Braden had given her some much needed self-confidence. Or maybe her ride in a race car had taught her life shouldn't be feared. Whatever the reason, two weeks ago she'd have never asked such a brazen question. But, damn it, she was tired of men pushing her around.

"Absolutely not," Ellington said, all righteous indignation. Dana didn't buy it for an instant. "Stewart is a friend, but I would never compromise the integrity of this firm by taking sides on an issue."

What the hell did that mean? She almost asked the question aloud, but she could tell by Ellington's expression that she'd get nowhere with her erstwhile boss, Mr. Steele.

"I see."

"I know that as two adults," Ellington said, "the two of you will act with utmost professionalism, despite your falling-out."

That just proved how little Ellington knew about Stewart.

"I'm not certain I agree with you on that point, Ellington, but nonetheless, I assume you're offering a severance package?"

"Actually, no," Ellington said brusquely. "As I mentioned, money is tight. Your termination will be effective immediately. All you'll receive are your remaining vacation and sick days which, as you know, are both at a minimum." He opened a drawer, fished out an envelope. "This is your last check. It represents eight hours of leftover vacation time and one week's sick pay, plus the hours you worked prior to your, er, trip last week." What he really meant was the week she'd taken off to prepare for her wedding, a wedding that had never taken place.

Almost two weeks' pay.

Ellington rose from his chair. "That's it."

"Yes, I suppose it is," Dana murmured, forcing herself to smile. "It was a pleasure working for you, Mr. Steele," she said, holding out her hand.

"Oh, ah, yes," Ellington said, seeming to be caught off guard. He clasped and released her hand in almost the same instant. "And you. I'm very sorry to see you go."

Sure he was.

"I'm certain you'll understand if I have security escort you from our offices."

Stewart must have made her sound like more of a crackpot than she'd thought. Amazing how one person could malign her character so completely in the space of a few short minutes.

"Of course," she said graciously, taking deep breaths in an effort to remain calm. What was she so upset about? She'd planned on quitting, anyway.

Yeah, but it was one thing to quit…quite another to be fired.

"I hope the firm, ah, rebounds," she added, giving him a look that she hoped told him she knew well and good there was no "financial crisis" at Steele & Steele. "I wish you and your brother the best," she said, referring to the other Steele, the one who was never at work and whose name was nothing more than paint on the door.

"Goodbye, Dana."

Five years of working her ass off had just been completely negated by one no-good, lying jerk. If only Ellington knew some of the things she knew about Stewart. He'd be showing him the door, too.

But she would be the bigger person. She wouldn't smear Stewart's reputation like he'd smeared hers, no matter that some of the things she knew about him could get him in serious hot water. Let them all wag their tongues. In time they'd learn who the bad person truly was.

"Good luck, Mr. Steele." *Be sure to watch prime-time news in a couple days. You might learn something interesting about your friend.*

It was hard to hold her head up as she went to her desk. That was all she had after five years. Alysa had the office, which had always been a sore spot for Dana. But it was her own damn fault, she realized now. She'd lived her life like the proverbial mushroom. Even her cubicle resembled the dingy warehouses where they grew fungus. Dana had a corner cubicle, one without windows, its dark gray walls lit only by her computer monitor.

But no more. From here on out she would put herself first. No more letting people push her around.

She almost slammed her fist down on the plastic tabletop. She would have, too, if she wasn't certain Stewart was waiting for her reaction from the safety of his nearby office.

Her phone rang.

Dana picked it up absently, opening the drawer to her right at the same time. It was the only space where she stored personal items. Well, aside from the photos she'd taped to the fabric-covered walls and the odd pencil and pen.

"Dana Johnson," she answered automatically. Crap. What the hell was she supposed to tell her clients?

"Hello, Ms. Johnson. This is Savanna Niles from *My-Lovematch*. How are you this morning?"

Dana straightened. "Terrific," she lied. *I've only just been fired. Any chance you can get me that two-thousand dollars I won a little early?*

"I'm so glad I caught you," Savanna said. "For some reason I didn't expect you to be at work this morning."

Probably because Savanna had expected Dana to still be at the race like any bona fide NASCAR fan. "Nope. I'm here." *For a few more minutes, at least. Until security comes upstairs and escorts me out.*

"Excellent," Savanna said in a cheerful tone. "I wanted to talk to you about the contest. As you know, you're the lucky winner of a date with Braden James."

The woman must not have a clue about what had happened in Vegas.

"So, you'll be receiving an all-expenses-paid trip to Napa compliments of *My-Lovematch*. You'll also be receiving a check for two thousand dollars. All of the tickets, the single event license that you'll need to fill out to get your HotPass, and the check will be overnighted to your address this morning."

"That's great," she said. She really needed the money, especially if she didn't find a job before rent was due next month.

"But as our contest winner, there are a few other things you'll be required to do. In the package, there will be a consent form. And, just so there are no surprises, I thought I'd go over the few things *My-Lovematch* will require as their contest winner."

Dana straightened, suddenly smelling a rat.

"What kind of things?"

"First," Savanna said in a pleasant voice, "and most important, we'll need you to do a photo shoot, as soon as possible."

"Photo shoot?"

"Yes. As you know, *My-Lovematch* is using the *Win A Date* contest as a way to generate publicity. We'll need some photos of you and Braden for press releases, advertising campaigns and any other unforeseen requirements."

"You'll be creating an ad campaign?" Dana said, her dread clearly evident.

"Oh, don't worry. We're not going to put you on billboards or anything. We'll be running some ads in a few NASCAR publications. You know, fun-looking ads. You and Braden hugging each other, or Braden holding you in his arms. Happy. That's the feel we're going for because people who use *My-Lovematch* live happily ever after."

She'd seen the *My-Lovematch* slogan before, although where she couldn't exactly recall. Now she was being forced to promote the idea. Terrific. As if *she* was the poster child for happily ever afters.

"And, since most magazines go to print three months before publication date, we'll need to get a move on this. Your date's less than twelve weeks away and we'd like to have the camera-ready artwork done by the end of the month."

"I see."

"So, when can you fly out to see us?"

"Where, exactly, do you want me to go?" Dana asked, hearing footsteps behind her. When she turned, she spied Stewart standing behind her, his black suit and dark hair making him look like one of the devil's own minions. Okay. So the jerk wasn't going to leave her alone. Fine. She'd give him something to get angry about.

She flipped him off. Childish, but it made her feel better.

He leaned in and whispered, "Anytime. Anyplace."

Revulsion made her lips purse. She covered the phone with her hands. "In your dreams." She uncovered the phone before he could reply. "How about we meet up this week?" she told the woman on the other line.

"Oh, wow. This week!" Savannah said. "I didn't expect you'd be able to get away so quickly."

"I'm completely at your disposal," she said with a seductive purr.

Stewart's eyes narrowed in such a way that Dana knew she'd succeeded in making him think she was speaking to Braden.

"Unfortunately, I'm not sure Mr. James has time to do something this week, but let me check with his PR rep. You never know. It's possible he might be able to squeeze us in. Why don't I call you back?"

"Great," Dana said with a false smile. She lowered her voice to a seductive whisper. "I'll be waiting for your call."

There was silence on the other end, then a hesitant, "Terrific," as if Savanna suddenly wondered about the sexual orientation of their contest winner. "I'll be in touch soon."

"Call me on my cell phone," Dana said.

"Oh, ah, sure."

"Bye, Braden," Dana said, hanging up quickly. If Savanna thought she was nuts, so be it, Dana didn't care. She relished the way Stewart stared down at her. Gone was the smug smile, and in its place was a look that could only be called righteous indignation.

"That was *him?*"

Dana nodded. "Yup. He sends his love." She crossed her arms in front of her. "Although you'll see that love in person when the two of you go to court."

Ha, she silently told him. *Take that, Stewart. I've grown a backbone since we broke up.*

"If we go to court," Stewart said, his black hair gleaming beneath the fluorescent lights, "I'll be the one pressing charges against *him.*"

She snorted. "Yeah, good luck with that. Incidentally, did you tell Mr. Steele about your impending criminal record?"

"Why should I?" he said. "His accusations are completely false, which will be proved in a court of law."

He was completely deluded. "Well, you better buy blinders for the jury then, because there's no way they'll find you not guilty once they see the security tape."

"I guess we'll see about that, won't we?" he asked, looking completely nonchalant. "Incidentally, did you tell your boyfriend about your change in employment status?"

"Of course," she lied, crossing her legs. She felt nausea bubble up inside her when he eyed her up and down. She'd thought he'd been joking earlier when he'd made his anytime, anyplace comment. Maybe not.

She locked eyes with him, saw lust deep in their depths.

Her jaw begin to ache, a psychosomatic reaction, she realized. "Actually," she said, trying to hide her revulsion, "we're both thrilled. We'll be spending more time together now. I'm hooking up with him this week." All true, although not quite for the reasons she hoped Stewart thought. "So, thank you." She gave him a blinding smile. "Since I assume I have you to thank for having me terminated."

He leaned toward her and said, "Oh, yeah. I flew back yesterday just in time to play a round of golf with our boss. Or should I say, your *former* boss. I convinced him of the wisdom of letting you go, especially since I threatened to leave Steele & Steele if he kept you on. It's no secret who the better CPA is in this organization, and who makes the most money for the firm. Guess it took him less than twenty-four hours to figure it out, too."

Despite suspecting as much earlier, Dana's temper boiled over to hear him confess. Almost… almost she told him she knew exactly *how* he made so much money. But she didn't. She might need that information later.

So she said instead, "Well, thank you for providing me with a vacation." Her free leg swung in a manner of supreme nonchalance. "I'm sure Braden and I will enjoy ourselves in the coming weeks."

They both caught movement at the corner of her cubicle. Dana recognized the gray uniforms of building security.

"Ah," Stewart said with a pleasant smile. "Here's your escort."

Dana's molars scraped together with what was surely an audible *criiick*. But she forced herself to relax, forced herself to smile. "Just a second, boys," she said without looking at the two men, "I'm disposing of some garbage right now."

She saw anger flicker in Stewart's eyes and, despite telling herself she had nothing to fear, she felt her cheek tingle in anticipation of his slap. Why not. It'd happened before. Twice.

But obviously he wasn't that big a fool.

"Goodbye, Dana," he said, stepping back.

"Goodbye, Stewart." She hoped it was forever.

CHAPTER SEVENTEEN

AS IT TURNED OUT, Braden couldn't meet with her that week. Dana heard back from Savanna while driving home, a pathetically small box of her belongings in the backseat. Next Monday, she'd been told. Braden would be racing in Virginia that weekend. They wanted her to meet with him there. So she'd be taking a trip to the East Coast. Dana told herself she should be excited. She might have been, too, except now that her humiliation about being fired had faded, she wasn't so certain flying off to see Braden was a great idea. What would she say to him? More importantly, what would he say to her?

She supposed she'd know the answer to those questions next week. Unfortunately, that meant staying in her apartment, alone, for the next several days. The prospect filled her with dismay.

She didn't trust Stewart.

The look in his eyes today…the things he'd said…

She had to leave town.

She drove. She didn't know where she was going; she didn't care.

She traveled north, wherever the mood struck. She didn't read the paper or turn on the TV. The only people she called were her mom and Roger. Her mom and stepdad were understandably concerned, but Dana reassured them that she would be fine. She cut them off before they could question her about Stewart, or about the interview. If they'd even *seen* the interview. She wasn't in the mood to chat.

Monday rolled around soon enough. She'd packed enough clothes that she didn't need to return home, just in case. Stewart might be waiting.

Dana boarded the commercial flight with a mixture of dread and anticipation. She dreaded the thought of facing Braden, but she knew him well enough to know he'd be nothing but a perfect gentleman. And despite the way they'd ended things, she *wanted* to see him again.

They flew her into Richmond, a tiny airport that looked like a private airstrip compared to LAX. Brown buildings were set against a green backdrop. Acres of lawn surrounded her. Lush green trees could be seen in the distance, clouds that looked to be the size of Mount Everest floating overhead. Thunderstorm, she surmised, gauging it to be a few miles away. The South was rife with them, or so she'd read. Actually, she'd read a lot of books in the past few days, mostly about NASCAR.

NASCAR was a sport with *very* dedicated fans.

And Braden, the man who'd protected her from Stewart and kissed her senseless, appeared to be one of the sport's biggest celebrities. She'd known he was famous, of course. At least on some level. But the breadth of it…the sheer scope of his notoriety. Now that she knew his face, she saw him everywhere. Advertising car products in magazines. Endorsing a brand of tires in a local newspaper. Drinking soda on TV.

But there was more to his celebrity than that. Among NASCAR fans, the man was a legend. A much loved legend, with devoted acolytes adoring him for his humility and his unassuming attitude. He rarely drove dirty, loved his fans and gave back to the community. Braden James was one of the good guys.

Or at least he had been until he'd met her.

The next morning, she followed the directions Savanna had e-mailed her. The whole way over Dana forced herself to take deep breaths. She could do this, she reminded herself. She'd faced far scarier moments—like confronting the man who'd done his best to destroy her.

The photo shoot was in downtown Richmond, in an old gray building that Dana would bet had been around since the early 1900s. Made of dark stone and at least five stories tall, it looked made to last. The studio was on the first floor. Dana let herself inside and immediately spied a reception desk with no one behind it. She heard voices so she followed them, bracing herself as she passed through a door that led to a studio.

There he was. He stood outside a perimeter of lights and photographic equipment. She had to look away before their gazes met. It didn't help. Tension straightened her spine. *Sexual* tension.

Oh, jeez. Her body remembered that kiss…all too well.

"Dana," someone said, breaking apart from a group to greet her. Dana recognized Elizabeth. "You made it."

"I made it," she echoed, looking anywhere but at Braden. Still, her heart was racing, its rhythm increasing with every breath she took.

"I'm so glad you came." Dana could have sworn the PR rep's gaze searched her own for cracks in Dana's brittle exterior. "And on such short notice. You know Braden, of course," Elizabeth said, motioning toward her client. "But I don't think you've met Savanna." She pointed toward a cute blonde that reminded Dana of Alysa.

Alysa who hadn't called her. Her rejection stung. They'd never been close friends, but, after their trip to Vegas, Dana had thought they'd grown closer. Obviously not.

"Hi, Savanna," she said, slightly embarrassed when she recalled the woman's confusion during their first phone conversation. "So nice to meet you." *I really am sane,* she wanted to add. *I was just trying to make my psycho ex-fiancé jealous.*

"This is our photographer," Elizabeth said. "Damien Renquest. He's shot all of *My-Lovematch*'s campaigns in the past."

"He does wonderful work," Savanna added. "You'll be thrilled."

Dana shook Damien's hand, and the photographer said in a high, nearly feminine tone, "Yeah, but I won't have to work hard to make this one look pretty." The hand she shook was limp. "She's stunning. Have you ever modeled before?"

"No," Dana said, uncomfortable with his praise.

Savanna beamed. "She is, isn't she? I can't wait to see what hair and makeup does with her. You ready for that?"

"Sure."

"They have clothes for you, too," Elizabeth said. "Red and white, *My-Lovematch*'s corporate colors."

"Oh, ah, terrific," Dana said, still unable to meet Braden's gaze. She'd known he'd wear his driving suit, but he seemed taller and larger than she remembered him.

"Well, good," Elizabeth said. "I'm glad you don't mind us dressing you. Of course, we had to guess at your size. But you can try the clothes on in the other room. Right this way."

Finally Dana found the courage to look straight at Braden.

It felt like being shot with a stun gun.

Every nerve sparked. Every goose bump popped. Every hair on the back of her neck lifted. The breath was sucked out of her. What she meant to be a fleeting glance turned into an unblinking stare.

"Nice to see you," he said. Then he turned away. He didn't even smile.

She was left standing there, alone, feeling like the biggest fool on planet Earth.

"You coming?" Elizabeth asked.

Dana turned away, numbed by his response. She told herself to get a grip. What was she so upset about? She'd been the one to tell him to leave her alone.

"Isn't this place cool?" Savanna asked. "We rented it just for this shoot, but it's going to be perfect…."

Dana barely heard her. As she followed Elizabeth and Savanna to a different area of the office, Dana admitted part of her thought this was all wrong. She'd imagined their reunion differently. Braden should have lit up when he saw her, made it clear that he was still interested in her, maybe even given her a hug. He'd done none of those things. Dana wondered if she'd been played. Or if his interest in her had been feigned to please his sponsor.

Maybe that was why she gave herself up to the

woman they'd hired to do her hair and makeup. Daisy was energetic with a wide smile and black hair streaked with wide swaths of red. Normally, Dana would shun such feminine attention from someone who looked like Count Dracula's wife. But suddenly she didn't care. An hour later she'd been washed, blown dry and curled, her hair having been left long. Her makeup had been done with a deft hand. And her clothes...well, that was the only time she'd grown nervous: When she saw what they'd picked out for her to wear.

"We were guessing at your size," Elizabeth said again. "But we have other dresses for you to try on, too, if this one's too big."

It wasn't the size that concerned her. It was the cut. Made of red fabric, it had a halter top, a style Dana usually avoided. The waist was tight, too, accentuating her figure—something else Dana tried to avoid. The skirt flared wide, the hem hung at uneven lengths so that it swished around her legs when she walked, exposing her lower thighs and knobby knees.

"You look breathtaking," Elizabeth said when Dana came out of the changing room.

"Damn," Savanna said. "I wonder if we shouldn't hire you to do some modeling for us."

Dana studied herself in a mirror. She'd never been fond of makeup, and, in her opinion, Daisy had gone a little overboard with the eyeliner and mascara, but the dress certainly flattered her trim figure and tall form. Her hair looked nice, too, her natural curls a mass of ringlets that framed her face.

What would Braden think?

She knew she shouldn't care, but deep down she admitted she *did*.

She cared a lot.

"DOESN'T SHE LOOK GREAT?" Braden heard Elizabeth say.

Max Arnold looked past him, and Braden watched as the man's eyes widened. Uh-oh.

"Hot damn," the CEO of *My-Lovematch* muttered. "I knew she'd clean up good, but *wow*."

Braden cringed, both at the crassness of the man's comments and at the way he eyed Dana. Braden's fists clenched.

"Dana, hi," Max said, moving forward. "Do you remember me? I'm Max Arnold. CEO of *My-Lovematch,* and boy, am I glad you agreed to take part in our *Win A Date* contest."

Braden didn't want to turn around, but like a motorist whose eyes were drawn to the scene of an accident, he found himself facing her.

He almost took a step back.

He'd known she'd look stunning. Of course he'd known that. But what he hadn't expected, what he was in no way prepared for, was the way seeing her made him feel. Though she tried to be brave, he knew by the look in her eyes that she felt scared and out of her depth. Lost and vulnerable. Maybe even close to tears. It was like he was a little boy all over again. Like he looked into his own eyes. He saw someone frightened and alone, exactly as he had felt whenever he'd been forced into a new foster family.

It tore at his heart.

"Nice to see you again, Mr. Arnold," Dana said.

"Max," the CEO of *My-Lovematch* said. "Call me Max."

She nodded, her eyes darting around the room as if trying to reassure herself that everything would be okay. "I'm really nervous," she admitted.

Only by sheer force of will did Braden stop himself from moving forward, from placing a reassuring hand on her back.

Hell, she hadn't even called. Not that he blamed her. None of them had expected the media frenzy that had erupted as a result of Melanie's touching story: the woman who'd won a date with one of America's biggest sports stars right after the devastating abuse she'd suffered at the hands of an ex-lover. No names had been mentioned, but it hadn't taken long to put two and two together. Braden had read her fiancé's name in more than one newspaper.

"Hey, Braden," Dana said, her gaze moving to

his and anchoring there like a ship at sea. "I guess this is it."

"You bet this is it," Max said, the big, boisterous man moving forward to take her hand. "Dana Johnson, you look ravishing. The American public is going to love you."

"They *already* love her," Elizabeth said. "When Melanie Murray aired that story, my phone started ringing off the hook. How many interview requests have you gotten, Dana?"

Braden saw her eyes widen, saw her look between Elizabeth and Savanna, her eyes radiating dismay. "They aired the story already?"

"Of course," Elizabeth said. "We were told it might be broadcast as soon as the Tuesday after the race, remember?"

"And they actually did it?" Dana asked. "I just thought—well, I guess I wondered if they would go through with it."

"They did. It aired on Tuesday," Elizabeth said.

She hadn't known, he realized. Good lord. She'd been completely clueless to the fact that the two of them were now front-page news.

CHAPTER EIGHTEEN

DANA FELT STUNNED. She'd known it was coming. But the fact that it'd actually happened threw her for a loop.

"There's no need to look so worried," Elizabeth said. "Melanie kept your fiancé's name out of it. And she made it pretty clear that Braden was protecting you when he got into that fight."

Dana's stomach dropped. She looked at Braden. "Did she?"

"Yes," he said.

Well, at least she had that to be grateful for. Sure, at the time it had seemed like a good idea to talk about her ex, but now that the story had actually aired…

Tell anyone and you're dead.

But she hadn't told anyone. She'd kept Stewart's name out of it. Sort of.

"The interview completely killed the story about Braden being an out of control race car driver," Elizabeth added. "He came out looking like a hero. They even talked about what he did for Belinda. Our phone's been ringing off the hook."

"And our Web site hits have tripled thanks to all the great publicity," Savanna added. "It was terrific publicity, and great exposure for the *My-Lovematch* brand. I can't believe you didn't know."

She hadn't wanted to know, Dana admitted.

Braden stepped forward. "Let's get started," he said to the photographer, glancing at his watch. "I'm sure Dana doesn't want to be here all day."

"You okay?" Elizabeth asked, coming over and patting her on the back.

"Fine," she said.

"All righty then," Damien said with a clap of his hands. "Let's get going."

It didn't get any easier from there. Damien asked Braden to step aside so he could get some head shots of Dana alone. Dana's frazzled nerves frayed around the edges even more as she took center stage. She hated being in the spotlight, everyone staring at her, the flash of Damien's camera causing spots to dance before her eyes. But the worst part was knowing Braden was out there, on the other side of the camera, watching.

"Just relax," Damien said.

She tried, she truly did. Dana wasn't prone to drinking, but suddenly she found herself wishing for a shot of whiskey.

You didn't mention Stewart's name. You'll be okay.

But she'd talked about an ex. People would assume that ex was Stewart. At the time, she hadn't cared. Now she sort of did.

Fool. You shouldn't care. Stewart deserves his fate…whatever that might be.

Yeah, but what about *her* fate?

"There you go," Damien said, even though Dana had no idea what she'd done. "That's better."

She assumed more poses, growing more uptight with each passing moment. Then Braden was asked to join her under the lights.

"Okay, you two," Damien said. "Let's see you have some fun. Dance a little. I want happy people."

Happy, Dana thought. Ha. She'd just been profiled by a major network, her dirty laundry aired for all to see. She had an ex-fiancé who scared the hell out of her. And a man she cared about, someone she'd thought was kindhearted and sweet, wouldn't give her the time of day.

"Come on, you two. Dance."

She tried. She really tried, but she felt like a fool as she moved around.

"Smile," Damien said.

Dana had to blink against the numerous bright strobes of light.

"Okay. Enough of that," Damien said. "You two won't be winning any dance competitions, that's for sure. Let's try something different. Braden, wrap your arms around her."

Dana's gaze jammed on Braden. He only looked in her direction for a moment, but it was long enough to see the displeasure in his eyes.

"Are you sure we need to do that?"

She saw Damien's head pop out from behind his camera. "We're trying to project romance. What's more romantic than having you hold her? Go on, Braden. Reach for her."

Dana tried to apologize to him with her eyes. It hurt when she saw his jaw tighten.

"Come here," he said softly.

"Just one arm for now," Damien said. "Give me a friendly smile, you two."

Dana did her best. She assumed Braden did, too.

"Perfect," Damien said, the camera flashing yet again. "Now pull her a little closer. Keep your smiles. No, no…not a forced grin. I can't believe how tense you two are. Relax. You look like you're about to get a rectal exam."

It was an apt analogy because she didn't think anything could make her as uncomfortable as standing next to Braden. Because she wasn't as indifferent to him as she pretended. Oh, no.

She'd told herself a million times in the past week that it'd been smart to walk away from him. Obviously, she'd been right. Look how quickly he'd forgotten her. Yet here she was wanting him to hold her, to tell her everything would be all right, to reassure her that she'd done the right thing by talking to Melanie Murray and that he'd protect her if Stewart came after her again.

Instead he kept his distance—or tried to. It nearly tore her apart.

"Okay, let's try a more romantic pose," Damien said. "Braden, pull her into your arms as if you're about to kiss her. Dana, look up at him with those big pretty eyes of yours. Stare at him as if you're besotted."

She couldn't do it, but Braden did as instructed, his big body turning toward hers, his arms slowly reaching for her.

She braced herself.

"Come on, Dana. Look up at him. He's not going to bite. I know you're embarrassed, but just think about the millions of women who'd love to be in your shoes."

She met Braden's gaze, long enough for Dana to note his eyes were completely devoid of emotion.

The smile she forced on her face wobbled a bit. She closed her eyes, trying to erase the image of his blank stare. When she opened her eyes, she forced herself to appear relaxed, happy, carefree.

"That's better," Damien said.

She softened her gaze and, before she could stop herself, she reached up and touched Braden's face.

He flinched.

"Perfect," Damien all but cried. "Dana, that's great. Braden, why don't you bend her over your arm?"

He'd flinched. *Flinched.*

Braden's arms tightened. She braced herself. He tipped her backward and managed his own stare of adoration.

She wished it wasn't an act. Only then did she admit that fact. She'd been away from him for a week and yet when he held her in his arms, it felt as if she'd never left.

"Good. Perfect," the photographer said, snapping away. "Now, swing her back up."

Braden pulled her to her feet so quickly she lost her balance. Dana almost fell. He started to catch her, but when he saw she was okay, he turned away instead.

But not before she *saw* it—desire. It flickered in his eyes like an animal half-starved and crazed.

SHE KNEW, DAMN IT. She *had* to know.

"That was great, Braden," Damien said. "Now pull her into your arms. Tight."

"Come on, Damien," he heard himself say. "Surely you've got all the shots you want? There's no need for me to make poor Dana uncomfortable."

"Come now, don't be coy." Damien waved his hand. "Just do it. Pull her to you."

"Braden," Dana murmured. She didn't say his name in warning, it was more like a plea.

He looked into her eyes.

He saw desire there. And sadness. And longing.

"Dana."

Slowly, ever so gently, she moved into his arms. Braden couldn't look away.

"Yes!" Damien yelled. "Yes, yes, yes. That's the look. Finally."

Braden's hand moved of its own volition. Without thought, he cupped her face.

"Perfect!"

It'll be okay, he told her with his eyes, because it was obvious that she was terrified. Not of him. No. She feared the repercussions of her interview. He just knew it.

I'll protect you.

Will you? she silently asked back.

"Yes," he murmured softly, his hand brushing her cheek.

She blinked. Braden's heart lodged in his throat when he saw tears in her eyes.

"Okay, people," Damien yelled, setting his camera down and clapping his hands. "That's a wrap. Great job, you two."

But Braden held on to her.

"Braden. You can let go of her anytime," Max Arnold said.

It was Dana who stepped away.

"I should change," she said quietly.

What had just happened?

"Good job, Braden," Elizabeth said, coming forward to clap him on the back. "What was all that about?" she murmured for his ears alone.

"I don't know," he answered.

"Well, you better figure it out because Max wants the two of you to go dinner with him."

"I don't know if that's such a good idea."

"Neither do I. But Max is the CEO of *My-Lovematch*. You *have* to go."

"Can't you tell him I have a prior commitment? Dinner at the White House? Church with the Pope? Coronation at the queen's?"

Elizabeth shot him a look of long-suffering impatience. "Don't be ridiculous. Nothing short of major surgery would get you out of this one."

"I think I might need an appendectomy," Braden said immediately.

Elizabeth swatted him on the arm. "Braden, what's wrong with you? This thing between you and Dana hasn't gotten out of hand, has it? 'Cause I gotta tell you, judging by the heated glances the two of you just exchanged, I'm thinking it has."

"What thing?" he asked, keeping his expression blank. Easy to do since he'd been practicing the look all day.

She shook her head. "Give me a break. You ought to know there's no secrets in the garage. Half the team saw you go off with Dana in Las Vegas. Word is you christened the cab of the truck."

"No," he immediately countered, grateful Dana wasn't within earshot. "We did not. Dana needed some privacy. That interview with Melanie Murray tore her apart."

He saw his PR rep scan his eyes. Elizabeth was like a sister to him. He swore sometimes she could see inside his brain.

"Nothing happened?" she asked. "Really?"

"Not the kind of nothing you're thinking about," Braden said, crossing his arms in front of him.

"But it almost did."

There she went again, reading his mind. "That, my dear, is none of your business."

Another cocked brow. "What's the matter? She turn you down?"

"Look," Braden said, trying to change the subject. "About this dinner. Does it have to be tonight? Can it be tomorrow?" After Dana was gone.

"She did turn you down, didn't she?" Elizabeth said. "Good for her. I knew I liked her."

"The dinner?" he prompted again. "Can we postpone it?"

"No," Elizabeth said. "We're going tonight. Max has to fly out in the morning for a meeting. Don't look at me like that, Braden. This isn't *my* fault. You're the one who didn't keep his hands to himself."

"I *did* keep my hands to myself. That's what I'm telling you."

"Did you, Braden?" Elizabeth asked. "'Cause I've got to be honest with you. I've never seen you act this way. Most of the time you're so busy sweet-talking women, they're half in love with you by the end of the day. But you never mean a word of it. I know you don't do it intentionally," she hastened to add. "It's just your way. But today, you're staring at Dana like you might actually care."

"I do," he admitted, shoulders sagging. Why bother denying it? "But she doesn't want anything to do with me."

"Well, from what I've seen today, you're wrong. That woman is definitely interested."

"You think?"

"I know."

"Shit."

"Shit?" Elizabeth said. "Shit what? What's wrong with getting involved with her?"

"Oh, a little something called an ex-fiancé. An ex-fiancé, I might add, that left more emotional scars on her than a flat tire on a fender well. Not to mention, he might pose a problem if she's dating again. I don't trust that man as far as I can throw him. He worries me."

"This from a guy who races cars for a living."

"Your point is?"

"You rarely scare easily."

Braden crossed his arms. "Yeah," he said. "So?"

Elizabeth's expression grew serious. "Look, Braden, there's something between you two. You might try and deny it, but I see it plainly as the nose on my face. I know she just broke up with that guy, but so what? You're more than enough man to stand up to him. What if this was meant to be?"

"You sound like a *My-Lovematch* ad."

"So?" Elizabeth huffed. "She's a nice girl. Probably one of the nicest I've ever met. She's unassuming. She has no idea how gorgeous she is, and it shows. Very down-to-earth. And smart. You should snatch her up."

"Right. She's single because she just got unsnatched."

The door opened. Braden glanced at the entrance and spied Dana making her way toward them.

"Then snatch her again," Elizabeth hissed up at him before turning to Dana. "We were just talking about you."

Braden tensed.

"Mr. Arnold wants to take you and Braden to dinner."

"Oh, no, I couldn't," Dana said. "I'm really tired. And tomorrow's an early start. I have a nine-o'clock flight—"

"It wasn't a request," Elizabeth said sternly. "Be there by five."

When his PR rep turned away, she shot him a triumphant grin.

There, she seemed to say. *I've taken the matter out of your hands. Deal with it.*

He just hoped he could…deal with it, that is.

CHAPTER NINETEEN

DANA DIDN'T WANT TO GO.

She pulled on a fresh pair of jeans and a poufy white blouse, one that hung off her shoulders and concealed her figure in a way Dana liked. She thought about calling Elizabeth, but she was tired of running away. She was taking a cab to the restaurant. Right now.

How many times had she vowed to face life head-on, only to turn tail and run when things got too tough? She'd almost let that fear stop her from racing with Braden that day, an experience that had become one of the most exhilarating of her life. She had a feeling spending time with Braden would be just as earth-shattering…if she was brave enough to take the plunge.

Her cell phone rang. Dana jumped. To her shock and dismay, Alysa's name showed on the display.

"Hello?" Dana said tentatively, the phone's plastic exterior cool against her cheek.

"Hello, Dana."

"Hi, Alysa, what's up?" She pressed the phone

against her ear so tightly that it hurt. Or maybe that was her heart.

"I know about the Melanie Murray interview." There was a lengthy pause, and then the softly uttered, "How could you do it, Dana? How could you betray Stewart like you did?"

Her betray *Stewart*?

"What the hell are you talking about?" Dana asked, anger finally getting the better of her. "Last I heard, *he* was the one who betrayed *me*."

"Yeah, but *he* didn't trash-talk you to the media. How could you do that? Everyone's in shock. Stewart's had to take a leave of absence. His clients are calling left and right."

"What do you mean? I never even mentioned him by name."

"You didn't *have* to, Dana. God, are you stupid? Everyone knew who you were talking about."

"Everyone at Steele & Steele," Dana said, stung by Alysa's words. "Nobody else."

"That makes it better?" Alysa asked. "You made him sound like some kind of wife beater."

"So what? He is a wife beater. Or a fiancée beater," Dana cried. The cab slowed. Were they there already?

"According to *you*," Alysa said. "But no one's seen any bruises."

"*You* have."

"So? You could have gotten them anywhere. The last thing you should have done was infer Stewart did it. Not on the national news. You've ruined him."

So? she almost cried out again. He deserved to be ruined.

The cab stopped. They'd arrived, and the driver looked back at her questioningly. Dana fished inside her purse, pulled out a bill and thrust it in his direction. She hopped out before the man could give her change, her brown leather satchel hitting her in the back as she bolted away.

"All I did was talk about my past. I never once mentioned Stewart by name," Dana repeated. She glanced at the front of the restaurant, where a blue neon sign announced its name. She turned left instead of going inside. "As far as I'm concerned, I've done nothing wrong."

"Then you're a bigger fool than I thought. It took less than a day for some reporter to get hold of his name. A *gossip magazine,* Dana. They called the office wanting background information on Stewart so they could glamorize your relationship with Braden. That's what the woman said. Jeez, Dana, are you *trying* to antagonize Stewart? He's furious. Rightfully so."

Dana stopped walking for a moment. *A gossip magazine?* Was Braden *that* famous?

Of course he was, she admitted. Just as famous as

a baseball or football star, and she'd seen plenty of stories on them in the gossip rags.

"He's crushed," Alysa added. "He really thought there was a chance the two of you could work it out. If your goal was to kick him in the teeth, mission accomplished."

"For your information, Alysa, Stewart got me fired. If he was truly trying to *work things out,* he was going about it the wrong way. He's a no-good, lying sociopath, one who's obviously got you and everybody else conned. But I know better. And you know what, that's all that really matters. *I* know the truth, and *I* got away from Stewart before it was too late."

Silence again. To her left, cars raced up and down a narrow street. She'd stopped in the shadow of a building. Maybe that's why she felt so chilled.

"Wow," Alysa said. "Life in the fast lane really *has* changed you, Dana. And not for the better. Maybe your new friends think it's okay to ruin someone's life, but I'm here to tell you it's not. Not for any reason."

"What new friends?"

"Aren't you with Braden right now?"

Dana stiffened. "Yes, but not for the reasons you think. I had to do a photo shoot for *My-Lovematch.* But so what? What if I was here with Braden? What if I chucked it all and threw myself into an affair with a world-famous race car driver? What if, for once, instead of worrying about how a man's going to treat me, I just enjoyed myself? As someone I thought of as a friend, shouldn't you be happy for me?"

"I am happy for you," Alysa said. "But I don't think you and I will ever be friends again."

Despite knowing that was the truth, the words hurt. Damn, how they hurt.

"I can't be friends with someone who betrays the people close to her. You've changed, Dana, and I don't like the new you."

"You've changed, too," Dana said. "The Alysa I knew would never treat a friend like you've treated me. I don't know what's gotten into you, but you're not yourself."

"Well, neither are you. See you around, Dana."

Dana glanced at the display.

Call Ended 16:42.

She dropped her arm to her side. She toyed with calling back, but what was the use?

Her hands shook. She blinked, eyes burning.

First Stewart and now Alysa. Well, she was better off without them. *You and I will ever be friends again.*

The burn in Dana's eyes turned to heat. She blinked against the tears.

"You okay?"

She stiffened.

"When you got out of the cab, you looked like death warmed over."

Braden.

She took a deep breath. "I'm fine." Even to her own ears her voice sounded clogged with tears. "Just a sneezing attack." She fumbled for the purse on her shoulder, reaching inside for a tissue.

"Dana," Braden said softly.

No. She didn't want him to be nice to her. Not now. Not when she was so close to tears. Damn it. Why did he always see her at her worst?

"I'm fine, Braden, really," she said, still not facing him. "Just go on back to the restaurant." She dabbed at her eyes. She still had on makeup from the photo shoot. The tissue immediately turned black. Damn, damn, damn. "I'll be there in a minute."

"Who just hung up on you?"

He moved to stand in front of her. She saw his shoes. She refused to let him see her face. "Nobody. It's not important."

"Was it Stewart?"

Her gaze slammed to his. "No. I'd be the one to hang up on *him*." She wiped at her eyes some more, hoping he didn't realize she'd been crying.

"Here," he said, taking the tissue from her.

"Hey," she said. "I can do that."

"You're smearing black gunk all over your face."

"Because I never wear makeup."

"I know," he said, gently cupping her face with one of his hands. "You don't need makeup."

The breath left her. Here was the man who'd pretended indifference all day. Who'd made her feel both rejected and wanted in a matter of hours. Who now tenderly dabbed at her eyes, the look in his green gaze so full of tender sympathy she felt her lashes glom up all over again.

"I think I'm having an allergic reaction to the makeup."

"Who hung up on you?" he asked again, his touch so very gentle and kind.

"Alysa," she answered softly.

"Why?" He swiped at a spot near her nose.

"She thinks it was wrong of me to talk about what happened with Stewart."

His hand stopped moving. She opened her eyes she hadn't even known she'd closed. His gaze bored into her own. "Stewart is an ass."

"I know."

"Then why are you crying?"

"I'm not crying."

His head dropped closer to her own. "Yes, you are."

"Why did you ignore me all day?"

Way to change the subject, Dana. And way to confront issues head-on.

"It's what you said you wanted," he answered. "*You* walked away from *me*, remember?"

"I never expected to see you again."

"You knew we'd see each other on our date."

"Yes, but that was months away."

"What difference does that make?" he asked.

"I'd have time to guard my heart."

His hand dropped.

"I was frightened, Braden," she admitted. "Afraid of how I felt about you. I'd just broken up with Stewart, just met you, and there I was ready to jump into bed with you. You're famous and good-looking and I'm scared to death of how I feel when I shouldn't be feeling anything for *anyone* right now."

"Dana—"

"No. Let me finish. I was supposed to have gotten married the weekend of the race, and yet there I was kissing you. It scared me to death. The way you make me feel *still* scares me.

"Did you ever think," he said, "that maybe this is right?"

"Yes, but I'm tired of being hurt, Braden."

Her words touched a chord deep inside. "I know. It's hard to trust people with your heart, especially when that heart's been broken."

"Who broke your heart?" she asked.

"Just about every foster parent I ever had."

This time she reached up to touch him, the pads of her fingers resting gently against his cheek. "I'm so sorry."

"That's okay," he said with a reassuring smile. "My childhood made me who I am today."

"A good man," she said. "Someone those foster families should be proud of."

"Oh, they are," he said with a wry grin. "Each one of them claims to be responsible for my success, even the bad ones."

"I'm sure you let them go on thinking that."

"No, I'll never forgive the bad ones."

She nodded. She understood him like no other woman had before.

"I'm scared," she said.

"Don't be." He stared into her terrified golden eyes. "Let's just go with this."

Those lashes fluttered. A pulse beat at the side of her neck. He could see it perfectly thanks to the shirt she wore, a soft, feminine blouse that left her shoulders bare. He wanted to kiss every inch of her exposed flesh.

His head lowered.

Those eyes of hers widened even more. He waited for her to pull back. He didn't know what he would have done if she had. But she didn't.

"Dana," he said softly. "I promise never to hurt you." He tried to show her he meant it with a kiss, his lips claiming hers as gently as possible. Her lips were warm, but they tasted of fear and uncertainty.

Don't be afraid, he silently told her. He felt her tension ease, her mouth soften, her lips part. A tiny battle won, but it was as if she'd touched him intimately. Perhaps, in a way, she had.

His hand lowered, moving to her waist, turning her without words to better fit the crook of his body. She went willingly, her head tipping sideways. Braden dared to increase the pressure, hoping and praying she'd open for him, wondering how he'd keep himself in check if she did.

She parted for him.

He began to shake. He wanted. God, how he wanted. To suckle her. To mimic the motion of his lovemaking with his lips. To turn her on in a way she'd never been turned on before. But he was afraid of moving too fast, worried she might get scared if he lost control.

She nipped his lower lip.

Braden couldn't take it anymore.

He pulled away, burying his hands in her hair, nuzzling the side of her neck.

She groaned and tipped her head sideways.

He couldn't believe how much he wanted to lick her skin. There. On the street. In broad daylight. Where God and everybody could see them.

It turned him on.

All day long he'd had to ignore his desire for her. Now he could set it free.

"Let's go," he said, after somehow finding the strength to come up for air.

"What? What do you mean?" she asked, her lips swollen from his kiss.

"We're hailing a cab."

"What about dinner?"

"To hell with dinner." He turned and looked up and down the street for a cab.

"Braden, Max Arnold is waiting for us."

"I don't care," he said, pulling her toward the curb.

"He's your sponsor."

"No. He *works* for my sponsor." Ah. There. Wait. His car was parked in front of the restaurant. Damn. She had him addled.

"He's the man who controls the purse strings."

He turned her toward his car. "I'll sponsor myself next year."

"Braden," she said, stopping and pulling on his hand.

He reluctantly turned to face her.

"We should go to dinner."

"No," he said. "I'm not going to wait for you."

She drew back. He saw it and remembered that she was no ordinary woman. He needed to slow down. To show her without words that he wasn't like the men she'd been with in the past.

"Don't make me sit through dinner after spending a whole day trying to resist your charms. I've been in hell. Take pity on me."

To his absolute delight, she actually laughed. "I don't think I've ever had a man propose a night of debauchery in such a charming way."

"Debauchery?" he said with a laugh. "Is that what we'll be engaging in?"

"That and other things," she said, her eyes lighting up. "I know I'm going to call myself crazy in the morning, but you know what? I don't care."

Elation warmed his insides. He'd done it. He'd broken through.

"Come home with me?" he said, holding out his hand. "End my misery?"

She took his hand. "Only if you end mine."

CHAPTER TWENTY

SEX.

That's what they were going to have.

She should be scared to death.

But as Braden walked her to his car, she found herself not terrified but exhilarated.

For once in her life, she would do something impulsive. And she wouldn't regret it. She would embrace it. She would do exactly as she threatened Alysa she would do. She would chuck it all.

She just wished she didn't feel like throwing up.

"Whoa," she said when she spotted the low-slung sports car—silver—parked parallel to the curb. "Nice rental."

"I didn't rent it."

Talking was good. It helped keep her mind off the inevitable. "What'd you do? Fly your own car out here so you could drive it around?"

"I live here."

Dana slipped inside the car, the smell of tanned leather filling her nostrils. Whatever it was, it looked like it belonged on a race track. "You mean, you live here part-time?"

"No. I live here year-round."

"But I thought all you drivers lived in North Carolina. Moorpark or something."

He helped her inside the car, his hand lingering in her own. Dana met his gaze.

Sex.

He radiated it. *Oh, dear.*

"Mooresville," he said once he'd come around to the driver's side. "But not every driver lives there. A few of us live in other states."

Her hands shook when she snapped her seat belt in place. "I had no idea," she muttered, although why her pulse would escalate just because he was taking her to a private residence, and not a hotel, she had no idea.

You'll be alone with him.

All alone.

Her right hand clutched the door in a way that had nothing to do with the fact that they were peeling away from the curb. Braden squealed the tires as if he raced toward a checkered flag.

"Do you, um…do you live far?"

"About an hour," he said. "Toward the west. Sort of between Martinsville and Richmond, two cities that have race tracks on the NASCAR Sprint Cup schedule."

An hour! She'd have a whole hour of sitting next

to him? Of second-guessing herself? Of worrying if this was the right thing to do?

"Do you have any neighbors?"

He shot her a perplexed look. "Dana, why are you suddenly as pale as a ghost?"

"Oh, I don't know. I was just thinking it's awfully rude to stand up the CEO of *My-Lovematch.* Maybe, since you live a whole hour away, we should eat dinner first. I am kind of hungry."

He pulled over.

"What are you doing?"

"You're worried about being alone with me, aren't you?"

"What?" She acted surprised when deep inside she wondered how he could read her so easily. "Of course not."

"You are, aren't you?"

"No, I ah…I just thought it'd be nice to eat dinner first since it's going to be such a long drive. An hour."

He'd stopped in a yellow-striped loading zone. Dana watched as a man and a woman opened the old-fashioned wood and brass door of a historic building nearby. The couple smiled into each other's eyes. Dana's stomach kicked. When the man bent down to give the woman a kiss on the lips, Dana had to look away.

Had she ever looked at a man like that? Somehow she doubted it.

"Dana," Braden said softly, resting a hand on her thigh, startling her. Ten minutes ago he'd made her sigh with his touch. Now she felt like bolting from the car. "Hey," he said gently. "Look at me."

She hated bossy men. She really did. And yet, reluctantly, she looked him in the eye.

"It's okay to be scared. I understand. But I promise you, if we get to my place and you've changed your mind, that's okay, too. We can take it slow. I have plenty of guest bedrooms. And you'll love my farm. It's a place of sanity in a crazy, insane world. I want you to see it."

She wasn't breathing.

She'd changed her mind.

"Dana?"

She jumped, brought back to earth by his hand cupping her face.

He always touched her so tenderly.

And his eyes. They were full of gentle understanding and compassion. Here was a man as different from Stewart as a poet was from a hit man.

She changed her mind right back.

"Yes," she said softly. "I'll go."

He leaned toward her, making sure she looked him in the eye when he said, "You're so brave."

"No," she said, her throat suddenly tight. "I'm not brave. I'm scared to death.

"I am, too," he admitted, giving her a gentle kiss on the lips. "But we'll work through this together."

He let her go and put the car into gear.

Dana knew then she was no fool after all.

"DID YOU KNOW," Braden said as he drove into his hometown, "that someone tried to name the town after me?"

"Doesn't it already have a name?"

Braden was relieved that she'd relaxed. She no longer looked ready to run the moment the car stopped.

"Yup. Lakeville. But that's so generic. They thought Jamesville sounded a little catchier."

Light brown eyebrows lifted. "You're kidding?"

It was dusk, that time of day when the sun cast a golden glow over everything, including her face. No longer were her eyes brown. They'd turned the same color as the leaves they drove beneath, a deep green bronzed by sunlight.

"Nope," he said, forcing himself to recall what she'd asked. "But it didn't pass, thank God. Not that I wasn't flattered. I was. But naming a whole town after me seemed a bit much. My fan base in town had to settle for an official Braden James Day once a year."

"Did you grow up here?" she asked.

He almost gave her the same flip answer he gave everybody else: that he'd never been in one place very long. Instead he found himself saying, "It's where I wish I'd grown up." He'd never admitted that to anybody.

"From the first moment I drove through town, I knew it was where I was meant to be. I was on my way to a race. Martinsville. My plane had to land in Richmond thanks to bad weather. I drove to the track, and since I had some time, I decided to take the scenic route. The rest, as they say, is history."

They were traveling along the top of some low-lying hills, near the edge of a state park. Tall trees caused sunlight to strobe light across the interior of the car. They were less than a quarter mile from the edge of Lakesville and Braden couldn't believe how much he anticipated her first glimpse of his hometown.

"Okay, wait for it," he said, although the words were for him, not her. "The trees will open up in just a moment. When they do, look down below."

She leaned forward, and Braden smiled. She had calmed down. She even seemed excited, her beautiful hair spilling over one shoulder as she clutched the car's armrest. He couldn't wait to bury his nose in that hair, to spread it out beneath her and watch her eyes fill with longing.

"Oh!" she exclaimed, the mouth he'd been fantasizing about dropping open. "Braden, it's beautiful."

It was Norman Rockwell brought to life—at least, that's what Braden had always thought. Down below, historic buildings dotted a grassy valley. It wasn't a big town, only a couple thousand people, but it still looked as it did a hundred years ago. A white church tower near the middle of town. Stone and brick buildings down Main Street. Stately homes beyond that. No stoplights, just a single glowing yellow light that warned people to slow down.

"My farm is on the edge of town, backed up to the state park. You can see the top of the roof if you know where to look." He pointed even though he doubted she'd spot it. "I had to wait three years for it to come on the market, and even then it felt like I had to be voted into town. A few of the old-timers were nervous about a celebrity moving to their turf. Around these parts, NASCAR is about second only to God."

They were almost to the bottom of the hill. The town disappeared from view until only the church spire was in sight. Then the trees thinned, and grassy meadows surrounded by wood fences framed the two-lane highway.

There it was.

"Hey," she said. "That's your face on that sign."

His grin stretched from ear to ear. "Yup. When they shot down renaming the town, my fan club suggested this as part of the alternative."

They zoomed past the white billboard that said: Lakesville, Home of NASCAR Star Braden James.

The picture showed him leaning up against his car. God only knows what they'd do if he ever changed sponsors. For years, he'd been meaning to deface his own picture with a giant handlebar mustache, one made out of dried corn husks so that it stood out from a distance. Maybe he could convince Dana to help him.

"It's surreal."

"What is?" he asked.

They were approaching the main drag, a quarter-mile strip of asphalt bordered on both sides by red-brick buildings. A few years back, the chamber of commerce had ponied up the funds for green-and-white awnings and baskets of flowers hanging down from old-fashioned lamp poles.

"I forget," she said.

"Forget what?"

"That you're a celebrity."

"Not really," he said. "A celebrity's someone who's recognized no matter where they go. That doesn't happen with me. Most of the time I get the, 'hey, you look familiar' routine. They always think they went to school with me or something. If I wear a ball cap and glasses, I'm good to go."

"You make it sound so easy."

They crossed beneath the flashing yellow light. "It is easy. Not the job of racing. That's never easy. It's a competitive business. But I've been lucky in my career.

I had early success and that set the stage for some good rides. I've been fortunate in my team owner, too. I don't think I'll ever leave Wallner Performance."

They'd already passed through town, farmhouses dotting the landscape. Once upon a time, Lakeville had been home to tobacco farmers. Times had changed. Now Lakeville was known for its production of hay, another high-priced crop, or so Braden had learned. The result was acre upon acre of open field.

"It's so pretty."

If she thought this was pretty, he couldn't wait until she caught sight of his place. He owned the largest of Lakeville's farms, and he could tell, the moment he slowed to make the turn through his massive iron gates, that it wasn't what Dana had expected.

"Isn't it great?"

Her mouth gaped open. "You've *got* to be kidding me."

"I know." He smiled. "Southern belles love this place."

It was an antebellum mansion, Dana noted, one with massive columns that stretched three stories. Lead-paned windows with dark green shutters dotted the front of the white facade.

"It's too bad it's getting late. I could give you a tour in my mini-tractor."

"Your what?" Dana eyed the two-story carriage house. He must use it as a garage, she thought, as, sure enough, fancy barn doors opened like Aladdin's cave as they approached.

"It's like a golf cart," he said. "Only better. It has a truck bed in the back."

"Oh." Her mouth had suddenly gone dry. Now that they'd arrived it seemed as if all her self-doubt returned with the force of a high-powered piston.

"Let's go inside."

Did they have to? Couldn't they sit in the car and continue talking? She'd enjoyed getting to know him on the ride over.

They'd come here to make love. She swallowed against a suddenly dry throat.

We can take it slow.

He'd meant the words. She believed that. As he helped her out of his car, her palm slid against his own. Something shivered up her arm, a current of energy that she labeled fear…at first. Only as he pulled her to her feet, their bodies brushing, did she recognize the truth.

She wanted him.

"Dana," he said softly. When she looked into his eyes, she knew that *he* knew.

"Did they keep horses in here?" she asked, eyeing the inside of the carriage house. Light spilled inside from the windows, scaring a cloud of dust motes into the air.

"They did." He didn't release her hand. "I kept the dirt floor in the event I decide to take up horse breeding."

"I didn't know you liked horses," she said, drawing toward him. She could have resisted, could have pulled her hand out of his, telling him without words that she wasn't ready. But she *was* ready. She was *turned-on*. She couldn't believe how turned-on. Never before had she felt such an attraction for a man. All he had to do was touch her and she was gone.

"Who hasn't dreamed of owning horses?"

"Who hasn't," she echoed breathlessly.

"Dana," he said softly. "I'm going to kiss you."

Her body pulsed at his words. "Oh, yeah?"

He leaned closer to her. "Please tell me that's okay."

She licked her lips. "It's okay," she said softly.

He didn't give her time to prepare. He pulled her to him in a way that could have terrified her given everything that'd happened to her.

She moaned her approval instead.

She opened for him immediately, sucked in the taste of him the moment she felt his tongue slide against her own.

He groaned.

She delved deeper.

Yes.

Wild. Crazy. Exciting. Kissing him was all those things and more.

He pulled his mouth away. She moaned. His lips found her throat. She bent her head back.

Slow down.

The words were a claxon call ringing in her mind.

He ran his tongue up the column of her neck. "Braden," she breathed, her fingers digging into his shoulders. "Please. Touch me."

He slipped his hand beneath her shirt, his big hands skating up her sides.

"I want to do things to you," he whispered. "Things that will drive you mad. That will have you moaning my name."

Yes!

"I want that, too."

"Do you?" he asked, his mouth nipping her throat. "Do you really?"

She gasped. As insane as it sounded… "Yes," she moaned. "Oh, yes."

She'd never been more certain of anything in her life.

"Take me inside, Braden. Take me now."

He did exactly that.

CHAPTER TWENTY-ONE

SHE AWOKE WITH A SMILE. Although to be honest, she wasn't fully awake yet. That suited Braden just fine. He pulled her against him again, remembering the look of wonder on her face.

He felt high.

That's what pleasing her did to him. He felt like he could leap tall buildings, slay evil empires, or please Dana, whatever the case might be.

He kissed her sweet, sexy lips, drawing back to see her reaction. She wrinkled her nose in distaste. He chuckled. Not the reaction he'd been hoping for.

Just as he'd fantasized, her hair lay around her head. He fingered a lock, debating with himself on whether or not to wake her up. He had a feeling she hadn't been sleeping all that well lately, so he slipped out of bed and padded to the bathroom.

An hour later he was showered, dressed and sipping his coffee on the balcony off his second-story bedroom, French doors open wide, a gentle breeze stirring the gauzy curtains.

Damn, he loved this place. He'd always dreamed of bringing a woman here who would love it just as much. Perhaps they'd have a few kids. Perhaps that woman was Dana.

The view was spectacular this time of day. Acres of grass sloped upward, like a green carpet. Property that belonged to the state of Virginia bordered his own and there were no homes in sight, just miles of trees that would never be disturbed. He grew hay in the spring, and the bottom board of his white border fence was barely visible between the thick stalks of grass. Soon he'd hire someone to cut it and the tangy scent of alfalfa would fill the air.

"Hey."

"Hey, yourself," he said, turning toward Dana. She stood behind him, a blanket tight around her, the hair he loved so much spilling long and loose down her back. She looked, he thought, like an actress, one in the midst of a morning-after-sex scene. Except the actresses he'd met over the years could never be as naturally stunning as Dana.

"What time is it?"

"Just before noon," he said with a smile. "You must be famished. I don't recall either of us eating dinner last night."

"Actually, I am."

He motioned to the tiny table that sat between the

two chairs. It held a plate of fresh croissants. "Have a seat," he said.

She clutched the blanket tighter and sank down. "These are good," she said after taking a bite, flaky bits of pastry stuck to her lips.

Braden couldn't resist. He leaned forward and smooched the crumbs away.

"Hey," she cried, but she smiled.

It felt as if the sun rose all over again.

Braden sat back, admiring the sight of her sitting there, the breeze picking up strands of her hair and tossing them behind her shoulders. He could get used to this, he admitted. It was too bad work would soon intrude. He'd gotten a scathing message from Elizabeth last night, one that perfectly conveyed how pissed off she was that the two of them had stood up Max. Braden had offered to take the man to dinner tonight, which meant heading back to Richmond where he kept his plane, and flying up to New York later that day. Unfortunately, he had some business to conduct beforehand in North Carolina. That meant a trip down south before he could head north.

"You want to hang out with me today?"

She shot forward suddenly. "My flight. Jeez. I missed my flight out of Richmond."

He rested a hand on her arm. "Relax. No big deal. I'll fly you home."

"Excuse me."

"I can take you home. Or my pilot will."

She looked floored. "You have your own pilot."

"Yes. And he comes with a plane. A jet, actually," he said with a smile. "A lot of successful drivers have jets. Makes it convenient if we're in more than one race on any given weekend."

"You have your own plane," she repeated tonelessly.

He laughed. He couldn't help himself. "It's no big deal."

"I can barely afford my car payment, but *you* own a jet."

"I also have a motor home, a ski boat, a bass boat, two homes—one here and one in Aspen, although the one in Aspen is really more of a cabin—and various other toys that I use from time to time."

She stuffed another piece of croissant in her mouth, wide-eyed.

"You're looking pale again."

"Again?" she squeaked, tearing off yet another piece.

"You looked that way last night, too, after you hung up with Alysa."

"Oh."

His smile faded a bit. "What's wrong?"

"Just how rich are you, Braden?"

He almost laughed. "Does it matter?"

She stared at him for a long moment. Braden was

shocked to note that she actually considered the question as if it might, indeed, make a difference in their relationship. Wow. Most women considered it a perk that he was worth millions.

"No," she said, setting the pastry down as if she'd lost her appetite. "I guess not."

"You *guess?*" he asked, her words startling a laugh out of him.

She didn't immediately respond. "I feel like a fairy-tale princess."

"Isn't that a good thing?" He reached for and then clasped her hand.

"It might be," she said, looking him square in the eye. "Until the clock strikes midnight."

He squeezed her hand. "Dana, I'm not going to turn into a toad."

She looked off in the distance. Braden continued to hold her hands. They were cold. "It's all so surreal. I meet you at a race, the next thing I know, you're offering to fly me home in your personal jet while we're having coffee at your multimillion-dollar estate. My head's spinning."

He leaned forward. "Dana, I understand why you're scared. Hell, I'm scared, too. Last night was…" He searched for words but couldn't find the right ones. "Last night was amazing." He saw her frown and hastened to add, "I know that sounds like a line. Something any guy would say to a woman after picking her up in a bar and bringing her home." He squeezed her hand again. "But I really mean it, Dana. I just can't think of a way to prove it to you except to ask you to stay with me. Go to the race with me this weekend. Hang out. Be my girlfriend."

He'd never asked that of a single other woman. He'd have told her that, too, except he had a feeling she wouldn't believe him.

"I don't want to leave," he added. "I can't stand the thought of you going home, not when I think I'm falling in love with you."

She jerked, her gaze slamming to his. "Huh?"

He released one of her hands and scooted his chair closer. This might be the single most important moment of his life.

"I'm falling for you, Dana. I know I am. Last night…" He tried to explain it again, and when he couldn't put words to how he felt, he tried a new tactic. His lips found hers. "Last night," he tried again, kissing her near the side of the mouth. "Last night." He cupped the back of her head. He put everything he had into that kiss, and some he didn't have. When she began to kiss him back, he knew he'd won. She opened her mouth. He lost it then, pulling her onto his lap before he could think better of it.

She pulled back. "You were saying?" she asked with a soft smile.

He smiled back. "I think it might be better if I just showed you."

And he did.

IT HAD BEEN, Dana admitted, the most amazing week of her life. No fairy-tale princess could have had it so good. That first day, Braden took her to North Carolina. Later, they flew to New York and had dinner with Max Arnold, who seemed to completely forgive his star driver when Braden offered to play golf with him. Next they'd spent time in Virginia, Braden showing her around his farm. He'd taken her everywhere with him: meetings, publicity appearances, interview requests. And between it all, he'd shown her without words just how much he cared.

It was heaven.

Then Alysa called.

Dana was packing for the race, Braden having gone to town to pick up their dinner. She almost didn't take the call. But against her better judgment, she found herself sitting on the edge of the bed and flipping open her cell phone. Probably some niggling ray of hope, some sad sprig of optimism that had her thinking maybe, just maybe, Alysa was calling to apologize.

She should have known better.

"I just thought you should know," Alysa said without a single word of greeting, "there's an article about you and Braden coming out in this week's *Celebrity!* magazine."

It took a moment for Dana to absorb the words and to realize that Alysa *wasn't* apologizing. She didn't even sound particularly friendly.

Still, Dana found herself saying, "How are you, Alysa?"

"Fine," her friend snapped back. "And this time, Dana, he won't come off sounding like some kind of golden boy."

"He being Braden," Dana clarified.

"Who else?"

She could almost understand Alysa tossing their friendship away. Well, not really, but at least Alysa had offered some sort of excuse. But the venom and loathing she heard in Alysa's voice...*that* she didn't understand *at all*. What had happened?

"Alysa, one thing Braden has said time and again—he can't control what the media says. As a result, he's immune to it all."

"So you admit you're still with him."

"Yeah," she said. "I am." *What of it?* But she didn't say the last aloud. There still remained some shard of hope that they could salvage if not friendship then at least civility.

"I suspect he won't be pleased to see you featured prominently in the piece."

"How so?" Dana asked, her hand clenching the

phone. The French doors were open. The happy chirps of a bird just outside the window contrasted with Dana's sense of dread.

"Let's just say the timing of your relationship with Braden is closely scrutinized."

"Alysa, you know better than anyone that I didn't plan this thing with Braden. It just happened."

"Just as Stewart didn't plan on being vilified by *you*."

Dana groaned inwardly. Not *that* again. She'd finally gotten the courage to watch Melanie's report, and while it mainly focused on Braden and his dedication to helping victims of abuse, Melanie had used portions of Dana's interview, too. Stewart hadn't come off in the best light.

Served him right.

"I didn't vilify him," Dana said. "Melanie Murray did that all on her own. *She* was the one who implied Stewart abused me. And in case you've forgotten, he *did* hit me, Alysa. Not once, but twice…as far as I'm concerned, that's two times too many."

She waited for Alysa to say something, perhaps express sympathy for Dana's plight. She didn't. All Alysa said was, "So now you get a chance to walk in Stewart's shoes. You get to experience what it's like to have people twist things around and imply things that aren't true. Have fun with that, Dana."

"You're too much," Dana said. "I can't believe you've bought into Stewart's side of the story."

Alysa sighed impatiently. "I don't have time for this. Unlike *some* people, I still have a job to do."

"Yeah, well, don't forget it was Stewart who got me fired from *my* job."

"Then you should congratulate yourself, Dana. You've gotten even with him in spades. It's too bad you're too hung up on yourself to apologize to him."

"What! Apologize—"

"Goodbye, Dana."

"Oh, no, you don't. Don't you go hanging up on me again—"

But a glance at the digital display confirmed Alysa was gone.

"Damn it," she cried, close to tears. But not tears of sorrow, tears of rage. How dare Alysa imply Dana had behaved badly? The only crime she'd committed was ever thinking Alysa could be a friend.

She wished Braden was home. She'd have him take her into town so she could buy the magazine Alysa had told her about. Not that she cared what it said.

Liar.

Well, so maybe she *did* care. She wasn't as immune to people saying things about her as Braden was. Maybe she'd *never* be immune. She wanted to know what was being said. Forewarned was forearmed.

She headed downstairs. Braden had an office there—one appointed with oak-paneled walls and maroon leather armchairs.

The flat-screen monitor sprang to life with a glow the moment she touched the keyboard.

She'd spent some time checking her e-mail the other day and so she knew exactly what to do. Dana's pulse rate escalated as she logged on. Ten seconds later she asked the browser for *Celebrity!* magazine's Internet address. The site came up instantly thanks to Braden's high-speed connection. She scanned the headlines, then the pictures on the page, looking for a photo of Braden. Nothing. Just shot after shot of movie stars.

Maybe Alysa was wrong. Maybe she'd just been trying to scare Dana.

Her palms were sweating by the time she used the site's search function. Again, nothing about Braden. Growing more curious, she looked up Braden's name on a search engine, thinking that a recent article, one from a magazine as popular as *Celebrity!,* would pop up. But it didn't.

Instead, she saw page after page of other information about Braden. She couldn't believe the sheer volume of it. Over four-million results.

Then she typed her name in with Braden's. That narrowed it down, but the number of links still shocked her. She'd become a hot topic among

Braden James fans—especially his *female* fans. Her hands hovered over the keys, fingers over the mouse. Should she click on one?

She did.

Braden James Seeing Dana Johnson.

That was the headline on the message board she'd found. A quick glance at the page's header revealed the site was exclusively devoted to Braden.

She began to read.

What does he see in her?
I can't believe he'd date a woman like that.
I hear she dumped her fiancé for him.

The words left her speechless. She might be new to fame—not that she considered *herself* famous— but she couldn't believe how rude people could be when they didn't know anything about her.

By the time she neared the end of the messages she felt ready to vomit. And then there, at the end of the thread, was a link to the *Celebrity!* article.

If you want the real story behind Braden and Dana, click here.

An acrid taste filled her mouth, one that had her swallowing reflexively, especially when she read the headline.

Superstar Not So Super

She told herself to stop reading, that with a title like that, it couldn't be good.

Forewarned is forearmed.

So she read, and if she'd thought she felt ill before she quickly learned she could feel even worse.

CHAPTER TWENTY-TWO

"WHAT ARE YOU DOING in the dark?"

Whatever the reason, Braden thought, it couldn't be good.

"Nothing," she said quickly.

How long she'd been sitting there, Braden didn't know, but it must have been awhile. The screen had turned black.

"I've been calling for you," he said, walking into the room. "I've got dinner in the kitchen."

"I'm not very hungry."

Something was wrong. During their time together Braden had learned one thing: Dana liked to eat. She seemed able to ingest whatever she wanted and never gain a pound.

He squatted next to her and rested a hand on her jean-clad leg. "What's the matter?"

She glanced at the computer monitor. Braden reached up and, on a hunch, pressed a key. The screen sprang to life. Just as he suspected, what she'd been reading was still there.

Superstar Not So Super

Celebrity! magazine, by the looks of things. He stood and leaned in so he could read better. He was used to the way reporters liked to spin stories, but even he was surprised by the hostile tone of the article.

"Is this what has you so upset?"

She nodded, her expression morose.

He tucked a copper-colored strand of hair behind her ear. "It's no big deal."

That snapped her out of it. "Braden, they've got it all wrong."

"So?" he said with a shrug, turning back to the computer and closing the article. "They *always* get it wrong. It's nothing to get worked up about."

"But the article makes it sound as if we intentionally smeared Stewart's reputation to make our illicit affair look better. *Illicit,*" she repeated. "That's the word they used. They inferred you and I were together before I broke up with Stewart, and that's why you got into a brawl, because Stewart came to Vegas to win me back."

He shrugged again. "The more sensational it sounds, the more magazines they sell. Or so the theory goes. It's just part of the deal when you're in the public eye. Let's go eat."

"That's it?" she said. "That's all you're going to say? *'Let's go eat'?*"

"I can say I'm sorry if you want me to."

"No, I don't. I want you to call the reporter who wrote that article and make him apologize."

"Dana," he said, squatting down next to her again. His stomach growled. "You can call reporters all you want, but they rarely *ever* apologize for getting their facts wrong. The days of ethical and accurate reporting are long gone, at least as far as the tabloid press is concerned. The sooner you realize there's nothing you can do about this kind of—" he pointed to the screen "—junk, the better off you'll be. If you try to right every wrong, you'll drive yourself nuts. Seriously, it's not worth the effort. It's taken me years to learn that lesson."

She looked away from him to the computer screen, then shook her head. "What about the nonreporters?"

"What do you mean?"

She pointed at the screen. "They're saying horrible things about me."

"Who?" he asked.

She turned to the computer, clicked open a window. His gut kicked when he saw the site's header: BODACIOUS BRADEN. He'd heard of the Web site infamous for its female members and its devotion to all things Braden James. To be honest, it embarrassed the hell out of him.

"Ignore them," he said, knowing immediately the tone of the messages she must have read. "That's all you can do, Dana. You wouldn't believe the things Lance Cooper's fans say about me, especially if I happen to nudge him during a race." He shivered theatrically.

Her brows lifted. "Seriously?"

"Seriously," he repeated. "It's nothing."

"They called me horrible names."

"And they will," he said. "The longer you and I are together, the worse it'll become. I've heard of blogs devoted to a driver's girlfriend...or wife, and not always in a good way." He patted her knee. "Just get used to it."

SHE WOULD NEVER get used to it, Dana thought when they arrived at the track that weekend. And it only got worse as the race events progressed. They'd arrived on a Friday, and Dana had preferred staying in Braden's motor home rather than venture out.

Now it was race day and they were making their way toward the garage, hand in hand, Dana trying without success to feel self-confident. She'd gone shopping days ago with a little of the money from her contest win, because she needed to be frugal until she found a new job, but she hadn't been able to afford the expensive clothes she'd seen other women wear in the garage. Braden had offered to pay, but Dana had refused and so she was wearing a brown, short-sleeved shirt and jeans, and wishing she'd been less stubborn.

"Wave," Braden said, turning in the direction of the fans who called out his name as they made their way toward his hauler. How the heck they spotted Braden from all the way across the race track was beyond her, but they did. And mixed in with those constant cries were the unmistakable calls of men yelling *her* name and saying, "You could have left your fiancé for *me*," or some other sarcastic variation thereof. Dana knew a lot of women would relish the attention, but not her.

"Well, I'm off," Braden said when they arrived at the hauler. "You going to sit out here?"

She nodded, knowing the routine by now. Braden would dash inside, change, practice, do interviews, whatever the moment called for, while she waited for him outside his hauler, usually sitting in one of the bar-height director's chairs.

"See you later then." He gave her a kiss. He turned, drawing up short when he spotted Belinda sitting in one of the chairs. "Hey, you."

"Hey, Braden," Belinda said, reaching up to kiss him as Braden leaned down. "You do good out there today."

"I will," he said with a confident smile.

Then he was gone, disappearing into the hauler to check in with Elizabeth.

"You look ready to vomit," Belinda said.

It was race day, and it was one of those beautifully mild spring days that would have lifted Dana's spirits had she been anywhere else. "I *feel* ready to throw up," Dana admitted.

"Relax," Belinda said. "NASCAR's done a lot to improve driver safety in recent years. Sure, there's always the possibility that Braden might get hurt out there, but the odds are slim to nil nowadays."

Dana wasn't about to argue the point. She didn't feel up to it.

A few minutes later Braden dashed out of the hauler, kissing her quickly before saying, "I'm off to give some prerace interviews. See you at the drivers' meeting."

"I don't know," Dana said. "You know how I hate to be in the way."

"You *won't* be in the way," he said with a smile. "I'm not taking no for an answer. I'll see you there."

He waved and jogged off.

"Guess the big man has spoken," Elizabeth said with a smile and a wave as she followed in Braden's wake. "See you later, Dana."

"Yeah, later," Dana said, though she doubted Elizabeth saw her answering wave. The PR rep was too busy trying to catch up with Braden.

"You want to walk around a bit?"

"I think maybe I'll hang out inside the hauler."

Away from the crowd and those curious eyes.

"You want to walk together to the drivers' meeting later?"

Dana paused after she stood up. "I'm not so sure I want to go."

Belinda looked shocked. As well she might. The woman made a career out of following Braden's every move. Not that Dana begrudged her that. She knew Braden looked upon her as a surrogate mother.

"Are you sure?" she asked. "It sounded like Braden really wanted you there."

"He won't miss me," Dana lied. "I'd just like to catch my breath before the race starts. You go on to the drivers' meeting. I'll be okay by myself."

"Wait," Belinda said before Dana could turn away. "Are you okay?" she asked, her dark eyes full of concern. "And don't hand me any of that, 'I'm just tired' bull-pucky. You look about as relaxed as a cat on the edge of a bathtub."

Dana shook her head. "It's nothing," she said. "I just need to get used to—" she waved toward the grandstands "—this. It's a little overwhelming."

As usual, Belinda's eyes missed nothing. "Something tells me there's more to it than that."

Dana hesitated before saying, "I'm really worried about Braden. I mean, I know NASCAR's been great about promoting driver safety, but that doesn't make it any easier for me to watch him out there."

Belinda didn't appear surprised by her admission. "I know," she said, nodding her head. "I worry about him, too."

"You do?"

"Yup," she said with an emphatic nod. "But you've got to let those fears go. Braden could crash just as easily out on the main interstate as he could on that race track. In fact, he's probably safer in his race car."

"You think?"

"I know," she said with another nod.

"That makes me feel better. I just have a case of prerace nerves, I guess. I'll be okay." She gave Braden's friend a wide smile.

But Belinda still looked worried. "I'm going to stay here with you."

"No," Dana said, laughing. "You go. Walk around. Enjoy the sights. I know how much you like that."

But Belinda didn't leave.

"Go on," Dana said again, waving her away.

Belinda's eyes narrowed. "Okay," she said, slipping off her chair. "But I'll come back for you later."

"No, no. That's okay. I'm going to hang here until Braden gets out of the drivers' meeting."

"You mean, you're really not going?"

"Nah," she said with a shake of her head. "Braden is working. Attending a drivers' meeting is his job and I don't need to distract him. He was just being kind when he invited me."

"What? Are you kidding? He wants you there, Dana. And I was only invited because Braden wanted me to bring *you*."

"That's not true."

"Dana," Belinda said with a smile. "I'm good friends with Braden, but not even *I've* been invited to a drivers' meeting before. It's sacred ground. He wanted *you* to see it, not me."

"Don't be ridiculous," Dana said, clasping Belinda by the shoulders. "You go. Tell Braden I'll catch up with him after the meeting."

"All right. Fine," Belinda muttered under her breath as she walked away and Dana was grateful for the respite. She liked Belinda, but she needed some time alone before the stress and tension of the race.

"Wow," someone said, only a few minutes later. "So this is where the famous Dana Johnson hides out. I wouldn't have figured she'd be hanging out by a bunch of tires. I thought for sure she'd still be in Braden James's motor home, or more specifically in Braden James's *bed*."

Dana stiffened. She knew that voice.

"Then again," Alysa said, "you never did like spending time in bed with men...or so Stewart tells me."

CHAPTER TWENTY-THREE

"WHAT ARE *YOU* DOING HERE?" Dana asked in shock.

Alysa smiled at her, but the grin didn't reach her eyes. "I was invited," she said, walking a few steps forward.

She looked stunning.

Like she fit in. White cropped pants hugged her trim figure. They were embellished with tiny rhinestones that sparkled beneath the Virginia sun. A stretch-knit top that almost exactly matched Alysa's beach-blue eyes glittered thanks to the silver thread shot throughout. Dana felt woefully underdressed by comparison.

"One of Braden's crew members asked me to come," Alysa said with a triumphant smirk. "So I came."

The tire guy, Dana surmised, the one Alysa had been flirting with in Vegas. "Good for you," Dana said, knowing the words had probably come off sounding snide, but unable to stop herself.

How had their friendship come to this?

How had someone she'd once cared about turned into such a bitter enemy?

"So where is the great man himself?" Alysa asked. "I've yet to see him today." She glanced around, as if expecting to see Braden pop out of a stack of tires like a birthday surprise. Within that gaze was a hunger, one that sent shivers down Dana's spine.

Alysa still wanted Braden for herself. "He's at the drivers' meeting," Dana said. And then, damn it, she heard herself ask, "You want to go over there with me?"

It was a peace offering, and she chided herself for throwing it out there. She owed Alysa nothing. If anything Alysa owed *her.*

"No thanks," Alysa said, her eyes growing harder. "I promised Jerry I'd be right back. He's going to let me walk with him while they push the car onto pit road."

But Alysa *wanted* to go. Despite every negative thing she'd said about Dana, she could tell by the look in Alysa's eyes that she would have gone if Jerry hadn't been expecting her back for a personal stroll with Braden's race car.

How had Dana never seen this side of Alysa before? She'd worked with the woman for nearly two years.

But then, hadn't it always been there? The casual affairs, the snide comments, oftentimes directed at Dana. Little digs that Dana now realized were meant to prick at her self-confidence and make her feel inferior.

"That sounds neat," Dana said, suddenly sad. "But maybe next time."

Alysa huffed in a way meant to convey disdain. "That's okay. I have Jerry. He can take me into a drivers' meeting."

Then why hadn't he done so? Dana wanted to ask. "Take care, Alysa. I'll see you around." Dana turned toward the hauler before Alysa could spot the emotion that no doubt filled Dana's eyes.

Horrible taste in men. Horrible taste in friends. Apparently, she was a poor judge of character.

Was she being a fool about Braden, too?

It was as if Alysa read her mind. "You know he's going to break your heart."

Dana stopped, even though she knew she shouldn't. *Walk on,* she told herself. *It's just sour grapes. Alysa can't stand that you're dating Braden and she isn't.*

"He's a frickin' famous race car driver, Dana. A woman like you will never be able to hold him."

Dana paused with her hand on the sliding-glass door. "You're wrong."

"He'll cheat on you," Alysa said. "Most celebrities do."

Dana shook her head. "Whatever," she said. "I'm not listening to another word." She turned toward the hauler.

"If you're not with him every moment of every day, he'll stray," Alysa called. "I know. It happens all the time."

"Yeah, right," Dana muttered, and she knew in that instant it wasn't true. Braden would never cheat on her.

He was in love with her.

And that realization was absolutely, positively terrifying, and completely and utterly liberating.

Braden James loved her.

Her.

"Watch out, Dana," Alysa called just before Dana slipped inside. "They'll try to steal him away. At every race, wherever he goes, some woman will be there, waiting, wanting to take him from you."

Dana turned on her heel and faced Alysa. "I'd like to see any woman try." She moved into the hauler and slammed the door closed. Dana smiled. No more Ms. Nice Guy.

"Have you seen Savanna?" she asked the first crew member she found, which was, ironically enough, Jerry—Alysa's new boyfriend.

"Yeah, she's inside the lounge—"

Dana didn't wait for him to finish.

"Dana, hey," Savanna said with a wide smile the moment Dana entered the cool interior. "I thought you'd be on your way to the drivers' meeting."

"That's not for a while. Besides, there's been a change of plans." She hooked arms with

My-Lovematch's marketing guru. "Do you know where I can get a Braden James T-shirt?"

"Yeah, sure. We have a few in the lounge."

"No. Not that kind," Dana said, having seen the shirts Savanna referred to. She needed something that screamed *Here I Am*. Something that proved to Braden that she finally understood what it was like to be loved by a good man, and to feel liberated because of it. "I'm talking about the girly kind. The ones with sparkles and stuff."

Savanna's brows lifted. "Ah," she drawled in the same Southern way as Braden. "You'd have to go outside for that."

"Outside?"

"Out of the infield. To a Braden James souvenir hauler."

"Oh," Dana said, disappointment filling her.

"I can have someone take you out there."

Dana straightened. "You can?"

"Yeah, sure." Savanna glanced at her watch. "Braden'll be busy for a little while yet. We can get there and back in a snap."

Dana felt hope. "You sure?"

"We can try."

"THERE SHE IS," Elizabeth cried in relief. Braden followed the direction of his PR rep's finger.

Braden had begun to think Dana had left the track.

But now he straightened in shock when he spotted Dana's attire.

She'd outdone herself.

For him.

He couldn't have been prouder as he watched her make her way toward him, every eye following her progress. Of course, those gazes were probably drawn by the radioactive glow emanating from her chest. It was his car number, shining like a disco ball on Saturday night.

"Look at you." He pulled her into his arms and planted a big ol' kiss on her lips. "I see now why you missed the drivers' meeting." Gone were his concerns about the coming race. He banished his concern about the track's slick surface and the new compound his tire manufacturer was using. In his arms was the one thing on earth guaranteed to calm his nerves.

The realization shocked him.

No woman had ever had that effect on him before. In fact, he usually preferred to be left alone prior to a race. Yet the whole time he'd been out on pit road— waving to fans, talking to his crew chief, doing interviews—he'd been looking for her. He'd even tried her cell phone, a sure sign of desperation. Now, as he held her, he couldn't believe how lucky he felt. Hell, who needed to win a race?

"How do I look?" she asked with a wide smile, stepping back.

Something had changed. It wasn't just her clothing, although that was nice. She wore a red top, one with sleeves that barely reached past her shoulders. The shirt hugged all his favorite curves. Her hair was loose, as he liked it, but it was tucked back by a pair of red glasses that had mininumbers on the lenses. If she'd suddenly produced a giant foam finger, he wouldn't have been surprised to see it carry his car number.

"You look great." He pulled her into his arms again. Now *this* he could get used to. The feel of her in his arms. The strength she gave him simply by being there. The sense of security that he hadn't felt in…well, that he couldn't remember *ever* feeling.

"Braden," Elizabeth said. "I hate to break up the party, but we really need to go."

He glanced around. Elizabeth was right. Several of the race teams had formed the lines that heralded the start of the national anthem.

He took Dana's hand. "Let's go."

She didn't walk with him right away and when he glanced down he realized why. She looked scared.

"Hey," he said. "It'll be all right."

She met his gaze. He could tell she grappled with her fear of crowds, something he'd learned about over the past few weeks, but she pulled herself together and mustered a smile. "I know."

Atta girl, he almost said.

Fortunately, his pit stall wasn't far away. They made it there before the singing of the famous song. He pulled Dana up next to him and ignored the television camera pointed in their direction, but he noticed Dana snuggled closer to him, as if hoping to shield herself from the camera's view.

"Let's play ball!" Pat, his crew chief, said when the song wrapped up, smiling at the guys. A few of them gave him high fives and Braden had to smile. Same old routine, and yet this time it felt different.

"Here we go," he said, squeezing Dana's hand. "Walk me to my car?"

"No thanks," she said. "Been there. Done that."

"Ouch," Pat said. "That had to hurt."

"Nah," Braden said. "She just doesn't want to make the other drivers jealous by talking about my skills where she might be overheard."

"Keep telling yourself that," Pat said. The red ball cap he wore shielded his eyes, but Braden could still see the amusement in them.

"No," Dana said, "I didn't mean that as an insult. I just hate the way people stare at me when I walk you to your car."

Pat laughed. "She's shy. Cute."

"I know," Braden said, tugging her to his side again. "It's one of the things I love about her."

Love.

The word came so naturally.

"Hey," he said. "I had our team manager purchase a headset for you. You can listen to me on the radio with your own earphones."

"I bet that just makes her day."

Dana glanced between the two of them and Braden could tell she was trying to decide if she should chastise Pat or laugh. "Actually," she said, "I'd rather go back to Braden's motor home and watch the race there." She smiled. "That way I can flip between it and my favorite soap."

"Ouch. I hate to ask, but which do you prefer watching?" his crew chief asked. "The soap or Braden?"

"The soap, of course."

She was going along with it, Braden realized. Good for her. "Don't go back. Watch the race from pit road. That way I can smile and wave at you during pit stops."

"As if you'll have time for that," she said with a smile.

"You might be surprised."

"Well," Elizabeth said. "It's time for Braden to go to work."

He waited for the look in Dana's eyes to change from one of amusement to fear. It didn't. Instead she stood on tiptoe and gave him a peck on the cheek. "Have fun."

"Oh, no, you don't," he said when she turned to leave. "You're not getting off that easily."

Her eyebrows drew together in puzzlement. "What do you—"

He jerked her to him. Dana gasped. He kissed her.

Hard.

Elizabeth laughed. Pat snorted. Braden didn't care. He was busy kissing Dana in a way that told everyone near them that she was his. Fans cheered. He saw a camera flash. Braden went right on kissing her. The only reason he stopped was because he was about to race.

"Wow," she said after he straightened.

"You think that was something," he said softly. "Just wait until *after* the race."

And though it was the hardest thing he'd ever had to do, he set her away from him.

Like Elizabeth said—time to get to work.

CHAPTER TWENTY-FOUR

"YOU'RE NOT NERVOUS, are you?" Elizabeth asked as they made their way back to Braden's pit stall.

"Actually, no," Dana said, having decided to watch the race from pit road after all. She couldn't abandon Braden after a kiss like that. "I don't know why, but I'm not."

"That's good," Elizabeth said. "Braden is a pro. You wouldn't believe how many of his ex-girlfriends freaked out before the race even started."

Ex-girlfriends?

"Not," Elizabeth quickly added, "that there's been a whole lot of those. I mean, Braden is no saint, but he's not exactly celibate, either."

Dana's eyebrows rose.

"I'm just making this worse, aren't I?"

Dana chuckled. "You are. But don't worry about it. Braden would have women lining up even if he *wasn't* a famous race car driver. I never imagined he lived the life of a monk."

"Actually," Elizabeth said, turning sideways as

they made their way through a group of people. "He's had remarkably few girlfriends."

"So you're saying he *does* live like a monk."

Elizabeth laughed. "Actually, I don't think I'll say anything else. I have a feeling I'm about to put my foot in my mouth. Besides. We're here."

They had arrived at Braden's pit stall, which looked almost exactly the same as it had in Las Vegas. Giant red toolboxes. Stacks of tires. And Alysa.

Oh, great.

She stood with Jerry, and she was looking in Dana's direction.

"You're welcome to sit up there," Elizabeth said, nodding toward a massive metal stand that Dana realized was also a toolbox with two small-screen TVs embedded into the sides—one on the left and one on the right.

"Are you sure that's okay?" she asked, glancing at Alysa.

"No one will bother you up there," Elizabeth said with a knowing look.

Ah. So, Braden's PR rep had picked up on the tension between the two of them. Why wasn't Dana surprised? Then again, it was pretty plain to see there was something wrong. Alysa kept glancing in their direction, the look on her face one of discomfort.

"Thanks," Dana said. "I think I'll take you up on the offer." There was a small metal ladder near the middle of the box and she assumed that was the way up.

"Hang on," Elizabeth said. "I'll go get that extra headset Braden was talking about."

Suddenly Dana was alone. She tried to ignore Alysa, she really did, but it was hard.

"Are you nervous about watching Braden?"

At first Dana thought someone else had spoken. It was hard to hear with all the prerace activity going on. Compressors hummed. Tools clanked. Voices droned on over the PA—not to mention the crowd across from the track. That's why she turned to make sure she recognized the voice.

Alysa met her gaze, eyebrows raised.

"Uh, yeah," Dana answered. "A bit."

"Don't be. Drivers don't often get hurt."

Were they actually having a conversation? One without arrows and barbs? "So I've heard."

Elizabeth came back with the headphones and, bless her heart, she gave Alysa the stink eye. "Here," the PR rep said. "It's already tuned to the right channel. All you have to do is turn it on when you get up there."

"Oh, are you going up on the pit box?"

Was that what it was called? A pit box? Leave it to Alysa to know. "Looks like it," Dana answered.

"Neat," Alysa said.

Dana didn't know how to respond. An hour ago she'd accepted that she and Alysa were no longer friends. Now it appeared as if that wasn't the case.

"Yeah, I'm kind of looking forward to it." She turned to Elizabeth. "Should I go on up now?"

The PR rep nodded. "You can climb up anytime. There's drinks in the cooler there." She pointed to an orange-and-white tub behind them. "Just ask one of the guys to hand you one if you get thirsty."

"Aren't you going up there with me?"

"Nope," Elizabeth said with a smile, completely ignoring Alysa. "I need to be down here where the press can talk to me."

"I see."

"Just go," Elizabeth repeated with a pat on her back. "You won't fall."

Famous last words.

"Wait," Alysa said as Dana turned away. "Can I talk to you for a moment?" Alysa glanced at Elizabeth. "Alone."

Dana's stomach clenched.

Elizabeth gave Dana a look, one that said she wouldn't leave if Dana didn't want her to.

"It's okay," she said to the woman who'd quickly become a friend. "I'll be fine."

But true to her word, only when they were alone did Alysa speak. "Look. I'll make this quick because I know the race is about to start. I wanted you to know that I'm sorry about what I said earlier." She looked away, shook her head. When she met Dana's gaze again there was something close to humility in her eyes.

Dana just stood there. She was still too raw to completely trust Alysa, but God knew she wanted to. She needed a friend. Someone who knew her before the glitz and glamour of NASCAR.

That's how it's always been, Dana, a little voice whispered. *Someone walks all over you, you turn around and forgive them and then they do it all over again.* Just why was Alysa being so nice? Did she see Dana as her ticket into NASCAR?

"Thanks," Dana said. "I appreciate that. Maybe we should talk more when I get back home."

"Speaking of that," Alysa said. "I thought I should tell you something else."

Dana went on alert instantly. "What?"

"I saw Stewart before I left town. He's back at work. He started saying stuff. Things I think you should know."

"What kind of things?" Dana asked. But she had to wait to hear Alysa's response because the crowd suddenly roared. Right after that, engines crackled to life.

The race had begun.

"He said he'd get even with you," Alysa said, all but screaming the words. "I thought he meant by talking to the press. But, Dana, I'm not so sure. He called me a few days ago. Told me you'd be in for a surprise when you got home. I was thinking about it the whole way here. The tone of voice he used." She shivered. "It really gave me the creeps."

Dana glanced toward pit road. Officials were waving cars forward. Braden would be out on the track in a matter of seconds. "Thanks for the heads-up," she said, wondering if she should believe Alysa or not. Sad to realize that their friendship had sunk so low.

Why would Alysa make up something like that?

To get you away from Braden.

"Just be careful when you get back home," Alysa said, following Dana's gaze.

So Alysa had finally witnessed firsthand how frightening Stewart could be. Too bad it had taken her until now to admit as much.

"Believe me, Alysa. When it comes to Stewart, I trust him about as far as I can throw him."

Alysa held her gaze, then she nodded. Something in her eyes made Dana think that maybe, just maybe, their friendship might be salvageable. In time.

"Have fun up there, Dana," she said. "I'll admit, I'm jealous."

"Thanks," Dana said with a smile. Maybe there really *was* hope after all.

THE BEST JOB IN THE WORLD.

Braden watched as the pace car entered turn

three of their last warm-up lap. He wasn't on the pole, but he was close enough to see the flashing strobe lights flicker.

"Looks like we're going green," his spotter said. Derrick had a bird's-eye view from atop the grandstands. "Watch that blue car in front of you. He's a rookie and he doesn't exactly have the best reputation."

"Got it," Braden said, even though he'd already been keeping an eye on the guy. Ricky Spears came from another division and he'd left a junkyard of broken race cars in his wake.

"Here we go," Derrick said, the words never failing to ratchet up Braden's adrenaline. "Green, green, green."

That was it. His motor roared to life. The inside of his car began to vibrate. The cries of the crowd became a distant memory as Braden raced by his pit stall. Dana stood there. She'd be worried. No need for that, he thought, turning the wheel slightly left. She'd soon realize it was business as usual out on the track.

But no day was ever the same. He should have remembered that. The rookie in front of him would be trouble.

"What the hell is he doing?" Braden asked no one in particular.

Everyone knew who he was talking about. Only one person was stupid enough to duck down the concrete apron of turn one and use the grass to pass.

Ricky Spears.

"Whoa, whoa, whoa," Braden said, backing off when the guy's back end began to wobble. If the yellow stripe on his bumper wasn't proof enough of his newbie status, the way he overcorrected and dove back up the inside of the track *was*.

"Look out high," Derrick said.

Braden was already on it. He checked up. So did the car to Ricky's right. Lance Cooper. But Ricky cut him off so bad the idiot's back bumper caught Lance's front end.

Lance began to spin.

From there it was like balls on a pool table. Ricky overcorrected once again, dove back down. Braden went to the brake. So did everyone behind him. A quick glance in his rearview revealed chaos. There was simply no place to go. Cars began to swerve to avoid hitting the rear bumpers of the people in front of them. Lance bounced off the wall to Braden's left.

Boom!

Braden heard it from inside the car. Debris flew everywhere. Lance began to drift, smoke billowing in his wake.

"Inside," his spotter cried, followed immediately by, "Outside," and then, "Watch out!"

Braden held his line. What else could he do? Lance shot down in front of him, a brief blur of red.

Spears finally got his car under control. He ended up alongside of him after Lance skidded across the grassy infield, out of the race.

"You okay?" Pat asked.

"Oh, *I'm* fine," Braden growled. "But that jerk-wad damn near killed Cooper."

"Calling for a caution."

Well, of course they were. They hadn't even gone a full lap yet, damn it all. That meant long minutes of cleanup and then even longer minutes waiting for everyone to line up. Damn, damn, damn. Totally unfair for those guys in the back. Judging by the carnage he'd glimpsed a moment ago, he would bet almost half the field had damage of some sort.

"What a jerk."

"Take it easy."

But Braden couldn't relax. Dana was probably flipping out. That was all he needed—for her to see him wreck the first time out. "Is Dana hyperventilating yet?" he asked.

He heard Pat chuckle. "Well, now," he drawled. "I can't say that she's breathing regularly, but she's hanging in there. 'Course, there's a few dents in the metal desktop where her fingers gripped the surface."

Braden chuckled, too. "Sorry, honey," he said. "I promise, no more excitement from here on out."

"Hey, now, wait a second," Pat said. "It'd be nice if you won the race. Haven't done that in a while."

That was true. It would be nice. And he was grateful to Pat for making light of the situation.

"I'll do my best," Braden said. "Just as long as I stay away from Ricky Spears."

As he predicted, it took a long time to clean up the mess. When it was all said and done, Braden was champing at the bit to get back to racing.

"Someone better tell that rookie to keep his car on the track this time," Braden said.

"Now, now, hold your temper," Pat said. "Remember there's a lady listening in."

"Sorry, Dana."

A moment or two of silence was followed by a tentative, "That's okay," and Braden smiled. Her first time over the radio. It was nice to hear her voice.

But his smile soon faded because, once the dust settled, it quickly became clear Lance wasn't the only driver taken out by Ricky Spears. Adam Drake had been caught up. Todd Peters, too. Just about everybody who was anybody. Granted, it wasn't like they were hip-deep in the Race to The Chase, but this might be one of races a driver pointed back to as a reason why they didn't make that Chase for the NASCAR Sprint Cup.

"Here we go," Derrick said again.

With Lance gone. Braden got to move up. As soon as the green flag waved, Braden stomped on it. His car shot forward. It was a challenge to hold the high line around turn one and two, but he managed it.

"Good move, ace," his spotter said as Braden dropped in front of Ricky, nearly skimming the back bumper of the car in sixth place.

"Had to do it."

It wasn't a very big hole that he'd wedged himself into, but as they entered turn three, the field stretched out like taffy. He held his line. The car directly in front of him started to pull away. The one to his right, up high, started to fall back. In a matter of a few laps, he'd moved up yet another spot.

The drone of his engine settled into a familiar rhythm. A deep-throated roar while screaming down the backstretch, followed by the popping protests of his exhaust as he braked. Martinsville was just over half a mile. Lots of speeding up and slowing down. Translation: close-quarter racing. He'd picked off two more drivers before they'd made it to lap fifteen.

"Inside," Derrick said, a yellow-and-black car suddenly blocking his path.

Yeah, Braden thought. Lapped traffic already. That was the flip side to racing on such a small track. Fast cars mixed with slow cars. Challenging.

"Eight nineteen on that lap," Pat said. "You're a tick faster than the leaders."

Braden didn't say anything. He was too busy trying to get around the lap car in front of him.

"Will someone tell this guy to move over."

"Flagman's doing that now," his spotter said. "Be patient."

Easier said than done. He glanced in his rearview again.

"Son of a—" He looked again. "How'd he get there?"

No need to ask who "he" was. Ricky Spears.

"He's been coming on strong in the last couple laps," Derrick said. "Been keeping an eye on him."

Terrific. Just what he needed. Three cars left to go before he took the lead, and now he had some over-eager young gun on his tail.

Don't think about it.

Braden focused forward. The grandstand continued to rush by, but Braden hardly noticed. If he could pass another car, maybe leave the kid behind…

It took all his skill to do exactly that. He was loose, not tight. But he'd rather deal with a wobbly back end than a car that wouldn't turn.

"Look out," Derrick said right as Braden's car shuddered.

Ricky. He'd "nudged" him.

"You're going down."

He gunned it. Ricky fell back, but not by much.

"Sure would be nice to see a caution flag," Braden said.

"Set up going away?" Pat asked, concern in his voice.

"No. I've just got Ricky Spears on my ass."

No comment. Braden hadn't expected one. Everyone knew what Ricky was capable of.

Braden tried everything in his power to lose him. No such luck. Worse, little by little the kid caught up. In a matter of laps he was at Braden's bumper again.

Thunk.

Damn.

He'd about wrecked him. "What the hell is your problem? Don't shove me out of the way. *Race* me."

Braden gripped the rubber-coated steering wheel harder, took a quick glance at the gauges. Normal temp and amps, but no button that would let loose a stream of oil thereby slicking up the track so Ricky would crash.

Ricky darted left. Braden had known the move was coming. What he didn't expect was *where* Ricky did it.

Right in the middle of turn two.

Son of a—

Braden tried to move left, but centrifugal force had him firmly in its grip. He could go nowhere. Eight feet. Five feet. Ricky slowly edged forward. Braden's back end began to dance around. Braden let up.

And then…

Boom!

CHAPTER TWENTY-FIVE

DANA COVERED HER EYES.

She opened them again. Out on the track, to her right, she could see Braden's car spin toward the wall. She shot out of her chair, as if that might help her see better. But even if she hadn't stood, she would have heard what happened next.

Bam!

The crowd roared. "Braden," she cried.

Pat stood, too. Beneath her, guys jumped up on the wall trying to see. Braden's car slid toward the infield. So did the car he'd collided with.

"Braden," Pat said. "You there, buddy?"

A long second of painful silence and then, "I'm here."

Thank God.

Dana collapsed into her chair. A flash of color caught her attention. The built-in TV monitor. The network broadcast showed a picture of Braden's car, still rolling.

"Better get out of there if you can," Pat said.

Dana watched in horror as, on screen, Braden's window net dropped. He moved around inside.

"Come on," she urged him, heart racing.

A hand emerged. She couldn't breathe as she waited what seemed like an eternity for the rest of him to wiggle out.

Braden popped free. He fell when he hit the ground. Dana gasped again. But then he was up, running away from his car, unbuckling his helmet. Another safety crew arrived, then an ambulance.

"We're done," she heard Pat say, his face filled with disgust as he caught sight of what was left of Braden's race car. "That stupid little—"

"Where are you going?" she asked when he turned away.

Pat took his headphones off. "Back to the garage. We'll take a look and see if anything can be done."

"But what about Braden?" she asked, horrified that Pat's only thought was for Braden's car.

"I'll have Elizabeth take you to the infield care center. You can meet up with him there."

"No. I meant is he okay?"

Pat drew back. "Oh, yeah. Sure. They take everybody to the infield care center. Even that idiot Ricky Spears." He nodded at the TV screen. They were showing a different car, the one that'd wrecked Braden's. Someone who didn't look old enough to drive stood next to it, helmet in hand as he surveyed the damage.

Then there was Braden.

He looked like he wanted to lunge for the kid.

Someone grabbed her foot. Dana glanced down. Elizabeth.

Come on, she mouthed, her words impossible to hear over the roar of the crowd and Dana's headphones.

Dana pulled off her headset, racing down the metal ladder far faster than she would have thought possible. "He wanted to hit that guy," she told Elizabeth.

"Who? Ricky?"

"Yes," Dana said with a nod, ducking her head as they made their way through the crowd.

"I'm not surprised. He once threw a steering wheel at someone as they drove by."

"Who?" Dana asked, having to stop suddenly to avoid crashing into a group of people. "Braden?"

Elizabeth guided her to the left and around the men and women standing in their way. "Yes," she said, "but he'll hold off on the track, or he'll get suspended for fighting." They crossed through an opening in the fence that kept people out of the garage. "Come on, we'll have to hurry if you want to see Braden before he goes into the care center."

"Is he okay?" Dana asked, thinking maybe Elizabeth was privy to information Dana wasn't.

"Of course," Elizabeth said, the two of them

nearly running. "He wouldn't be looking daggers at Ricky Spears if he wasn't all right."

"Does he get upset like that often?"

"Not often, but he's no different from other drivers. He hates being taken out by irresponsible rookies."

Put that way, she could kind of understand why Braden was so upset.

They arrived at a small white building. An ambulance had already pulled up in front of it, the back doors opening.

"Braden," she cried.

But she wasn't the only one awaiting his arrival. A film crew raced ahead of her, their camera pointed in the ambulance's direction, some guy with a sound boom following closely behind, the thing pointed at Braden like a lance at a jousting match.

"Braden, did you want to comment on the incident with Ricky Spears?"

"No," Braden said, his eyes sweeping the crowd. He spotted her.

Dana smiled, mouthed the words, *Are you okay?*

I'm fine, he mouthed back, but just then a second ambulance pulled up and Dana didn't need her degree in mathematics to figure out who was inside.

Ricky.

The camera crew swiveled in the second driver's direction. They were rewarded for their efforts by Ricky's immediate finger pointing. He yelled, "What the hell is wrong with you, James? You so desperate for a win you feel the need to take me out?"

Dana felt an instant surge of anger on Braden's behalf.

Braden was to blame?

She didn't think so.

"Let's get you inside," Elizabeth said to Braden. "Folks, Braden'll be out momentarily to give a statement."

"I don't need a moment," Braden said. "I'll give you one right now."

"Braden—"

But Braden ignored his PR rep. "You're a danger to yourself and others, Spears. I don't know who thought you were ready for this circuit, but you're not. Go back to Go Karts, or bumper cars or whatever it was you drove before arriving here."

Spears lunged, and Braden was pushed back. Dana winced, called out Braden's name in warning. Someone, Dana didn't know who, stepped between the two men. An official of some sort grabbed Braden by the arm and swung him toward the infield care center. She didn't hear words, but she saw the man whisper something in Braden's ear as he held a hand out to keep Ricky at bay. Whoever he was, he must be important because both drivers instantly stilled.

"Come on," Elizabeth said, motioning Dana forward.

When she reached him, he smiled. "Bet that wreck gave you a few gray hairs," he said with a smile.

"You could say that again."

Someone. A nurse, Dana assumed, said, "First room on the left."

Dana moved to follow Braden.

"Ma'am, I need you to wait outside."

"But she's with me," Braden said.

"You know the rules, Braden," the woman said. "No one but immediate family allowed inside the room, or those whose names are on the list, not until after we check you out fully."

"But she's my girlfriend."

"I don't care who she is unless her name is on the list."

"Who cares about the stupid, flippin' list?"

"Braden," Elizabeth warned. She looked at the nurse. "I don't think any of us thought to add her."

"It's okay," Dana said. "Braden, go. I'll wait out here. It'll only be for a minute or two."

He looked like a little kid ordered to the principal's office.

"Go," she ordered again. "Elizabeth can report back to me. That is, if her name's on the list," she said wryly.

"It is," Elizabeth said.

"Stupid list," he said.

"Go," Dana ordered again.

He turned away reluctantly, but not without muttering, "This better not take long."

Dana almost smiled...almost. Truth be told, she was grateful for the time alone...and for the chairs around the perimeter of the room. She almost didn't make it to one before her legs gave out.

Dear God, she couldn't do this.

She straightened suddenly.

She couldn't do it because she loved Braden too much.

HE DIDN'T TRUST THE look on her face.

"She's upset," he told Elizabeth as they walked down a short hall, the interior of the ICC so cool compared to outside that goose bumps sprouted beneath his fire suit.

"Of course she's upset," Elizabeth said with a glance toward where they'd left Dana.

"No," Braden said, ripping apart the top of his fire suit as they were shown to a room. He knew the routine. "She's upset at me for getting upset."

"This isn't over," Ricky called to Braden as the door was opened by the nurse.

"Bite me, Spears," Braden called back. Not terribly inventive, but it was the best he could do under the circumstance.

The door closed.

"I need you to strip out of your uniform," the nurse said.

"I know, I know," Braden said, feeling abnormally testy. He was usually pretty compliant when it came to a routine visit to the infield care center, but today he felt impatient. "Just as long as you don't expect me to strip naked."

The nurse gave him a frown of disapproval very reminiscent of the social workers he used to deal with. "Doctor will be here in a moment."

Because speed was of the essence. If his car wasn't a total pile of junk—which Braden suspected it was—they would want him back on the track as quickly as possible.

"Turn around," Braden told Elizabeth the moment they were alone.

"Braden, really. I know you've got a tank top and boxer shorts under there."

"Yeah, but I don't want your husband getting all weird when he finds out you've seen me naked."

"You're not going to be naked," Elizabeth said, but she turned toward the window anyway. "And, really, I'm always here for these things. Why so shy all of a sudden?"

"I don't know," he mumbled, slipping out of his uniform. "Must have something to do with Dana." Dana, who'd been forced to wait outside for him. Damn it...

"You know she's going to have to get used to you wrecking from time to time," Elizabeth said, his PR rep obviously psychic all of a sudden. "It comes with the territory."

"Yeah, but I don't think that's what she's upset about," he said, slipping on the light blue examination robe.

"No?"

"Nope. You can turn around now." Braden hopped onto the paper-coated exam table, the thing crinkling beneath him. Damn. That'd hurt a bit. Must have jammed his ribs.

"What do you think has her upset then?" Elizabeth asked, a blond eyebrow lifted in question.

It occurred to him then that his PR rep was about the closest thing to a best friend he had. He didn't know what he'd do if he ever changed teams. Probably see if she'd come with him. "I think she's upset because I lost my temper."

The other eyebrow lifted to join the first one. "Drivers are always losing their temper. Hell, I was almost decapitated once when someone-who-shall-remain-nameless flung his helmet."

"And you've never forgiven me for it, either," Braden said with a wry grin.

"But back to Dana."

Elizabeth was silent for a moment. "You want me to talk to her?"

"About what? About how I lose my temper from time to time? No thanks. I don't think that'll help my case."

"You really think she's wigged out?"

Braden considered the question. "Maybe," he said. "Maybe not."

But any further discussion was cut off by the doctor's arrival. He spent the next few minutes undergoing a complete physical and neurological exam. As expected, all was well. Just some minor bruising.

"They've asked Ricky Spears to report to the principal's office," Elizabeth said, scrolling through messages on her cell phone while Braden slipped his legs into his uniform. "And Pat just texted me. It's going to be a while before they can get the car back on the track. That's it so far. Should I go get Dana—"

"Can I come in?"

They both looked up.

"Dana!" Braden exclaimed, the top half of his fire suit hanging around his waist. "Elizabeth was just about to go get you."

"The nurse told me everything's normal," she said, her expression unreadable. "Or as normal as possible...for you."

"Ha, ha, ha," he said, opening his arms.

She came forward. "I was so scared."

"I'll be outside," Elizabeth said.

Braden patted her back. "It's all right. I'm okay. Really. They wouldn't let me go back to racing if they thought there was a problem."

"I know," she said, drawing back so she could meet his gaze. "I could tell the moment you lunged at that other driver that you were fine."

"Dana. About that—"

"Shh," she said, resting a hand against his mouth. "I know. You were frustrated."

He had her at arm's length now, the sleeves of his uniform dangling to the ground. "At the other driver. Not at you or anyone else."

"I know," she said. "I was just… I was just…" She shook her head a bit. "I guess I was taken by surprise. I've never seen you angry."

"It's part of racing," he said. "And, unfortunately, it probably won't be the last time you see me that way."

"I know. I guess I was, I don't know, freaked out about it, especially after what Alysa said."

"What'd she do to you now?"

She looked toward the door. They could hear voices on the other side. That punk, Ricky, by the sound of it. "Should you be getting back in your car?"

"No," he said. "It's too badly damaged. It's going to be a while." He dropped his head lower. "Now. What'd she say?"

He watched her chest expand as she took a deep breath. "Nothing about you. Just that Stewart was up to no good."

"That's nothing new," he said. "He's been on the warpath for weeks."

"She said it was more than that. But that's not the point, Braden. It got me thinking. I need to confront him. To tell him to lay off. And I think I know exactly how to get him to leave us alone."

"How?"

"Just some information I uncovered a little while ago. It ought to scare him enough to back off."

"Do you think that's wise?"

"Do you think driving a car nearly one-hundred-and-eighty miles per hour is wise?"

"No," he answered instantly. "But it's fun."

"Confronting Stewart won't be fun."

"That's why I'm going with you."

"You can't," she said, nibbling her lower lip and shaking her head. "Elizabeth showed me your schedule. You won't have time to go with me."

"I'll make time."

He took a deep breath. "Why do you feel the need to see that bastard alone?"

She took her time framing an answer. "Because I'm tired of running away, Braden. That's what I did. I ran away. To you. I'm still running away. I haven't been home in weeks. And I do have a home,

Braden. And a career. Or at least I *used* to have a career. And I will again. I'm not going to give up everything just because some idiot thought it was okay to hit me whenever he lost his temper."

"I don't want you to do this alone."

"Fine," she said. "We'll meet in a public place. I'll make sure someone is there to watch over me. From a distance. But I'm going back home."

"I'll clear my schedule and go with you."

"No," she said, lifting her chin.

He looked into her golden eyes and saw something that he'd never seen before, something that made him feel as if he rode in a car with a punctured tire. "This isn't just about Stewart, is it?"

He saw her swallow, saw her square her shoulders. Her eyes met his head-on. "No, Braden, it isn't."

"You're breaking up with me, aren't you?"

"No," she said quickly. "Of course not."

"Why don't I believe you?"

She shook her head, turned away from him. Outside, cars rolled by, the sound getting louder and louder—like a locomotive gaining momentum.

Green flag.

The room suddenly brightened. She'd parted the blinds. Cars flew by, going so fast they were like ghostly shadows.

"Look out there," she said, her voice filled with

awe. "All those people, cheering. For you. Or they would be if you were out there."

"Smoke and mirrors," he said, closing the distance between them. "You know that better than most. Away from here, at my farm, I'm just Braden. And I love you."

The blinds snapped closed. The room darkened. She turned. "Do you?"

"I do." He reached for her, clasped her hands. "I love you, Dana. I know this is going to sound trite, but it's never been like this with another woman."

"I know," she said in a soft voice. "I can tell by your eyes that it's true."

"Then stay with me," he said. Waiting, hoping she would say the words back. When she didn't, he tried not to feel too disappointed. "Move in with me. Permanently."

The room had quieted, but the roar returned with a sudden vengeance only to fade just as quickly.

"I'm not so certain that's a good idea."

"What? Why not?"

She took a moment to answer. "We have so much more to learn about each other."

"Such as the fact that I blow up at other drivers sometimes."

She huffed out a breath. "This isn't about that."

But it was. She might not admit as much to herself, but it was.

"I want to go home," she said. "I *need* to go home."

"Will you be back?"

She opened her mouth, closed it. "Yes."

"I don't believe it," he said.

She blinked, looked away, emotion flickering across her face like sunlight through wheel spokes. "Just give me some space, Braden," she said. "I refuse to rush into something right now."

"Dana, don't do this."

"I have to, Braden."

"No, you don't."

"Yes," she said with a tip of her chin. "I do. Too many times I've flung myself headfirst into stuff. When I was younger I thought I was ready to..." She looked away for a second before lifting that chin of hers once more. "I thought I was old enough to know when I was ready to be intimate with a man, but I was wrong, and it was a horrible experience. In hindsight, I should have waited. I thought I was ready for marriage, too, but I was wrong. I've been wrong about so many things. I even hate being a CPA."

"You do?"

She nodded, and he noticed then that she'd started to cry. "I don't know what made me think I'd like working with numbers. Except I'm pretty sure I *wasn't* thinking. Go to college, everyone said. Get a degree. I had that scholarship, so I opened up the book with the college class list and there it was on the first page. Accounting. But not this time. This time I'm going to take a step back. Really think about what I'm doing. About where it is I'm going. Not just about this, but about my whole life."

Though it pained him to admit it, he understood.

"If this is meant to be, Braden, I'll be back."

He looked out the window, listened to the roar of the crowd as the cars circled the track once again. "You picked a fine time to leave me."

A tear wobbled near the top of her check, hovering there before it fell. "I know," she said, her voice clogged with tears. "I'm sorry," she said, wiping at her cheek. "So sorry."

"Hey," he said, pulling her into his arms. "I understand. It's okay."

It wasn't. Not really. How was it that she didn't know that what they had was special? Real. But if he pushed her now it would do more harm than good. So he held her.

"I should probably leave," she said a long while later. "You need to get back to work."

"Elizabeth will come get me when it's time."

She wiped at her face again. "Delaying this won't make it any easier."

He nodded. "When will I see you again?"

She considered his words, her lower lip beginning to tremble. "I'm not sure," she said. "Maybe on our date."

"Our date? That long?"

She wiped at her eyes again. "I don't know, Braden. I just don't know. Maybe before then. Maybe…"

Not ever.

She didn't need to say the words aloud for him to hear them. "I wish you wouldn't do this," he said. But he knew it had to happen. She was like a horse, one whose spirit had been broken. Only with time and patience would she learn to trust again. What was the saying? If you love something…

"I'm sorry," she said, reaching up on tiptoe to kiss his cheek. "I'm really sorry."

"Dana," he said, reaching for her again.

"No, Braden," she said, holding up a hand. "Let's not make this any harder than it already is."

But it didn't have to be hard. That's what he wanted to tell her. Instead, he held the words back. Sometimes in order to win a race, you had to wait until the last lap to take the checkered flag. What was it his crew chief called it? Slow burn. He needed to burn it slowly for Dana.

"Goodbye, Braden," she said softly. "Be careful out there."

God help him, he hoped he didn't burn out in the process.

CHAPTER TWENTY-SIX

BELINDA SHOWED UP while Dana was taking her things from Braden's motor home.

"I hear you have to go back home for a little while," she said, her dark eyes looking into Dana's own as if trying to glean all of her secrets.

"For a little bit," Dana echoed, unsure of what Braden had told her.

"Uh-huh." Belinda's jaw was so tight it was obvious she didn't approve. "And you had to do it while Braden was in the middle of a race?"

So that's what this was about. Belinda didn't like that she'd potentially ruined Braden's concentration on race day.

"The sooner I leave, the better," she said, and to that end, Dana continued to pack her things. Belinda watched from the entrance, arms crossed, eyes clearly disapproving.

It didn't take Dana long. There hadn't been a lot of time to collect mementos. A miniature snow globe with the city skyline from their trip to New York. A sweatshirt—light yellow—with the word *Charlotte* emblazoned across the front. A mint-green baseball cap that he'd bought her to wear while out of doors on his ranch.

"Do you mind me asking why?" Belinda said as Dana made her way to the front door, tears in her eyes.

"It's not permanent," Dana mumbled, a black duffel bag that she'd pilfered from Braden slung over her shoulder.

Belinda stopped her as she tried to scoot by. "You're making a mistake."

"Am I?" Dana asked, wondering how much of Belinda's concern was about Braden's happiness and how much was about her being his biggest fan.

"What you have with Braden," she said, "I know it's new, I know it's sudden, but it's good, Dana. Everyone can see that."

Everyone but you.

That's what the words implied. "If that's true then it'll all work out. You'll see."

She tried to slide past Belinda again, but Belinda didn't move. "What are you waiting for? A carriage and six white horses? The pumpkin? A fairy godmother to tell you that you're going to live happily ever after?"

"I don't know," Dana said, looking Belinda square in the eye. "But I do know this. Holiday romances barely ever last. It may feel real at first, but it's not.

I'm trying to do the right thing here. To give us space. I know my timing sucks, but it's what needs to happen. For my sake and Braden's. It has nothing to do with wanting to live happily ever after and everything to do with being realistic."

Belinda still didn't let her pass. Dana thought she would say something else, something that might wound her to the quick. Instead, her eyes filled with sudden sympathy.

"I understand. Women like us, we've seen the ugly side of human nature. It's hard to trust again. I know. I get it. But I'm asking you to trust in Braden. He will never, *ever* do you wrong."

Dana felt her shoulders sag. "And I'm telling you I can't right now, Belinda. Not just for my sake, but for Braden's sake, too."

"You're panicking."

"Maybe," she said, remembering how she'd felt when she'd seen Braden's temper flare. "Or maybe not. Maybe, for the first time in my life, I'm looking before I leap. That's not such a bad thing. Please try to understand."

The older woman continued to study her. But then, slowly, her posture changed. "You could have waited until after the race," she grumbled.

"Would it have made things any easier?"

The woman finally let her pass, and Dana heard a barely audible "Probably not."

Dana turned to face her. "Take care of yourself," she told the woman as she hugged her goodbye.

"I hope you know what you're doing," Belinda said, holding on to her so tightly Dana had a hard time breathing.

"I hope so, too," she mumbled back.

Later, while she was at the airport, Dana watched Braden finish the race. She stood outside a bar while waiting for her plane to board and watched his car number scroll across the bottom of the screen. He was an astronomical number of laps down, but at least he wasn't in last place.

"Too bad he wrecked so early, huh?" a man with a Boston accent said while she was standing there, hoping for a glimpse of Braden on the television screen. Only then did she remember what she wore. The red shirt.

"Yeah," she said, turning back to the TV. "Too bad."

"Were you at the race today?" the guy asked.

"Ah, yeah," she said. "I was."

"Aw, man. You lucky dog. I love racing. If I'd timed my business trip right, I could have gone there myself, but I blew it. You want to sit and have a drink? You can tell me all about it."

He was hitting on her. She should have known. "Actually, no, my flight's about to leave. I just wanted to see where Braden was before I got on the plane."

"Too bad. You look really familiar. I was hoping to figure out why."

"I get that all the time," she said, turning away. "Have a safe flight."

"You look just like Braden James's girlfriend," the guy called. "That's what it is."

Crap. "Imagine that," she said.

This would be her life, she realized. If she stayed with Braden she would never be plain old Dana Johnson again. She'd be Braden James's girlfriend.

She would cease to have her own life.

Was that what this was about? she asked herself as she boarded her plane. Was she suddenly afraid to lose her own identity? Or was that just a convenient excuse to get away?

The whole way home she tried to figure it out. And when she landed, she had to resist the urge to pick up the phone and call him. To tell him she was sorry for her miserable timing. And even sorrier for her miserable hang-ups that had prompted her to leave him. When she opened up the door to her apartment, she'd half convinced herself to do exactly that.

And then she got a look at the place. Actually, she *smelled* it first.

"Holy—"

It was trashed. No, not just trashed, *ruined*. Her family room, normally tidy, had been completely destroyed. Her couch had been ripped to shreds, the insides spilling out like fuzzy blood. The coffee table that she'd smacked her chin on when Stewart had knocked her to the floor was on its side, gouge marks embedded into the oak surface as if someone had tried kicking it apart. A large plant she'd nourished throughout the years lay on its side, its root ball kicked apart, black soil scattered about. Books had been tossed from their shelves.

In shock, she moved to her kitchen. She halted at the doorway, her mouth agape. Everything had been taken out of the cabinets. Noodles lay scattered like confetti, the sugary cereal she loved so much was bright spots of color. Her refrigerator lay open, the source of the stench now evident. Milk had been poured onto the linoleum floor, as had leftovers and ketchup and whatever else Stewart could get his hands on. And it was Stewart—of that she had no doubt. The door had still been locked and she could see no immediate sign of forced entry.

In a daze, she headed to her bedroom.

"Oh, no."

It, too, had been destroyed. Absolutely devastated. Artwork had been pulled from the walls, smashed. The cherrywood bed frame that she'd saved up for months to buy had dents all over it—as it it'd been hit with a hammer. The matching dresser had been tipped over. Drawers had been opened, the contents tossed out, then the drawers smashed on the floor. The bedspread had been torn to shreds. And on her cheval mirror to her right, someone had written *BITCH* with a black marker.

She backed away, not because she feared someone was still inside. No. Because she just couldn't take it anymore. In that instant months of anger and frustration and despair coalesced inside her so that she gasped, then exhaled, a sob nearly choking her.

That bastard.

That lowdown, stinking *bastard*.

"Damn you." She cried, but not tears of self-pity, tears of rage. No more would she let that man push her around. No more would he be able to get away with behavior like this. She should have called the cops when Stewart hit her the first time. She would call the cops now. With any luck they'd get fingerprints, not, she admitted, that they would do any good. Stewart would merely claim that he'd been a guest in her apartment and that's why his paw prints were all over the place.

Bastard.

She'd get even with him.

She almost called Braden, but if she did that he'd be on the first plane to California. Scratch that, he'd have his own damn pilot fly him out. This was her problem. She'd never met life's challenges head-on. She had ducked her head under the sand until it was almost too late. But not anymore. She needed to fix her own problems before she allowed herself to lean on someone...like Braden.

Unfortunately, she'd been right. There wasn't much the cops could do. They knew, as she did, that Stewart would deny everything. They promised to go talk to him, but they were painfully pessimistic about their success.

That was okay, though. There was more than one way to skin a cat. She'd told herself earlier that she might need to use her wild card...the time to do that was now. She just needed time to plot everything out. By next week Stewart was going down.

She could hardly wait to watch it happen.

A WEEK WENT BY. A week during which Braden called no less than seventeen times. She learned a lot about him during those phone conversations, always rejecting his pleas to come back to Virginia. This was a test, she told him. A test of loyalties. His and hers. A test of his patience. A test of her independence. A test of his heart. But she almost cried when she read the card that accompanied a dozen red roses.

I love you.

Yes, he did. And she loved him, too. But before they could be together she needed to deal with Stewart.

They met in a public place as she'd promised

Braden she would. An Italian restaurant, which Dana found hysterically appropriate given that she felt she was about to break someone's legs Mafia-style.

The overpowering scent of garlic and oregano would have stirred her appetite if she hadn't already lost it. The place was tiny, only room for twenty or so tables, brick walls on either side and an L-shaped bar in the left-hand corner. Tabletops were covered by slick vinyl—red and white—a glass vase with a single carnation in the center of each. It was the kind of place where you could talk discretely, not because it wasn't crowded—it was—but because it was always so packed you had to concentrate to hear what was being said to you.

"I wondered if you might stand me up," he said with a smug, pretentious smile as she took a seat opposite him.

"Now, Stewart, whatever would make you think that?" she asked with a sweet smile.

It amazed her. She didn't fear him. Not the least little bit. Perhaps it was the public place. Perhaps it was her newfound confidence. Perhaps it was knowing that she had a man like Braden waiting for her, a man who would always love and protect her. Perhaps it was that she was too angry to feel fear.

"Your message sounded ominous," he said.

How had she ever found him attractive? His nose was too perfect. His black hair so in place she longed to mess it all up. And those eyes. She'd seen fish with more character shining from their depths.

She flagged a waiter who'd been passing by. "Martini," she said to a kid who didn't look old enough to drink, much less wait tables. "Extra dry."

Stewart's gaze had turned quizzical when she faced him again. "My, my, my. We've acquired a taste for alcohol, I see."

"No," she quickly contradicted. "I've just always wanted to order one and today seems as good a day as any."

"Liquid courage?" he asked sarcastically.

"Actually, no. It always looks so melodramatic when the heroine tosses a drink into her dinner companion's face, and martinis are always the drink they toss."

"My, my," he said. "We're full of piss and vinegar today, aren't we?"

"Pissed, yes," she said.

"And what have you got to be pissed about?" he asked.

She almost laughed, except if she did, he'd no doubt hear the irritation in her voice. So she cocked an eyebrow in his direction. "Eight thousand dollars worth of damage to my apartment and furniture. A closetful of clothes that have been shredded. I particularly liked how you broke the heels off my shoes, too."

He leaned back in his chair and assumed the relaxed air of someone completely free of guilt. Yeah, right.

"Ah, yes. That's right," he said. "You blamed me for a recent break-in you suffered. I spoke to a detective about that."

He acted as if speaking to the LAPD had slipped his mind. "Yes. I heard. You denied any involvement."

"Really, Dana, you need to stop blaming me for all your troubles."

Their waiter plopped down two glasses of water, some of the liquid sloshing over the side. That was the only thing that kept her from leaning forward and giving Stewart a piece of her mind. But the moment their waiter left, she rested her elbows on the table, cocked her head and said, "And you really need to stop thinking of me as the same, gullible fool I was six months ago when you beat the crap out of me and I let you get away with it."

"Why, Dana. I don't know what you're talking about."

"I beg to differ," she said, trying to match his pompous attitude. "You thought I was stupid enough to keep my mouth shut that second time. Were you surprised to see that I'd armed myself? Granted, the baseball bat I'd stashed beneath the couch wasn't my first choice, but I'll never forget the look on your face when I hit you in the shins."

"What do you want?" he asked, his voice deadly calm.

"CalCom," was all she said.

If she hadn't been watching him closely, she would have missed the way he flinched at the mention of the local conglomerate's name. She tipped her head sideways before saying, "I may not be as great with numbers as you are, but I'm not an idiot." The sip of water she took felt as cool as her mood.

"I have no idea what you're talking about."

He was nervous. For the first time in their relationship, *she* had the upper hand—and it felt good. "You shouldn't use message pads at home, especially the kind with a duplicate backing."

"You're grasping at straws," he said, leaning forward in a brazen attempt to throw her off the scent. "You're making this up as you go along."

"Who uses carbon message pads at home? I asked myself. I mean, that should have been the first sign that something was seriously wrong with you. You're so anal, it's not even funny."

"I think we can both agree this conversation is going nowhere. Obviously, it was a mistake to meet."

"On the contrary," she said. "This conversation very definitely has a point. But I have to admit, I almost didn't catch what you did. If I hadn't noticed the tiny bits of paper stuck in the margin, I would have never looked further. But those little pieces stuck in the spiral binding like cotton candy to a stick, and they got me curious. I wondered what could be so important that you'd tear out not just one message sheet, but the whole damn page? It wasn't like you. You're usually so precise in your record keeping. And, okay, at first I thought it was all about another woman. Boy, I was off base, wasn't I?"

He sat across from her, and she could have sworn he'd paled.

"So I got curious. I looked a little further. As it turns out, you forgot something." She leaned forward and rested her chin on the bridge of her laced fingers. "You forgot to remove the page behind it, which isn't usually a problem, but when you forget to use that little cardboard thing, you know, the separator that keeps your pen from bleeding through to the next page? Well, when you forget to do that a person can read what you've written on the next page. Which I did."

"Look," he said, leaning in so close she could smell his cologne, a scent she'd always hated. "I don't know what you *think* you saw—"

"I *saw*," she quickly interrupted, "what you'd written. CalCom. Going public. Need new CPA."

"I wrote that after the offering."

So now he suddenly remembered what CalCom

was. "No, you didn't," she said. "I kept the message book. Didn't you notice it was missing? Oh, wait, that's right...I bought a new one the next day so you wouldn't notice.

"I kept the book and everything written in it. I'd planned to confront you with it, but I never could gather up the courage. Gee, I wonder why. My arm still hurts on some days. But that was the beginning of the end. And isn't it ironic? You beat the crap out of me, but that's not what made me want to leave you. I decided I couldn't live with a man who had the ethics of a shark. The proof was right there in front of me. There was even a message from Myer and Masterson, the firm you called to represent them because, of course, our CPA firm couldn't do that, not when you planned to make a fortune by buying CalCom's stock cheap and then doubling, maybe even tripling your investment when it went public. Haven't some high-profile people gone to jail for just that kind of thing?"

"Dana, that's enough," he said. "I trashed your place. There, I admit it. And it's over between us. I even admit that. Give me the book and I'll be out of your life forever."

"No," she said.

"Excuse me?" he asked, ever the cocky jerk.

"Stewart, I'd like you to meet a friend of mine," she said, motioning to her right. The place was crowded, but the man in the dark gray suit stood out, especially when he stopped near the edge of their table. "Agent Blackstone, meet my ex-fiancé, Stewart Jones. Stewart, Mr. Blackstone is from the securities fraud division of the SEC and he has some questions about CalCom's IPO, and the millions of dollars you made trading on insider information."

"You bitch."

"I know," she said with a wide smile. "Took me a while, but I finally found my claws."

She stood up, giving Agent Blackstone a wink. "Have at him." She leaned in. "By the way, I already gave him the book."

"This isn't over," he hissed right back.

"Oh, yes, it is," she said. "Because the way I figure it, you're going to jail, and by the time you get out, I'll be long gone."

He tried to stand up. Agent Blackwell shoved him back down. "Mr. Jones," he said, flashing his badge. "I'd like to ask you some questions. This is Agent Camarillo and he'd like to ask you some questions, too."

Dana eyed the two men and smiled. "Have fun," she said, before turning around and leaving the restaurant. If she could have high-fived someone on her way out, she would have done it. As it was, she couldn't resist doing a little stomp-the-feet jig on the sidewalk outside.

Yes!

She'd done it. She hadn't chickened out. Hadn't let fear overcome her.

Her cell phone beeped. She glanced down. Now that she was out of the restaurant she could hear it. She glanced at the display, not surprised to see an incoming text message from Braden.

DID U GET THE FLOWRS?

Dana smiled. Almost…almost, she picked up the phone to call him. Instead she let her fingers do the walking…literally. YES, she typed back.

She stood outside the restaurant for a moment, tipping her head back and inhaling deeply. She felt so relaxed.

So at peace.

Her phone beeped again. R U READY TO COME HOME NOW?

Home. Virginia. Braden.

Was that where her heart belonged?

She looked up at the smog-filled sky just before sending a text message back: C U IN NAPA.

CHAPTER TWENTY-SEVEN

C U IN NAPA.

BRADEN READ THE DISPLAY and shook his head.

"What'd she say?" Elizabeth asked.

They were in Arizona and, as usual, it felt close to a hundred degrees...even with the sun on its way down. "It says, 'See you in Napa.'"

He looked up. They were outside his motor home, the two of them heading out in an hour or so for a race-related party at a local hotel. He wasn't exactly in a partying mood, but he had an obligation. The event was sponsored by one of his associate sponsors.

"Well, that's promising," Elizabeth said, her green eyes as bright as the little blue wildflowers he'd seen dotting the desert. "I mean, at least she didn't say what the hell are you doing sending me flowers?"

He leaned back in his red director's chair, the frame creaking beneath him. The aisle between his bus and the one next to his was pretty narrow and they had a modicum of privacy in the shade beneath an overhead awning. A TV screen flickered to his right, one built into the side of the bus. One of the creature comforts of owning a million-dollar motor home: outdoor television.

"Yeah, but Sonoma is weeks away," he said, leaning forward to rest his arms on his legs. The sun had started to go down, the sky the color of an Easter egg, all blues and purples and oranges. Nothing like a sunset in the desert. "I mean, I don't think I can wait that long."

"Well, that's too bad 'cause you need to wait," Elizabeth said.

"Did I miss the party?"

They both looked up. Belinda, her red outfit an ode to all things *My-Lovematch.com,* made her way up the aisle. Red ball cap. Red shirt. Red pants. Even red shoes.

"We're not leaving for another hour," he said morosely.

"I know," she said, "but judging by the look on your face, I would have guessed someone died."

"Who died?" someone else asked. Braden looked past Belinda. Pat, his crew chief, came up the aisle next, his salt-and-pepper hair still wet, a red polo shirt with *My-Lovematch.com* printed on the pocket still clinging to his body in places—as if he'd pulled it on while still wet. "I thought we were all going to a party together, not a funeral." He stopped before them and stretched. "Hey," he asked when his mouth stopped contorting. "You got any food in this joint?"

"You know I do," Braden said. "Help yourself." He didn't really have an appetite.

"Okay, but first, who died?"

"Dana sent him a message," Elizabeth explained, looking somehow smug as she sat across from him. "She wants to meet him in Sonoma."

"Yeah?" Pat asked. "Isn't that good news? I mean, at least she didn't dump you over the phone or something."

"If it was good news," Braden asked, "why would she make me wait so long? Sonoma is weeks away. I think she's dumping me. She's just giving me time to get used to the idea."

"Not necessarily," Belinda said, sitting down in one of the matching lawn chairs. "If she was dumping you, she wouldn't be talking to you at all. You two have spent *hours* on the phone."

"Food," Pat said. "My tummy's growling. Don't think I can wait another hour and a half."

"My love life is in shambles and all he can think about is his stomach," Braden grumbled.

He mustered a smile. The older woman was the closest thing he had to a mom, and he loved her to death.

"Braden," she said, "the woman's in love with you. She may not know it yet, but she's in love."

"I think Braden is right," Pat called from the doorway. "Why make him wait so long? I mean, talking on the phone is great, but it's not *being* there for someone."

"See," Braden said to his female counterparts.

"Don't listen to him," Elizabeth said. "The only thing he knows about is cars."

"I heard that," Pat called from inside the motor home. A moment later he returned, a bag of corn chips in hand, the plastic rustling like static on a radio. "Mmm," he moaned in ecstasy. "Just what I need in this heat. Salt."

"She's scared," Belinda said, getting the conversation back on track. "And I don't really blame her. She just got out of a bad relationship with that Stewart guy and then—*bam*—she meets you. I actually think she's being smart to give you two some space. How many women would do that?"

"None," Elizabeth provided, motioning Pat over. "Usually they're too busy trying to snare the big famous race car driver. Give me some of those," she said to Pat.

"Good point," Belinda said, nodding in Elizabeth's direction. "You're beating them off with a stick. But Dana's different. She was never after you because of who you are. She clung to you because she needed kindness in her life, and a loving hand. But it all happened so fast. She's right to worry it might not last. I, for one, am not worried at all. She doesn't know you as well as we do. We all could tell things were different with her. I've never seen you chase after a woman like you chased after her."

"Me, neither," Elizabeth murmured, her mouth full of corn chips. "Usually, it's 'keep 'em away from me.' Not, 'hey, find out what hotel she's staying at so I can track her down the same day I meet her.' I knew right then we were in trouble."

"And I knew the moment you put her up on that pit box," Pat said. "You've never let a girl sit up there before. Hearts broke all across America when they flashed her image up on that TV screen."

"Give me a break," Braden said. "My fans don't pay attention to who's up on my pit box."

Belinda and Elizabeth exchanged glances, Belinda saying, "He's so naive."

"No," Elizabeth corrected. "He just hates being a sex symbol. He's in denial."

"Whatever," Braden said, leaning back and crossing his arms. Between the two motor homes, he could see one of the other drivers pass by, the man hand in hand with his wife. Adam Drake and his wife, Rebecca. Now there was a classic example of a nice guy ending up with an equally nice woman. Shouldn't he be so lucky? Wasn't he owed some serious karma with all the work he did behind the scenes? And with his tragic childhood, *tragic* being the media's favorite word to use when describing it.

"The point is, Braden," Belinda said in her best I'm-your-mother-so-you-better-listen-to-me voice, "Dana's being sensible, and in a day and age where a lot of women are far from that, you should appreciate her all the more."

"What if she doesn't show?" asked the big stick-in-the-mud, otherwise known as Pat.

"Not show?" Elizabeth repeated, tiny daggers shooting from her eyes. "Are you kidding? She'll show."

"I don't know," Pat said, ever the pessimist. As a crew chief, that was his job. Braden had told Pat earlier that he thought they had the winning car. Pat's response: Don't wreck it then.

"I think Braden is right," Pat said. "That's an awful long time to give her. She might change her mind."

"See," Braden said, leaning forward and pointing in his crew chief's direction. "I'm not the only one that thinks that way."

"Pat's an idiot," Elizabeth said.

"Hey," his crew chief cried.

"No offense," Elizabeth said. "But he's a man. You guys just don't get it. Dana's in love. I'll bet my new scanner that she shows up in Napa with open arms."

"I'll take that bet," Pat said, pointing back at her with a chip that he plopped into his mouth a second later.

"Wait for her," Belinda advised.

"If you love something, set it free," Elizabeth added.

"If it comes back to you it's yours. If it doesn't, shoot it," Pat said.

"Hey," both women cried.

Braden chuckled. Not a ha-ha, that was so funny kind of laugh. No. He felt at peace. He may not have a real family, but the people surrounding him were more special to him than anything else on planet Earth. All he needed was Dana by his side to make it complete.

"Have faith," Belinda said. "She'll come around."

But whatever Braden was about to say was cut off by Elizabeth's cell phone ringing. When she glanced down at her phone, Braden saw her brows lift.

"Speak of the devil," she said in awe.

"What?" he said, shooting forward and reaching for her phone. "Is that Dana?"

"Hey," she said, darting out of her chair so fast the thing fell over.

"Let me talk to her," Braden ordered.

"No," Elizabeth said. "You two do enough talking on the phone."

DANA WAITED FOR THE phone to pick up.

"Come on," she muttered. She didn't think she had the courage to leave a message—

"Hello?"

"Oh, thank God," Dana said immediately, then wished she hadn't. "I was afraid to leave a message."

"Hi, Dana," Elizabeth said, sounding very happy-go-lucky. Dana heard voices in the background.

"Is Braden there with you?"

"He was," Elizabeth said. "But I've beaten him away. What's up?"

Now that she had Elizabeth on the phone, Dana didn't know what to say. Her skin tingled with the aftereffects of adrenaline. Suddenly Dana felt more like a child on her way to the principal's office than someone who needed help. "I think..." she said. "I think..."

"Yeah."

"I need your help," Dana said in a rush.

"I kind of figured as much," Elizabeth replied, sounding amused.

C'mon, Dana. It's no big deal. Just ask *her.*

"I've asked Braden to meet me in Napa."

"I know," she said. "He just told me."

"The thing is, Elizabeth, I don't think I can wait that long."

"That makes two of you then."

Dana closed her eyes. She'd started walking after her infamous meeting with Stewart and when she spied a park bench up ahead, she sat. Actually, it was a bus stop, Dana's back covering up some guy's smiling face, but she didn't care.

"Is he okay?" she asked softly.

"He's fine. Wants to see you pretty badly, but he's hanging in there."

"I can't see him yet," Dana said. "I had to give us some time. You understand that, don't you?"

"Actually, Dana," Elizabeth said. "I do. We all do. You're being smart."

"What if he meets someone else?"

"Believe me, Dana, he's not even looking. Besides, the two of you are on the phone so much he doesn't have time to look."

Dana smiled. "Yeah, I guess that's true."

"It is true." Then her tone changed, "What'd you need my help with?"

Dana's smile faded a bit. "It's about Napa...."

As THE WEEKEND OF the big race drew nearer, Dana's nerves were stretched thin. She didn't turn on the TV. Didn't take a peek at the Internet. She completely disconnected to the point that when at last the big day arrived, she felt ready to vomit.

"Welcome aboard," the pilot said as he helped her settle into a plush leather seat on the jet *My-Lovematch.com* had sent to pick her up. "Can I get you anything before we take off?"

Yeah, a defibrillator, Dana thought, because her heart felt as if it might jump out of her chest. "No. Thanks. I'm fine."

But she wasn't fine. Not at all. Her hands dug into her lap even though Dana told herself to stop it. She wore a black silk dress and had even gone so far as to have her hair professionally piled atop her head, but if she wasn't careful, she'd end up looking like a doggie chew toy.

Oh, God, she thought as the jet took off. She didn't think she could do this. Her stomach dropped to her toes, and not because they were suddenly airborne. The plane had two rows of seats and she searched the little pouch in front of her for a barf bag. She never ended up needing it, but she clutched the white receptacle the whole way, the thing as wrinkled and worn as she felt by the time they arrived.

But if she'd been nervous before, that was nothing compared to the way she felt when the plane came to a halt and she looked toward the private terminal.

Camera crews.

Not a lot of them. This was, after all, just a human-interest story. But she recognized the logo of more than one major network, and Dana felt like sliding under her seat.

"Good luck," the pilot said once he opened the door for her.

"Thanks," she said. *I'm going to need it.*

What if Braden stood her up? What if this whole thing turned out to be a joke...on her? What if she

*got to the restaurant and Elizabeth was there, a look
of sorrow on her face...*

No.

She would not think that way. She *would not.*

"Dana," one of the reporters called, "have you
spoken to Braden?"

"Dana, what if he's not at the restaurant?"

"Dana, what does *My-Lovematch.com* think of
all this?"

Dana had no idea. Actually, they were probably
wringing their hands with glee. Sure, it wasn't that
her date with Braden would make the six-o'clock
news, but their little contest had turned into a public
event thanks to the press release she'd had Elizabeth
send. *My-Lovematch* must have been thrilled. She
just hoped it didn't end badly.

What if he stood her up?

No, she quickly reminded herself. Elizabeth
would have called if that was the case.

But not necessarily, a little voice warned. She'd
told Elizabeth she wanted the press there, whatever
the outcome. She'd told her she needed the press
there as a way of showing Braden that she was
committed—absolutely committed—to staying with
him no matter who might be watching, or what came
their way. This was it for her. The weeks of waiting
had taught her that.

Outside the single-story building, a limo waited.

Dana ignored the voices calling out to her and slid inside, the door closing with an atmospheric pop.

"We'll be there in less than twenty minutes," the driver informed her.

Fifteen minutes. Would her life be different after those fifteen minutes were up? Would she walk into the restaurant and find Braden? Or an apologetic Elizabeth?

She closed her eyes. Refused to think about it. Whatever happened, she would know soon.

Braden, please be there.

Vino, it turned out, was on a bluff, one of those jagged cliffs that offered a stunning view of Napa and all its green-leafed splendor. She'd seen pictures of the vineyards—who hadn't—but standing for a moment outside that restaurant, a warm breeze tugging at her ankle-length skirt, she suddenly felt at peace.

He was here.

She knew he was. Could feel it deep inside. It was an unexpected feeling, so amazing that at first she thought she was crazy. It was just wishful thinking on her part.

But, no.

He was here. She knew it in her heart.

"Sorry I didn't meet you at the airport," a harried voice said. "I meant to, but I got hung up here at the restaurant. I can't believe how many people are inside. It's crazy."

Dana turned. Elizabeth's smiling face greeted her.

"I'm so glad you're here," the woman said. "We're all so excited." She hugged her. Dana hugged her back and knew in that instant that the two of them would be friends. Good friends.

Elizabeth leaned back and said, "We've got more camera crews inside. The ones from the airport have followed you here, too. I don't know if you've been keeping track of the news coverage, but it's really something, Dana. It seems like all of America is waiting to hear the outcome of this date. It's like some kind of impromptu reality show."

Is he inside?

She wanted—oh, how she wanted—to ask. To know for sure that her intuition was right. But she didn't ask. Elizabeth wouldn't look so damn happy if he'd stood her up.

They entered the restaurant, and Dana was almost immediately blinded by lights.

"Dana, do you want to say a few words before you go in there."

"Dana, what if Braden proposes?"

Proposes?

"Dana, what will you do after the date?"

Proposes?

"Not now, folks," Elizabeth said. "I told you—after the date. Right now Dana needs to have dinner with her love match."

Love match.

The term seemed so old-fashioned. She'd never noticed that before.

"We cleared out the place," Elizabeth murmured. "Cost *My-Lovematch* a fortune, but they don't care. This is great. They want to have dinner with you and Braden tomorrow."

Tomorrow. Would there be a tomorrow? First she had to get through today.

Elizabeth guided her toward the back of the restaurant. There were windows on all four sides. Tables covered with white linens and sparkling glasses like empty sentinels. Ahead stood an archway, the entrance to another part of the restaurant.

"You ready?" Elizabeth asked.

Dana nodded. Was she? Was it possible to ever be ready for such a moment?

"You look stunning."

Dana grabbed Elizabeth's hand. "Thanks for everything."

Elizabeth was grinning again. "I'm not going to say the last few weeks were easy. Braden has been a bear...a lovable bear," she quickly amended. "There's not a mean bone in that man's body. I hope you know that."

"I do."

"Good. Now go put the poor boy out of his misery."

Dana felt tears come to her eyes. She felt so lucky

in that moment. So very lucky to have met Braden and, in the process, gained a new friend.

"Go on," Elizabeth said, and she saw tears sparkling in the PR rep's eyes. "You're going to make me cry if you keep looking at me that way."

"Thank you," she said again.

"Just go, would ya?" Elizabeth said, giving her a playful tap on the shoulder.

Dana went. Her feet made no noise on the plush beige carpet. She tried to distract herself with the view, even more spectacular from inside as the restaurant seemed to be perched on the edge of the bluff.

Then he was there.

He stood next to one of the windows, hands in his pockets, white shirt glowing in the sunlight.

"Hello, Dana."

Suddenly, she couldn't see for the tears in her eyes. And she wanted to see. Boy, did she ever want to see. Because in Braden's eyes she saw something precious and rare.

Love.

"Oh, Braden," she said softly.

And then he was coming toward her. And she was running. He pulled her to him, lowered his head and Dana laughed in delight just before he kissed her. Hard.

She was giggling and sighing and clutching at him and thinking what a fool she'd been to wait so long. Why had she kept them apart? Hadn't she known it would be like this? Couldn't she tell?

He drew back after a long while, but only so he could draw back and say, "You, Dana Johnson, better never do this to me again."

She'd forgotten how handsome he was. And how much she loved his Southern accent. And how extraordinarily masculine he smelled. And how good it felt to be in his arms.

"I'm sorry," she said. "So very sorry. I should have never left Virginia—"

"Shh," he said, interrupting her apology so he could rest a finger against her lips. "You did what you had to do. I understand."

She loved him all the more because of that. He loved her despite all her idiosyncrasies, her hang-ups and her letdowns.

"I don't deserve you," she said softly, a hot tear splattering on her cheek.

"Yes, you do," he said firmly. "You were long overdue a good man."

She laughed a little. Or maybe she choked on another tear. She didn't know. "I love you, Braden," she said. "I really do."

"I'm glad to hear that because I have a little question to ask you."

He let go.

Dana froze.

"I've been carrying this thing around for weeks. Been riding in my car with me, even. In my pocket, of course, but once I bought it, I couldn't seem to let it go."

A box.

A little black box. And inside…

She gasped.

"Like that, do you?"

What looked to be a five-carat diamond, one so cleverly cut it sparkled like a million galaxies. "It's beautiful," she said, her hands lifting to her cheeks. This couldn't be real.

But it was.

He sank to one knee.

"Oh, Braden."

"Dana Johnson. Will you marry me?"

She couldn't speak for a moment, not because she was afraid to answer, but because she was so overcome with emotion that it was all she could do not to let out a ragged sob. "Yes," she managed to gasp. "Oh, yes."

He stood. She laughed. Hysterical laughter because he'd slipped the ring on her finger and it felt good and heavy and…*right.* Then he kissed her again and they were both laughing and crying and Dana knew she'd found the most perfect man in the world.

OUT IN THE LOBBY, Elizabeth had to wipe tears from her own eyes. She'd heard their conversation. They'd all heard it. Behind her, she heard someone say, "And so there you have it, folks. It looks like a wedding for Braden James and his fiancée, Dana Johnson. A true happily ever after—one we all hope, here at KEXL, will last forever."

Elizabeth thought it probably would…and she couldn't wait to watch it happen.

EPILOGUE

"YOU LOOK STUNNING."

Dana stepped back from the mirror and had to admit she didn't look half-bad. She turned. "Thanks."

Alysa smiled, though it was a wobbly grin at best. "Dana, about last year."

"Shh," Dana said, her wedding dress rustling as she crossed to Alysa's side. "That's all in the past. What's important is that you're here now. Today." The day she was wedding famous race car driver Braden James.

"I know, but I just want to tell you." Alysa glanced away for a second, and when their gazes met again, there were tears in her eyes. "I'm sorry for everything I did. Everything I said. I was such a—"

"Brat?" Dana finished for her, unable to resist a small chuckle. "That's okay. I knew you'd come back to your senses."

"Still. You've been so nice to me. And I wanted to tell you." She stopped for a second, pressing her lips together as if she fought back a sob. "I wanted to tell you that Braden ended up with the right girl. The perfect girl. The *best* girl."

Dana's eyes burned. That wouldn't do. That wouldn't do at all. She hated putting makeup on and she refused to do it all over again. "Thanks, Alysa."

"I hope you know how much our friendship means to me now. You didn't have to be nice to me out on pit road, but you were. Always. Even when I was so rotten to you."

"Like I said." Dana clasped her friend's hand. They'd grown close over the past few months. Not as close as she'd grown to Braden's PR rep, but close enough that Alysa had been asked to be a part of her wedding party, her gold dress stunning with her blond hair. "It's all in the past," Dana said. "You're here now. That's all that matters."

Alysa moved forward. Dana opened her arms, peace sluicing through her as they embraced.

"And it's you I have to thank for convincing me to enter that contest in the first place."

"You ready?" someone said.

Dana pulled back. Elizabeth stood there. Her own golden dress equally stunning. "As ready as I'll ever be," Dana told the woman who'd become her best friend.

"Good, because I think Braden is about to come up here and get you if the ceremony doesn't start soon."

They were in Napa, at the restaurant where it'd all started. She was in a room, one to the side of the building, tall windows giving her a glimpse of the vineyards beyond. Cut into the side of the bluff was a terraced garden. Spacious, stunning and more importantly, private. Dana had known it was perfect the moment she'd spotted it.

"Let's put him out of his misery," she said to her friends with a smile.

Alysa was still wiping away tears, but Elizabeth beamed, stepped forward and lowered Dana's veil. They'd gone traditional for the wedding. As such, Dana wore a white tight-waisted gown that made it look as if she actually had cleavage. Its wispy skirts reminded her of a fairy tale.

She *was* in a fairy tale. One where she and the prince would live happily ever after.

"Dana, look this way," someone yelled as she stepped outside.

"Are you nervous, Dana?" another person yelled, a TV camera pointed in Dana's direction.

"Where are you going after you exchange I dos?"

The media. They were ever present in their lives, but that was okay. Dana had come to terms with that. "I'll never tell," she said to the woman who'd asked.

"Careful," Elizabeth said as she began to descend the steps leading to the carved-out terrace. Then, ever the media manager, Elizabeth turned back to the press. "Give us some privacy, people. We promise to give you photo ops after the ceremony."

Amazingly, the media adhered to their wishes. "Congratulations," someone cried out.

This was it, Dana thought, gingerly descending the steps, the world seeming to be coated with powdered sugar when viewed from behind a veil. Lush foliage grew to her left and right, everything opening up at the bottom of the steps. Her stepdad—a man who'd clearly been touched when she'd asked him to walk her down the aisle—waited for her there, his steel-gray hair smoothly swept back, a wide smile on his face. Her stepfather wasn't a NASCAR fan, and so when he leaned down and said, "I still say you should have set your cap for a quarterback," she didn't take offense.

"I know, I know," she said. "But maybe one day Braden and I will have a little girl. *She* can date the quarterback."

Her stepfather drew back and smiled. "Your mom and I would like that," he said, with a squeeze of her hand. "Boy or girl, we'd be happy for you. We want to watch your children grow up in a loving household, and we want to be doting grandparents."

Dana felt her eyes burn. "Thanks," she said.

He patted her hand again and Dana realized her mom had found a perfect man to marry, too. He loved her mom, just as she loved Braden. "Here we go," she said, glancing to where her mom sat near the altar. Row after row of chairs had been set up on a grassy lawn, each one of those seats filled. From her left, a string quartet suddenly stopped playing. Dana took a deep breath, one that froze because when the music stopped, a man turned.

Braden.

He stood in front of a lattice trellis, red blooms dotting the foliage. Red flowers were everywhere. And white. Braden's team colors. Dana had done that on purpose. Max Arnold, one of the wedding guests, had been thrilled.

"Be happy," Roger said, just before the familiar strains of the bridal march began.

"I will be," Dana said,

Yes, she would be, Dana thought, walking forward. Elizabeth and Alysa had already taken their places, not that Dana really noticed. She had eyes only for one man. Braden. Her darling Braden. A man who'd held her through the worst time of her life. A man who'd given her a shoulder to cry upon, and wings to fly when the time had come. A man she loved with every speck of her heart.

"Congratulations," Roger said, lifting her veil and giving her a kiss.

"Thanks," she said, smiling at her mom, who looked stunning with her brown hair piled atop her head. Dana had left hers long and loose, just like Braden liked it. Then her dad stepped out of the way, and Dana locked eyes with Braden again.

I love you, his eyes clearly said.

I love you, too.

She didn't hear the rest of the ceremony. Didn't notice Alysa crying her eyes out next to her. Didn't see Pat, Braden's crew chief, wipe at his own eyes a time or two. The only gaze she held was Braden's, the only time she moved was when it came time to exchange rings, and then a moment or two later, to kiss the bride.

"Pucker up, Mrs. James," Braden said as he stared down at her.

"Lay it on me, Mr. James," Dana quipped right back.

He did.

It was the prefect wedding kiss, one filled with patience and love and ever-present understanding. One that burned, slowly, Dana melting into Braden's arms.

She didn't hear the crowd erupt. Was oblivious to the helicopter that suddenly flew overhead. All she saw was Braden. Braden her husband. Braden her lover. Braden her soul mate.

"Now *that's* a love match," someone cried out.

Braden drew back and chuckled. He looked in Max Arnold's direction, his eyes aglow as he said, "Yes, sir, it certainly is."

And it was…one that lasted forever.

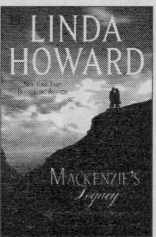

REQUEST YOUR
FREE BOOKS!

2 FREE NOVELS
FROM THE ROMANCE/SUSPENSE
COLLECTION PLUS 2 FREE GIFTS!

YES! Please send me 2 FREE novels from the Romance/Suspense Collection and my 2 FREE gifts (gifts are worth about $10). After receiving them, if I don't wish to receive any more books, I can return the shipping statement marked "cancel." If I don't cancel, I will receive 4 brand-new novels every month and be billed just $5.74 per book in the U.S. or $6.24 per book in Canada. That's a savings of at least 28% off the cover price. It's quite a bargain! Shipping and handling is just 50¢ per book.* I understand that accepting the 2 free books and gifts places me under no obligation to buy anything. I can always return a shipment and cancel at any time. Even if I never buy another book from the Reader Service, the two free books and gifts are mine to keep forever.

185 MDN EYNQ 385 MDN EYN2

Name	(PLEASE PRINT)	
Address		Apt. #
City	State/Prov.	Zip/Postal Code

Signature (if under 18, a parent or guardian must sign)

Mail to **The Reader Service:**
IN U.S.A.: P.O. Box 1867, Buffalo, NY 14240-1867
IN CANADA: P.O. Box 609, Fort Erie, Ontario L2A 5X3

Not valid to current subscribers of the Romance Collection,
the Suspense Collection or the Romance/Suspense Collection.

Want to try two free books from another line?
Call 1-800-873-8635 or visit www.morefreebooks.com.

* Terms and prices subject to change without notice. Prices do not include applicable taxes. Sales tax applicable in N.Y. Canadian residents will be charged applicable provincial taxes and GST. Offer not valid in Quebec. This offer is limited to one order per household. All orders subject to approval. Credit or debit balances in a customer's account(s) may be offset by any other outstanding balance owed by or to the customer. Please allow 4 to 6 weeks for delivery. Offer available while quantities last.

Your Privacy: Harlequin is committed to protecting your privacy. Our Privacy Policy is available online at www.eHarlequin.com or upon request from the Reader Service. From time to time we make our lists of customers available to reputable third parties who may have a product or service of interest to you. If you would prefer we not share your name and address, please check here. ☐

BOB09

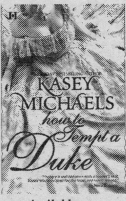
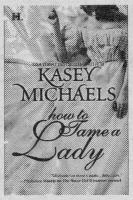

pamela britton

77222	ON THE MOVE	___ $6.99 U.S.	___ $6.99 CAN.
77242	TOTAL CONTROL	___ $6.99 U.S.	___ $8.50 CAN.
77187	TO THE LIMIT	___ $6.99 U.S.	___ $8.50 CAN.
77103	ON THE EDGE	___ $6.99 U.S.	___ $8.50 CAN.
77098	IN THE GROOVE	___ $6.99 U.S.	___ $8.50 CAN.

(limited quantities available)

TOTAL AMOUNT	$ _____
POSTAGE & HANDLING	$ _____
($1.00 FOR 1 BOOK, 50¢ for each additional)	
APPLICABLE TAXES*	$ _____
TOTAL PAYABLE	$ _____

(check or money order—please do not send cash)

To order, complete this form and send it, along with a check or money order for the total above, payable to HQN Books, to: **In the U.S.:** 3010 Walden Avenue, P.O. Box 9077, Buffalo, NY 14269-9077; **In Canada:** P.O. Box 636, Fort Erie, Ontario, L2A 5X3.

Name: _____

Address: _____ City: _____

State/Prov.: _____ Zip/Postal Code: _____

Account Number (if applicable): _____

075 CSAS

*New York residents remit applicable sales taxes.
*Canadian residents remit applicable GST and provincial taxes.

HQN™

We *are* romance™

www.HQNBooks.com

PHPB0909BL